M000206051

Ghost of the Guadalupe

Lockwood
The Accidental Sheriff
Beware a Pale Horse
Trouble

Sioux Sunrise
Paint the Hills Red
Grit
Cut Nose
The Long Walk
Coldsmith

Ghost of the Guadalupe

Ron Schwab

Uplands Press

OMAHA, NEBRASKA

Copyright © 2023 by Ron Schwab

All rights reserved. No part of this publication may be reproduced, distributed or transmitted in any form or by any means, including photocopying, recording, or other electronic or mechanical methods, without the prior written permission of the publisher, except in the case of brief quotations embodied in critical reviews and certain other noncommercial uses permitted by copyright law. For permission requests, write to the publisher, addressed "Attention: Permissions Coordinator," at the address below.

Uplands Press
1401 S 64th Avenue
Omaha, NE 68106
www.uplandspress.com

Publisher's Note: This is a work of fiction. Names, characters, places, and incidents are a product of the author's imagination. Locales and public names are sometimes used for atmospheric purposes. Any resemblance to actual people, living or dead, or to businesses, companies, events, institutions, or locales is completely coincidental.

Ordering Information:
Quantity sales. Special discounts are available on quantity purchases by corporations, associations, and others. For details, contact the "Special Sales Department" at the address above.

Uplands Press / Ron Schwab -- 1st ed.
ISBN 978-1-943421-68-8

Chapter 1

KATHLEEN RYAN BRUSHED away some of the army of lice from the straw mattress on her wobbly bed in the Albuquerque jail. The blanket was also littered with rat turds, obviously deposited by the rodents that had checked out her sleeping place during the night. She was surprised to learn at sunrise a few hours earlier that despite the taunts of the jail's other occupants, she had dropped off into a deep sleep sometime before midnight.

She sat down on the bed, glad that she was wearing baggy denim britches, although she was sure she felt the lice crawling up her legs. She figured they were nesting in her long black hair and scalp, too.

She desperately needed to piss, but the chunky, young man in the adjacent cell was sitting on his own bunk ogling her like she was a prized horse, this despite the loose garments that hung like a scarecrow's clothes on her slight frame. At no more than a few inches over five feet tall, Kat had never weighed as much as 110 pounds. She brushed her fingertips tentatively over her swollen closed right eye and the painful, bruised cheek bone where Louie Gaynor, who claimed she was his common law wife, had hammered her with his fists, bloodying her nose as well.

This was her punishment for refusing to fornicate with the disgusting, stinking man who had not bathed for weeks and whose face was adorned with a scraggly, knotted beard that was blond when she last saw the washed version a year ago. He was a bearlike man, mean as a grizzly, who did not take no for an answer. She had been planning to leave him but had no funds, no horse, and no destination in mind. He would have killed her in an instant if he tracked her down in Albuquerque.

Gaynor, twice her own eighteen years of age, a foot taller than her, and a solid 250 pounds or more, had dragged her into the bedroom, ripped off her clothes, and quickly had his way with her before falling away and descending into a drunken slumber. She had retrieved the hatchet she used for decapitating chickens from the back porch of their three-room cabin, just a mile east of Albuquerque, returned to the bedroom, and driven the butt-end twice into his forehead. She wished now she had used the blade end of the weapon because she had failed to kill the bastard.

It had been her misfortune that Buford Walters, formerly deputy city marshal and presently acting marshal, was Louie Gaynor's best friend and had stopped by the house with a full whiskey bottle to drink and gossip not a half hour later. It also happened to be the usual supper hour when Buford expected to grab a free meal. When she had told him that Louie was sleeping, Buford had just laughed, bullied his way through the door, and gone into the bedroom to roust his buddy.

Thus, Kat was now confined to the city jail, awaiting determination of her future. Louie was taken to a local physician's five-room hospital, still breathing the last she knew. She supposed she should be grateful. If he survived, she might avoid hanging. But she did not intend to wait around to learn the outcome.

Kat had a plan. Buford had left an hour earlier to visit the hospital which was nearly a mile distant. She waited for Buford's return. He would have ridden his horse, the red roan mare she had always admired, and the critter would be hitched to the rail out front. There was no way Buford would have walked. He was a man of average height with a belly the size of twin watermelons that lopped over his belt. He was only a half dozen or so years older than Louie, but he could barely walk across the street without stopping to catch his breath.

There were four cells in the jail maintained by the city marshal, two of which were occupied by cowhands who had been dragged in last night by the acting city marshal. Both had been engaged in a brawl at the Last Hideout Saloon and had evidently been in drunken stupors when Buford arrived and did not have sense enough to escape with the others through the doors and windows. The inability to vacate the saloon determined who was awarded a night in jail.

It annoyed her that Buford had not had the decency to at least leave a cell vacant between her and the new guests. Regardless, she could wait no longer. She pulled the slop bucket out from under the bed, turned so that her backside faced the other prisoners, who were located nearer the entrance to the cell block, and dropped her britches and cotton drawers. She squatted, supporting herself on the side of the bed and relieved herself. There was no paper with which to tidy herself, so she stood and pulled up her underpants and britches, carefully placing the bucket against the wall opposite the cell door.

The task completed, she sat down again facing the other cells that lined one side of the hallway. She saw that her nearest neighbor was still seated on the bunk, now rubbing the crotch of his faded denims with a crooked grin on his face. Beyond him stood his string bean partner, bug-eyed with his fingers clutched to the cell bars. She glared at them, and the skinny one turned away, retreating to his own bunk. The near neighbor appeared oblivious, lost in his dreams.

Several minutes later, the hall door opened, and Marshal Buford Walters waddled in, heading directly for her cell at the far end. He stopped at her cell door and stood there, staring at her with a taunting grin beneath a brushy, salt and pepper mustache that badly needed a trim. "Ain't you going to ask about your husband?" he said.

"He's not my husband, and I don't much care about him."

"You really are a feisty wench, ain't you? Well, Louie's done woke up. Doc Timmons says he likely won't see again out of that left eye, and he ain't going to be so purdy anymore with part of his skull bone above that eye caved in some. He ain't talking a lot of sense yet, but he told me to keep his little breed here till he gets out of the hospital. That might be two or three days yet."

"You're taking your orders from Louie? I thought you represented the law. I didn't kill the dumb bastard. I want out."

"Well, you maybe got out of a murder charge and won't hang, but the prosecutor could likely come up with a book of charges that would send you to the territory penitentiary in Santa Fe. They got a new one just getting started, but that place they got now ain't much more than a hog barn, and they don't do good keeping the men away from the women they got there. You would likely be a busy lady."

"So, Louie gets out of the hospital. What then?"

"He comes to take you back home, and the happy married couple takes up where they left off."

"And the law will just let him beat the hell out of me?"

"I'd say you're ahead on the beating business. Not unreasonable that he might even things up a mite. Now, I'm going to go over to The Biscuit House and have me some breakfast. If you don't raise any more ruckus, maybe I'll bring some back for the three of you."

The stocky cowboy said, "Ain't you going to let me and Clem out?"

"Not yet. Before noon maybe. You got money for a fine?"

The string bean called Clem said, "I thought a judge set fines."

"Judge Roker can do that if you want to wait a few days."

"How much is the fine?"

"I'd say five dollars would do."

"That's all I got."

"You are a lucky man. And you can get breakfast for your five dollars. We'll settle up when I get back." He turned to the other prisoner. "What about you, Harold? Do you got money for the fine?"

"Almost. I'm two bits short."

"I guess that will do this time. I'm feeling on the generous side today."

Kat said, "I want my slop bucket emptied."

Buford said, "In due time." He started to leave.

She said, "If you don't take it now, I toss my water in the next cell. I'll give my horny neighbor a piss bath."

"You know, I can see now why Louie can't help but give you a good beating now and then. I just might give you a whack or two myself, if you don't shut that sassy mouth of yours." He sighed. "But all right, I'll take your damned bucket. Put it up near the door." He pulled the key ring from his vest pocket, selected the cell key, and inserted it in the lock. A quick turn of the key and a tug, and the steel, barred door creaked open.

She put the bucket down some five feet inside the cell and stepped off to the side.

"I said to push it up to the front," Buford said.

"I didn't understand."

"Stupid bitch. Never mind." He stepped inside the cell and bent over to grab the bucket handle.

Like a gust of wind, she snatched the Colt from his holster and slammed a hip into his buttocks launching him forward onto the bucket. He dropped onto the concrete floor, his face falling into the bucket contents. Kat had already closed the door and locked it with the key that was still lodged in the lock. She raced down the hallway, ignoring the threats and expletives that trailed her.

Before exiting the building, she looked outside to confirm that the roan mare was hitched there. She was, and it was Kat's good fortune that the bonus included a holstered rifle in a saddle scabbard. Kat dropped the pistol on the marshal's desk and walked out the door, taking the keys with her, strolling like she was headed for a casual Sunday ride. She mounted and trotted the horse east down the rutted wagon road that headed toward what Louie Gaynor now claimed was his ranch. She assumed she had little time to gain a decent lead from any pursuit, but she would require provisions for wherever flight was taking her, certainly at least several canteens of water. She gave the key ring a toss along the roadside and nudged the mare into a gallop.

Chapter 2

KAT RYAN'S MOUNT did not protest the new rider, but Kat supposed the roan was carrying less than half the load to which the critter had been accustomed. She had put together a bedroll and filled two canteens with water that were now slung over her saddle horn. Stale biscuits and two handfuls of beef jerky were stuffed in the saddlebags along with spare cartridges she had found at the house for Buford Walters's Winchester. She also had something over five dollars in coins in the saddlebags, more money than she had ever possessed at one time in her life. Of course, Louie would be enraged when he learned she had raided the little stash he kept in the old boot in the closet.

It was several hours past noon, she estimated, and they were following a creek that headed southeast as near as she could tell. Her goal was Texas, but she was uncertain where after that. El Paso maybe, if she could figure out how to get there. She spoke fluent Spanish, her mother having been Mexican, and she might blend in well in the border town. She assumed that New Mexico lawmen would not be looking to chase her down in Texas. She hoped there would not be posters out on her. Louie would not have any money to fund a reward, so it seemed unlikely.

She considered her position. She had attempted to kill Louie and had not denied it. She was now a horse thief and had stolen a saddle and rifle, not to mention a jail break and locking the acting marshal in his own jail.

She questioned how much success Buford would have in raising a posse, since he was something of a town joke with a reputation for ineptness. Louie would certainly try to track her down, but he evidently would not be fit for some days, and she hoped to disappear by then. Buford might even join him considering the humiliation she had inflicted upon him.

Poor Buford. He had been serving as deputy city marshal when Marshal Milton Yarberry was arrested by the Bernalillo County sheriff for shooting and killing a man named Harry Brown during an argument over a woman. Yarberry was claiming self-defense although the other man was unarmed. Most folks thought he would be acquitted because the former outlaw, the first to wear a city marshal's badge in Albuquerque, was needed to deal with the lawlessness that had erupted there in recent years.

Buford's acting marshalship was by right of succession, but if Yarberry was convicted, the town fathers would likely find a different replacement, especially after this morning's fiasco. Yes, Buford would have revenge on his mind, too.

How her life had changed in three years' time since her mother Juanita's sudden death from an unknown cause. She had appeared overflowing with her usual, unflagging energy while planting her garden on an April afternoon. That evening, she and Kat were preparing supper, and Juanita had found it necessary to sit down and rest a spell. She did not eat supper and later commenced coughing up blood. Kat's father, Flinn Ryan, insisted that if Juanita was not improved by morning, they would summon a doctor. She died before sunrise.

The Ryan family had resided on a tiny ranch of less than a hundred acres that barely supported two horses and several goats. Kat's father was a carpenter when sober and eked out a subsistence livelihood despite losing jobs during intervals when he was on a drinking binge. In contrast to Louie, he was not a mean drunk. He just retreated into isolation and silence for a week or two at a time when he surrendered to the demon that seemed to own him. When sober, he was a kind and cheerful sort, hardworking and skilled at his craft.

After Juanita's death, the binges had grown longer and more frequent and then the bank called in his delinquent mortgage. When Louie Gaynor heard about Flinn's financial dilemma, he befriended the Irishman and bought the property, paying Flinn a bit over the mortgage debt and agreeing to a restriction in the deed allowing Flinn Ryan to occupy the residence for his lifetime. A month after the transaction closed, Flinn Ryan was murdered in an alleyway adjacent to the tavern. With the passage of just over a year's time, Kathleen Ryan had become a sixteen-year-old orphan.

She had taken over her mother's household duties and the livestock chores after her death, but Kat had little work experience outside the home. A day after Flinn Ryan's death, Louie had appeared at the home and offered to pay for burial arrangements and agreed to allow her father to be buried on the ranchero adjacent to her mother and two infant brothers.

Having access to no funds, she accepted, worrying that the man was not simply being kind but feeling she had no choice. Several days later she was preparing to head for town and seek work of some kind. At least she had an eighth-grade education and was better than most at reading, writing, and numbers. And she was fluent in two languages.

Before she departed the house, Louie appeared again. "We need to talk, Kat," he said, a grim look on his face.

"Well, certainly, come in." She owed this man. What else could she do?

They entered the house, and he said, "Can you spare a cup of coffee?"

"Of course, it will take a few minutes. Why don't you sit down at the table."

She could feel his eyes scrutinizing her body as she made the coffee, and it made her uneasy. When she finished, she put a mug in front of him and poured a steaming cup of the brew and sat down, noting that his eyes were still fixed on her bosom.

"You wanted to speak with me?" she said.

He tried the coffee, pressing the cup to his lips, but finding it too hot, set it back down. "Yep. You need to decide some things."

"I don't understand."

"I paid for your pa's burial costs. Just saying."

"Yes, and I am very grateful. I will try to pay you back when I find work."

"And when your Pa got hisself kilt, you lost the right to live here. I'm planning to move in."

A wave of panic swept over her. "I had not thought about that. You are wanting me to leave then?"

"Not necessarily."

"I am confused."

"You can stay and keep my house for me. Do what you've always done. And warm my bed nights."

"You are asking me to marry you?"

"Ain't necessary. But I want you to be my woman. Live here with me and do the things a wife does. Had a wife once. Bitch took off with another feller."

She did not know what to say. After she left school, her life had been isolated. She had made few friends and had no experience with boys. But where would she go? Her mother had told her once that many orphan girls ended up in whore houses. "I guess we can try it," she said.

He stood up, forgetting about the coffee. He took her hand. "We will start now. Take me to your bedroom."

That first time had been painful but over quickly. It had never taken Louie more than a few minutes to satisfy himself all those countless times. It occurred to her now that she had ended up a whore, selling herself for a place to live. Thankfully, she had never conceived a child.

She had learned a few months later when Louie came stumbling home in a drunken rage that he had bought the ranchero because it was speculated that the new

Atchison, Topeka and Santa Fe Railroad was interested in the land for its main line to Albuquerque. Other land had been purchased for that purpose, and Louie's dream of a fortune died. That was the night of the first beating she had endured.

Only later did it occur to her that Louie may have murdered her father. The killer was never apprehended, and Flinn Ryan's right to live on the land could have impeded sale to the railroad. Her father's death was possibly destined the moment he signed the deed. Louie likely had planned to inherit her with the property from the beginning. She supposed she would never know for certain.

Late afternoon, she reined in the mare near a stream that appeared to erupt from a sandstone-walled butte not more than a hundred yards distant. Her father had always cautioned her about drinking creek water. Perhaps she could find a place to fill her canteens there in the morning. The mare could drink here, and decent grass grew along the stream where the horse could be staked out to graze. Such grazing was generally prized in this semi-arid land. Studying the landscape beyond the stream and creek, she viewed flatlands dotted by mesquite and agave and tufts of dry, brown grasses.

She had chosen this spot because of a bit of concealment offered by a cluster of sumacs and potential cover of three trees she judged to be pinon. The day had been warm and sunny, but in May the nights could turn downright chilly in this country.

After the horse was unsaddled and staked out, she rolled out her blankets under the pinon branches and plucked a biscuit and two jerky strips from the saddlebags. She would need to ration frugally until she figured out a strategy for procuring food. She had hunted often with her father and shot a good number of rabbits and even a few deer. Fortunately, she had thought of bringing a skinning knife. No pots or pans, but she had matches and most things could be roasted.

For a few minutes, she pondered the perils ahead. Apache. It was 1882, and many, but not all, were on the reservations. Outlaws. Of course, starvation was likely a greater risk than those hazards.

Strangely, for the first time in years she was unafraid. She must be insane, but she felt like she had embarked on a great adventure. For now, anyhow, she was free. She understood why people would die for that. She decided that she would willingly do so, too.

Chapter 3

ROMAN HAYES LEANED back in the rocker on the covered veranda that extended the entire eighty-feet length of his "Triad," as he called it. The structure was constructed of native limestone with thick walls to withstand summer's heat, winter's cold blasts, and Mescalero attacks. He had no idea who had built the imposing fortress-like building that stood impervious to time except for the burnt-out roof and interior. When he arrived some sixteen years earlier following his service in the Confederate Army, he had assumed that Mescalero or other Apache had done that damage.

He suspected that Spaniards of a century or two earlier might have been responsible for erecting the buildings. Whoever had built the Triad and other structures had been master craftsmen. The buildings had not only endured but were architectural wonders of a sort, making him think of the pyramids of ancient Egypt that so much was being written about these days.

The Triad lay just outside of one of the many canyons that sliced into the base of the New Mexico side of the Guadalupe Mountain range. Except for the privy, the other buildings, also stone, lay some fifty feet into the canyon. These included a stable far larger than he needed for his few horses and the mules. There was also ample shelter there for his ten-cow herd if a nasty winter storm struck. Two other buildings almost as large as the stable were available for warehousing, but one was more than enough for his needs.

The Triad had three sets of steps and three doors along the railed veranda. Roman had carved out a residence with two small bedrooms in the center section. Connecting doors gave Roman access to his medical offices on one side and the trading post, twice the size of either of the other sections, on the other.

It was a tad past high noon, and the shadows from the mountains that framed the Triad were starting to surrender to a scorching sun. Roman did not mind. He thrived in heat, but he tugged his battered hat lower on his forehead to ward off the glare. Some believed that after death man was reincarnated into another form. If so and given a choice, he would become a desert Gila monster and spend his days on a rock basking in the sun.

He watched a dust cloud in the west inching its way along the mountain foothills. He hoped that the dust source was Conor Byrne's big Studebaker wagon pulled by two mule teams. His young partner would likely have a string of four or five mules trailing behind, all loaded with bags of salt dug and bagged by Mexican miners at the salt flats southwest of the Guadalupe, mostly on the Texas side of the mountains.

Roman's eyes turned to his big Australian shepherd-mix dog rolling in the dirt at his favorite spot in front of the Triad. Why Loafer chose the well-used place, Roman had no idea. There was not much but dirt and sand for miles out there broken up by patches of mesquite, agave, sage, yucca, and other desert-thriving plants. Just behind him, the canyon hosted a contrasting world of grasses and water, even a few willow trees. At the far end of the canyon, several acres of oaks and ash thrived, providing him with a source of firewood. He sometimes wondered if prior occupants of the residence had planted the trees, since some were ancient.

Loafer must have felt his master watching him, because he got to his feet and trotted up the three steps and placed his nose on Roman's lap, asking for some ear scratching. Roman loved the male dog and complied. Loafer's mother had been the Australian shepherd, but an invading lothario had got into her pen several nights while she was in heat. A rancher north of El Paso owned three bitches and a male and was planning to enter the purebred market for the valued cow dogs. For Loafer's mother, he would be forced to wait for another litter. A friend from the war years, the rancher had talked Roman into taking one of the pups off his hands. He claimed the father was a wolf, but Roman doubted it.

The breed was growing in popularity, although the early breeding of the dogs started in California, not Australia. Loafer carried most shepherd traits with medium length hair, black-speckled fur and random patches of rust-brown markings intermingled.

The dog enjoyed sleeping, not being inclined to hunt, and sought no confrontations with surrounding wildlife. Sometimes he barked when strangers appeared near the Triad, but Roman could not count on Loafer as a watchdog. Not once had he alerted Roman when the Ghost visited. Roman suspected the two might have formed an alliance. Loafer generally lived up—or some might say down—to his name, but he did hang close to Roman, following him as he carried out his daily chores. Loafer was a good friend that he could talk to without fear of being challenged about any wisdom he might be offering the world.

"Conor will be here in about ten minutes, Loafer. I'd better get up and open the warehouse doors so he can drive the mule team and wagon in." Roman abandoned the chair and headed toward the main warehouse located some thirty yards beyond the Triad, nearer to the mountains' base and almost parallel to the big stable. He walked at a brisk pace with an erect posture that belied the weariness that plagued him more these days. His weathered face and closely cropped white beard and hair might cause some to guess his age at significantly more than his sixty years, but this man of average height and sturdy frame still put in a good day's work without complaint.

He opened the wide doors at both ends of the stone building so that Conor could drive the wagon in, unhitch the mule teams, and lead the critters out the opposite door. Roman and Conor had torn part of the end wall away and installed the rear exit door so a loaded wagon could be sheltered there for a time and later pulled on through without mastering the logistics of a turnaround within the limited space.

Loafer barked, and Roman turned and saw Conor and his mule caravan had arrived and angled toward the warehouse. When Conor reached the warehouse, he waved and grinned at Roman and reined in his team. "Good afternoon, Doc. I've got the salt. Now we've got to sell the stuff."

"Welcome home, Conor. We will sell it, and soon." Roman went to the rear of the wagon and untied the string of five mules that had followed it and led the critters off to one side before waving Conor inside.

While Conor unhitched the two mule teams, Roman began unloading the bags of salt from the pack animals and stacking the fifty-pound burlap sacks adjacent to the building. Each mule carried six bags. They would move the salt bags inside later after all the mules were put up in the stable.

Conor Byrne came out of the warehouse leading the four team mules just as Roman finished unloading the other mules.

"I guess I timed that right," Conor said.

"Moving the stuff into the warehouse is the hard part. I've got plenty of beans and some bacon I fried up for sandwiches. Fresh bread and an apple pie Maria brought over, hoping you might show up to eat it. That gal's baiting a trap for you. I suppose you have figured that out by now."

Conor grinned sheepishly and shrugged. He was a lean, sinewy man who stood an inch or two over six feet. His reddish-brown hair turned coppery in the bright sun, and his fair complexion had turned tan with the outdoor life here. Roman always watched his young friend's hazel eyes. They talked and revealed a lot about the speaker. He liked what he saw there and had early on judged Conor to be a man he could trust. There were too few of that kind in his experience.

Roman said, "You like Maria, but you're not sure about her, right?"

Conor shrugged again. "Let's get these critters put up and see about that apple pie."

Later, the two sat on the veranda, Loafer cozying up to Conor as a result of bacon treats the young man had passed to him while he watched the men eat a late lunch. "Wish I had me a dog like this," Conor said. "I would sleep better if I had a watchdog, and I could put him to work with the cow herd I'm building."

Roman said, "Loafer's a good dog, but I don't count on him as a watchdog, and I don't think he's got a notion what to do about cattle."

"You've got to train him."

"Hmph. What's that about teaching an old dog new tricks? Loafer and I are both what we are. Too late for changes."

"What about the salt? I've got a little more than fifteen hundred pounds on the Studebaker, so we should have more than a ton and a half altogether."

"Decent sized chunks?"

"Three to five pounds, I would guess. Average of a dozen chunks per bag."

"Cheapest cost for us would be to charge by the bag, say ten dollars. Balance the chunks out, so if we can get forty or fifty bags full, we would get over twenty cents a pound and walk away with four or five hundred dollars. The Cahill ranch would snap that up. They're hurting for salt up north of here."

"Seems expensive for cattle," Conor said.

"Critters do better with salt access. That's why I suggested you always hold some back for your animals. Of course, our salt load won't furnish a fraction of what Cahill and other ranchers need. I've been told John Cahill is running nearly a hundred thousand head of cattle on their land that covers a strip a hundred fifty miles long and fifty miles on each side of the Pecos River. Sounds a bit farfetched to me considering the acres it takes to feed a critter out in this country, but I suppose there is some grass nearer the river."

Conor said, "Doc, we could send a wagon a day up that way if we figure out how to make it pay."

"That's what we are experimenting with now. John Cahill's headquarters is just south of a settlement called Roswell that consists of a few adobe buildings that are used for a trading post and a sleeping place for passers-through. I saw several houses scattered about when I was there, but it's centered on a trading post established by a man named Van Smith who named it Roswell Smith's Trading Post for his father. That's where we would want to unload, maybe get the storekeeper there to be our agent, pay him five percent to market the salt to Cahill and anybody else that wants it. That will be your job. See if you can hire Diego Munoz to go with you. It will take at least three days, each way. I'll keep looking after your place and livestock while you're gone."

"I will need a few days at the ranch."

"The salt and mules won't be going anyplace."

"Doc, I need to head home, but there is a bit of gossip I picked up down at the salt flats. Probably nothing to be concerned about, but there is talk that some tough look-ing hombres have been calling on settlers in the south-east part of the territory."

"And?"

"They are giving notice to move out, claiming that other folks own the lands by rights of old Spanish land grants. Could that be a problem here?"

"I don't see why it should be. After the war, when the carpetbaggers took over Texas, I purchased over twenty thousand acres here from a Mexican rancher who starved out. The place had been in his family for thirty years. I sold you five thousand of that—which we need to get surveyed out. I sold another two thousand split up between eight different Mexican families. The remainder, except for three thousand acres to cover the canyon and building site, I am holding for you till you say you are ready to buy."

"I'm sure it is not a problem. I just felt I should let you know."

Conor's eyes told Roman that the young man was not so certain.

Chapter 4

Conor Byrne rode Stoic, his iron-gray gelding, into his barren ranch yard, which included a two-room, weathered-board shack and a three-stall stable and hay shed that tended to sway in a windstorm. The cedarwood horse pen outside the stable was the sturdiest structure on the place, but the enclosure offered mostly inedible cacti, foxtail, agave and yucca for horse pasturage.

Most days, Conor staked his two horses out near a stream that tumbled down the mountain slopes and through the foothills that backed his house on its journey to the Pecos River some thirty miles farther east. A variety of grasses grew along the watercourse, enough that he could harvest hay for winter feeding of both horses without turning them loose in the canyons where his fifty-cow herd tended to graze. He hoped that the stream portended a decent water well for the place someday. Doc

Hayes had sunk a good one not far from a stream that edged his building site.

He dismounted and caught sight of a rider approaching his place from the east. He supposed that would be Maria Sanchez. He wondered if she had a watchtower and a spyglass at her parents' home a few miles to the northeast. She always knew when he was home. He sighed. He was tired and did not feel like entertaining a guest this evening.

He liked Maria and enjoyed the food she prepared for him, but he could not say with certainty that he was in love with the nineteen-year-old Mexican woman who was in the market for a husband. She was the eldest of nine children, and he suspected sometimes that she was desperate to escape the crowded Sanchez household where she shared a room with three sisters and bore much of the child-rearing responsibility. Besides, she was quickly moving into spinster territory.

There was a shortage of women in this country, and it was not unusual for women to start marrying by their sixteenth birthdays. It was not that Maria could not have married. There were young neighbor men who had courted her, but she always said she was choosy about her prospects, that she wanted a man with ambition and a future. Evidently, Conor was one of the chosen—for now.

Conor was not immune to Maria's voluptuous beauty, however. Ample breasts and full-figured, she was an enticing specimen, and her pouty lips and seductive, dark eyes could reduce a man to an obedient dog. At the thought of her now, he changed his mind about being too tired for company. Perhaps she would join him for a bath in the stream before they coupled in his bed.

If she stayed the night, he usually tucked a dollar in her shirt pocket before she dressed. He knew the family needed money, and she had never seemed offended. No mention of the money was ever made by either, but he could not help but wonder if the dollar was part of the incentive for her visits. He did not care. He was reasonably confident she was sleeping with no one else. Still . . .

Maria galloped her father's sorrel mare into the yard, reined in, and dismounted. The baggy, ragged denims and the faded, green shirt that revealed just a hint of cleavage somehow only made her more alluring. She led her horse over to him and lifted her chin for a kiss. She was a few inches over five feet tall, so he lowered his head and obliged.

She stepped back and seemed to be appraising him with those dark eyes. She spoke English with only the slightest hint of an accent. "We will put up the horses and then we can go to the stream and bathe. I brought tamales and churros. You can make coffee and then I will give you a shave and haircut before we go to bed. I plan to stay the night if things go well, but Padre complained about it, as usual. He fears I am going to hell."

She had taken command as she was inclined to do. For a good meal and a few romps in bed, he was not about to complain. He sensed a warning in her words "if things go well," though. "I could shave myself," he said.

"Of course, you could, but I like pressing the blade against your throat."

A strange comment. He changed the conversation. "Let's get the critters put away."

Later, invigorated by the mountain stream's icy waters and conveniently naked, they had taken advantage of the blanket spread on the ground near the stream. He liked that she was far from a passive participant in their lovemaking.

Now, feeling stuffed and contented by his second good meal of the day, more than he had enjoyed in over ten days traveling the wagon road, Conor submitted to the haircut. Until he saw the mass of hair gathered on the floor, he had been oblivious to the mop that had collected on his scalp over three- or four-months' time, although he guessed it had been covering his neck lately.

Now, Maria, after lathering his face, was shaving off the beginnings of a beard.

Normally, since his days at West Point, Conor kept his face clean shaven, but on the trail he tended to abandon such habits. There were always many camp chores, including animal care, that took priority, not to mention the need to keep a lookout for outlaws or renegade Apache.

"We must talk," Maria said, as she swiped the straight edge down his cheek.

Those words made him apprehensive, especially with a blade just several inches from his throat. "About what?"

"It is time for me to know your intentions. I have been visiting for almost a year now. Padre says it is time. I cannot argue with that."

"My intentions?" He felt the blade move slowly under his neck. He hoped it was his imagination that it was pressing more harshly than necessary to remove the whiskers. He reminded himself that there was more growth than usual.

"You have never asked me to marry you, but we do the things that married people do."

"Well, we are not the first to do that. I guess I haven't given much thought to marriage. I am just getting started in the ranching business and am hardly able to support a wife and family."

"You have never said you love me."

"Well, I like you a lot. I'm not sure what love is. You have never said you love me for that matter. I thought we were content to just enjoy each other's company."

"What we do makes babies. It is only a matter of time before I am with child."

"That's true, I suppose."

"What would you do if I told you I am with child?"

A shiver raced down his spine. "Are you?"

She was silent as she finished the shave. After the last blade swipe, she tossed him a wet rag. "You may wash your own face." She picked up the small mirror off the table and held it up for him.

He felt and looked human again. "Thank you. As usual, you did a fine job, better than any barber I have encountered."

"I am not with child."

Instant relief arrived. He told her the truth. "If you were, I would marry you. It would be a matter of honor. I believe in responsibility."

"Honor but not love?"

"Love is more complicated. I would have to think about that."

"You have no intentions of marrying me?"

"I did not say that."

"I did not have an education like yours, but I attended Doctor Hayes's school on the two days weekly that he offered for five years. I read and write, do numbers better than most. I am not ignorant."

"I never thought you ignorant. You are an intelligent woman."

"I want more than this shack you live in, but I think you are capable of more. Do you have money?"

He did not consider the question any of her business, but he answered it. "No. I still owe Doc Hayes a significant balance on my note for the land. I am partnering with him in the salt business, and we hope to expand freighting. He would like to run his own regular wagon for general store merchandise from Santa Fe instead of waiting for the rare wagon to come this way or travel for the small selection of goods in El Paso. I have considered processing our salt for preserving meat and such, maybe even for table use. I am studying on it. I know I am years from making a living in ranching. That may never happen here; the land acreage required to support a cow is so great."

"If you cannot make money here, will you leave? With your education, I am sure you could find a good position in a big town or city."

"I love it here. I would have to be starving. This is my home now. But I expect to do well enough in time. I am patient, and I do not quit."

"At least you have ambition. I think I could live with that for now, if you could build a decent place to live."

"Money is important to you?"

"Yes. I have no intention of being poor. A man from Santa Fe stopped at our house recently asking questions about our land and how we came to own it. He and I talked for a long time before he moved on. He said I should go to Santa Fe or El Paso. Speaking both Spanish and English fluently, he said I could find work there and meet a man worthy of me—his words, not mine. As you know, my family settled in Texas long before Texas became a republic in 1836. My grandfather was at Sam Houston's side at the battle of San Jacinto. Texas became a state in 1845, long before I was born. I am as American as you."

"I never thought otherwise, not that it would have made a difference. Tell me about the man from Santa Fe. Why was he interested in your property? Did he say?"

"He represents people who might be interested in buying the land. Padre showed him the boundaries, which are marked by stones and trees and such."

"Did he make an offer?"

"No, but he hinted that it might be enough for Padre to start a new life on better land that will grow something more than cactuses."

"Did he give his name?"

"Ignacio. Nothing else. He said he would be back after he reported to his bosses in Santa Fe. A month, maybe two. He was in his early thirties, I would guess, and well spoken. He spoke English like that was his first language. Quite handsome, I might add."

Conor was discomfited by this news. Was the Santa Fe Ring stretching its tentacles toward the Guadalupe?

Maria said, "You did not answer my question about your intentions."

Conor sighed. "I must think about it. I want to be honest with you, and you are entitled to know."

She said, "I am going home. I can saddle my horse without your help. If you wish to marry me, come to our house and ask me. If I am agreeable, then you may ask Padre for my hand. If not, this will be my last visit. I will miss you, but less than you might think." She started for the door.

35

Conor stood and followed her. "Maria, we should talk some more. It's dark. You should not be riding home alone. Wait till morning."

She paused and turned toward him, her eyes smoldering with anger. "I am finished waiting, and I am done being your whore for a lousy dollar. I told you how it must be. Just decide." She spun, heading out the door and slamming it behind her.

Chapter 5

KAT RYAN HAD lost count of the days since she departed Albuquerque following her jail break. She thought it was approaching a week now, but it felt like more. She knew she had been travelling more south than east. Still, she suspected she was off course for an El Paso destination. She had been fearful of losing sight of the watercourse which she assumed would eventually lead her to civilization, and at the very least, assured her and the roan mare, which she had taken to calling "Toughie," of ample drinking water.

The mare seemed to be holding up well enough, ferreting out grass patches along the creek banks. As for herself, she knew that she was on the brink of starvation. She had killed, skinned, and roasted two rabbits after her scant provisions had been consumed several days out. This had been supplemented by a few handfuls of bitter juniper berries and the roots and leaves of occasional dandelions that fought for their share of the increasingly sparse growing spaces.

She was growing weaker now as each day passed. This morning, it had taken all her strength to insert her foot in the stirrup and lift herself into the saddle. A wave of weakness had struck her, and she almost fainted before she nudged Toughie onto the trail.

It was midafternoon and she was nearer the mountains that had been nothing but dark shadows against the sunrise this morning. Distances could be deceptive when it came to mountains, though. She could be anywhere from five miles to as many as twenty from their base, she supposed. She liked the idea of seeking refuge in the mountains, but she knew no more about survival there than on the desert lands. She speculated these mountains might be the Guadalupe. She had been fascinated with maps as a schoolchild and had pretty much memorized the maps of New Mexico Territory and West Texas. She just was uncertain where she was located on the map now.

If these were the Guadalupe mountains, she would need to abandon the creek and angle southwest. Perhaps she would pick up a wagon trail that would lead there. And what would she do when she arrived penniless and starving? She had a good horse, saddle, and tack if someone would buy the merchandise without asking too many questions. She winced at the thought of giving up Toughie. She had become attached to this horse that was not even rightfully hers, but she would do what she had to do to survive.

Kat realized now, however, that she had been so focused on escape she had not given much thought to what she was going to do with her newfound freedom. Was she simply on a journey to another kind of hell?

One decision was suddenly made for her when she tossed a look over her shoulder and saw dust clouds kicking up on the trail behind her. There were several riders she guessed, certainly more than one. Of course, it could be anyone, but she struggled to think of a favorable possibility among outlaws, Apache, or Buford Walters and a posse.

She reined the mare off the trail, picked up the pace, and headed for the mountains. Fortunately, the mount had been given ample rest and not been pushed the last few days. The riders behind her rode like they were on a mission, which gave her increased cause for worry.

As her mount raced across the barren flatlands toward the mountains, Kat tossed a look over her shoulder and saw that the riders had left the creek trail and were following her, confirming that she was their quarry.

Off the trail, the pursuers had spread out some, and she could now count three distinct swirling clouds of billowing dust. If she could beat them to the mountains and find higher ground with stone cover, she might have a chance to hold them off. Better yet, she might find a hiding place there, although she feared she might be forced to abandon Toughie.

Alone in the mountains without a mount. She erased that thought from her mind. It was too late to plan beyond the next minute. She tapped her moccasined heels to the mare's flanks and urged her ahead and nearly toppled from the saddle when the roan shot ahead like a bullet fired from a rifle. The horse's speed surprised her because she had not pushed the critter to this point.

She was encouraged when she realized the mountain foothills were nearer than she had estimated. Within a half hour she hoped she could start seeking cover. She turned in the saddle again to check on the riders. They had not closed the gap, but one rider had disappeared. Her eyes scanned the landscape in all directions, but she could not see any sign of the missing rider. If he had just fallen back, perhaps with a lame horse, that was all to the good. Kat doubted she had a guardian angel watching over her, however. She feared she had not seen the last of that rider.

Abruptly the ground turned rougher, creased now by dry ravines and gulches and marred by occasional rocky hillocks and dunes. The footing more treacherous, her pace slowed, but she figured her followers would be slowed some, too. The ground was gradually sloping higher into the foothills and soon high, steep rock walls and ragged escarpments confronted her. There were breaks in those walls, though, a good number of them. A rider and horse could escape through one of those, but which one and where would it take her?

The two riders were still coming on, but they did not seem to be pushing their mounts, only concerned with keeping her in sight. And where was the third rider? As she approached the rising walls ahead, she could discern no trail that led her into the higher reaches of the mountains, which stretched now as far as the eye could see. She reined the mare toward what appeared to be a schism in the wall.

As they broke through the opening, she found herself in a narrow canyon with sheer, towering walls broken intermittently by what seemed to be jagged holes that she guessed to be cave entrances. She could see no exit ahead and no stream that might escort her somewhere and doubted it would lead her through the mountains in any event. She went deeper into the canyon searching for a likely place to make a stand. It worried her that darkness was coming on, possibly prematurely because of the shadowy canyon and the rising mountain above which would block the sun's last light.

Perhaps the black of night could work to her advantage, but she shivered at the notion of a night in this place stalked by the demons who were pursuing her. She would prefer a showdown in the sunlight, death, if that was her destiny, with the sun shining on her face and a chance for her spirit to find its way out of here.

As she rode along the edge of the northeasterly canyon wall, she spied her fortress just ahead, a mass of stones and boulders that had obviously been deposited from a landslide some years past. If she could nest there, she might fend off the men for a spell, maybe find out who they were and why they were trailing her, not that it mattered all that much.

She staked out Toughie in a patch of brown grass fifty or sixty feet beyond the boulders to keep her out of the likely path of gunfire. The mare had to be thirsty, and it saddened Kat that she could not find the horse a source of water. She had only a third of a canteen full herself and was fighting off the temptation to quench her own thirst. She scrambled upon the landslide remains and found a cluster of boulders that would offer cover from three sides. The canyon wall would not be far behind her.

She leaned her Winchester against one of the boulders and surveyed her surroundings. She had lost sight of the two riders for a spell but now she saw them not more than a hundred yards distant. They had dismounted, and it appeared a bulky man might be looking her way with a spyglass. It could be Acting City Marshal Buford Walters, given his size, but she could not make out a face. The other man stood back some distance suggesting that the big man was in charge.

Feeling a surge of energy at the prospect of confrontation, Kat snatched up her rifle and dropped down behind the boulders where she would be blocked from a telescope's view. She peered between gaps in the rocks to watch the stalkers. The two men mounted their horses now and were riding slowly in her direction. They reined in their mounts when they were within twenty-five yards of her stone fortress. Even in the fading light, she recognized Walters now with his pendulous belly and shaggy mustache and a gray Stetson pulled low on his forehead.

The other rider she could not recall having ever seen before unless it was without the red beard that covered his face. Both were easily within her shooting range, and Buford Walters confirmed her low opinion of his intelligence by moving in so close. He was the easier of the targets, so she levered a cartridge into the rifle chamber and raised herself up on one knee, lifting her head and shoulders above the top of the rocks, and aimed.

Walters yelled, "Hold up, missy. Hear me out or you will wish you had."

She froze. "Say your piece, buffoon." She supposed she was not helping her case by the taunt, but she could not hide her contempt for the man. Besides, he intended to take her back dead or alive unless he died first.

"Now you just put that rifle down and come out peaceful-like. You don't give us no trouble, and I promise the law will go easy on you, get you back home to your man in no time."

She squeezed the trigger, the rifle cracked, and Walters howled, sliding off his mount. He was on his knees on the ground, grasping the side of his face. Damn, she had hit the fool, but it wasn't a kill shot. She was out of practice. She readied the rifle for another shot, one that would take this man out of her life forever, but she had to take cover when the other rider started firing her way.

Walters hollered, "You just signed your death warrant, bitch."

She rose and got off a wild shot, ducking back behind the boulders as the two men both started firing at her. It appeared that her shot at Walters had been wasted. She decided that darkness was her only friend now. If she could hold Walters and his companion off another half hour or so, perhaps she could slip away to Toughie and make a break for it.

Of course, she had not a clue where her destination might be. She was certain, though, that not even Buford Walters would be stupid enough to give her another clear shot. She could not withstand a siege if pinned down here. Her water was nearly depleted. She could not let the horse die of thirst. She figured she could walk to the mare and get into the saddle, but that would suck out what little strength she had left.

"Kat Ryan, do you hear me?"

Buford again. She did not reply.

"You hear. I know you do. I got something to say, and then I ain't talking no more. This feller I got with me is Joe Hadley. He's a deputy U.S. Marshal. You are dealing with big trouble if you resist arrest. Kill a deputy marshal, and your neck gets stretched. If you want to surrender, just throw down the gun and walk out with your hands in the air."

Her first instinct was to fire the rifle, but the sun had just disappeared over the mountain tops, and the black shroud of nightfall was descending on the canyon quickly. She would be shooting at shadows. Also, she decided it was better to keep them guessing. She wondered if Buford was lying about the other man being a deputy U.S. Marshal. And did it matter? She could not see how her law problems could get much worse anyhow. She doubted Buford would want to take her back alive, but if Hadley was a federal law officer, he might see that she was not harmed when taken into custody.

She started to get up and make a dash for her horse when something wrapped around her neck and yanked her backward. Like a vice, it tightened. She could not breathe, and she was too weak to do anything but flail helplessly. She could no longer take in air, and her head felt like it was spinning. This must be what it is like to die, she thought before blackness overtook her.

Chapter 6

Kat heard voices and wondered for a minute if she was in the afterlife. Figuring she had no chance for heaven, she assumed it must be hell, and the soreness in her neck and shoulders felt like it. But she recognized Buford Walters's booming voice, and she doubted he had completed his journey to that destination just yet.

Buford was obviously quarreling with somebody, and she kept her eyes closed and listened.

Walters said, "Joe, you got no say in this. I hired you on to help me find this woman. I decide what to do with her."

The other man said, "You ain't even got no authority here. You ain't even an acting city marshal since you got fired. Bet you won't be a deputy for long. You said we was just going to take Kat Ryan back to Albuquerque for the law to deal with her. I needed work so I said I'd help.

I ain't never raped or beat a woman. I done some low things but not that low."

"Then get your ass out. I don't need you no more. Me and Cold Eyes will finish the job."

"Are you taking her back to Albuquerque?"

"Maybe. In due time. We're going to make camp here for a few days and rest up some, have some fun."

"You still owe me a double eagle. Give me my gold piece and I will be on my way."

"You didn't finish the job."

"You got the woman. I'm finished. I want my money."

"You going to keep your mouth shut?"

"If the woman comes back unharmed."

"Here's your damned double eagle."

There was a prolonged silence except for footsteps on the rocky ground, which Kat assumed were those of the man who had demanded his payment. Then the roar of two gunshots echoed through the canyon walls, and she heard the moans of a man in agony . . . and then a third shot.

"Get him out of here, Cold Eyes," Walters said. "You can have his horse and tack, but I want his money. It come from me in the first place. That critter's worth five times what he's got in money."

"I take horse but want woman, too."

"You can have her after I'm done with her. She's mine tonight and tomorrow. You can have what's left of her and then take her to Mexico and sell her to a whorehouse like we talked."

"Not like wait. You hurt too much, and I not find buyer."

"I won't kill her, and she will still be able to spread her legs for you. By the time you get her to Mexico, she'll be fit for sale. She's a beauty, if you get her cleaned up some, maybe steal a dress someplace to make her look more like a woman, she will sell. Of course, she could pass for a kid. I hear they pay extra for them."

Kat opened her eyes just enough to survey her surroundings. She lay on a bed of small stones and sand near a cluster of creosote bushes. A small campfire spat and crackled no more than twenty feet away. A squat, long-haired man, hair bound by the cloth headband worn by many Indians of the Southwest and wearing calf-high moccasins, stood on one side of the fire. Walters stood on the other facing him. The body of the man just shot was sprawled not more than a dozen feet beyond him.

The Indian said, "Woman wake."

How did he know? He turned her direction and was walking toward her, and she squeezed her eyes shut.

She sensed him kneeling beside her before he tore back her shirt and placed cold fingers on her breasts.

"Open eyes," he commanded.

She obeyed and was met by an appraising stare that made her heart skip a beat. Cold Eyes. She understood the reason for his name instantly. He was obviously the man who had slipped in behind her and choked her into unconsciousness. His fingers were now traveling the length of her body, pausing at her crotch before working down her inner thighs. Thankfully, he had not stripped her of her garments, but she knew that would be happening too soon. It sounded like Buford expected first poke, though.

The Indian stood up and turned away, addressing Buford Walters. "Woman like little girl. Tits like pinyon nuts. Skinny like starving cougar. All bones, no meat."

"Don't matter none to me. Now, you git. Set up camp within hollering distance after you get rid of our friend Joe someplace."

"Do not like this place. Ghost no like Apache. Me Chiricahua. Guadalupe home to Mescalero. Then ghost come, most leave."

"You ain't making no sense. Ain't no such things as ghosts. Now get rid of that body and keep your distance till I'm finished with the woman."

"Take horse. You kill man. I not take body. Ghost maybe follow." He untied the dead man's horse from a low-hanging cedar branch, mounted his own and led it away. "Wait till morning. Be back for woman. Maybe take with me."

Walters yelled after him, "You no-good, worthless redskin. You can have your turn with the woman, but you ain't taking her that soon. Do you hear?"

Kat heard him mumbling to himself for several minutes before he sauntered over to where she lay with a big grin spread across his face. "Well, howdy do, Miss Ryan, or is it Missus Gaynor? Old Louie always claimed you was his wife in all the ways that counted. Don't know what the hell that meant."

Her mind raced. Normally, she could outrun this lard barrel, leave him behind in the dust, but she barely had the strength to walk. She felt so dizzy, she was not certain she could even get to her feet. And if she did escape, he would yell for the Indian. If she could just figure out how to kill the oaf.

"Hey, girl. Say something. We got to get reacquainted here. You made me look like the town clown when you broke jail and took my horse. I'll never live it down, may even lose my deputy's job when the marshal gets through his trial, if he gets off for killing that other feller."

She still refused to respond until the toe of his booted foot drove into her ribs, and she could not help screaming at the excruciating pain.

He reached down, clutched her hair and yanked her to her feet like a rag doll. He tore off her shirt, exposing her breasts and torso. "Now you listen to me. You are going to come with me to where I've got my bedroll laid out. Then you are going to get out of them britches and get ready for a treat."

She could not restrain herself. "Good luck. I doubt if you can even find your tiny pizzle in that lard you carry on your belly."

His fist drove into her nose, and she heard the crack before she felt it cave, and she fainted again. When she awakened, cold and shivering, she realized that she lay naked on some blankets. Groggily, she tried to recall what she was doing here. Then she saw Buford standing above her, naked below his waist, struggling now to get onto the ground beside her to take care of business. She closed her eyes; she did not have the strength to resist. He could have her, and she hoped he killed her afterward. If not, she would find a way to kill herself. It no longer mattered. She was just tired. She sent her mind to another place.

She thought she heard screaming and then a choking, coughing sound like a person vomiting, but she could not open her eyes and did not care. Whatever nightmare had come to her could not be worse than the reality of what she faced. Sleep eased the pain, so she claimed it.

Chapter 7

LOAFER'S INCESSANT BARKING rousted Roman Hayes from his sleep. Usually, the big dog shared the bed and fought with him over sleeping space during the night's slumber. There was a hinged hatch in the back door that allowed Loafer to squeeze in and out during the night. Doc did not like the arrangement, since a raccoon wandered down from the mountains to pay a visit on occasion, and, of course, Loafer never challenged the visitor. Still, it was better than getting out of bed every time the dog took a notion to relieve himself or seek another sleeping place.

He lit the kerosene lamp and checked his timepiece on the bedstand. It was almost five o'clock, and sunrise was likely an hour away. He lived an uncharted life, anyhow, never knowing when the sporadic patient would show up at his door or when a traveler or one of the locals might need supplies. He got up and pulled on his britches, snatched yesterday's cotton shirt from the back of the nearby chair, then socks and boots. He would clean up and change later after morning chores.

Now his priority was to see what was troubling the dang dog. The racket was coming from out front, so he hurried to the door and stepped out onto the veranda. Loafer was standing just outside the doorway next to what appeared to be a bundle of blankets. Then Doc saw the long, black hair and a bloody face half-hidden by the blankets. He rushed to the heap and knelt, pulling the cocoonlike blankets back. A naked girl, quickly amending his thoughts to "woman" upon a more thorough examination of his emaciated visitor. Apparently unconscious, but the gentle rise and fall of her chest told him she was breathing quite normally.

He detected no injuries beyond red and swollen ribs and a nose that was obviously broken, the flesh surrounding it bruised and puffy. Purplish-blue skin about her cheek and one eye suggested that this was not the first time she had been assaulted.

A horse whinnied and he looked up and for the first time noticed two saddled horses, a red roan mare and a sorrel gelding hitched to the long rail that fronted the Triad. What in blazes? He shook his head in disbelief. He needed to get this young woman inside and on one of his two patient beds. He should examine the ribs more close-ly and tend to the mangled nose, get her into one of the cotton robes. In her near-starved condition, he doubted she would weigh a hundred pounds, an easy enough load for him twenty years ago, more of a challenge these days.

He got to his feet and started to bend his knees to lift her when he saw the deerskin pouch a few feet from her head. He picked it up and loosened the drawstring to peer in. He had a strong stomach, but it was the sur-prise that came near to making him gag. Two human tongues, brown-crusted now from the blood that had covered them, a silver deputy city marshal's badge, and a rawhide cord strung through a single bear claw and two gold Spanish doubloons, the message that the Ghost of the Guadalupe had visited this morning, no doubt deliv-ering the injured young woman and horses. That would explain why Loafer had not started barking till his friend disappeared.

He closed the pouch, deciding he would deal with the contents later, perhaps putting the tongues in a jar of alcohol till he otherwise disposed of them. For now, he stuffed the pouch in his trouser pocket. Clumsily, he scooped the woman into his arms, feeling his back pop when he straightened, and carried her into the house with Loafer trailing. She was thrashing some and her head tossing about by the time he deposited her on the bed.

He pulled a cover over her after he had her settled in the bed. He glanced at her face and was surprised to find her eyes were open and that she was studying him with curiosity. "Good morning," he said.

"Thirsty," she said in a raspy whisper.

"Quickly solved." He turned and went to the sink in the residential section of the Triad, pumped a big glass of cold water from his handpump, and returned to the patient room. He set the glass down on the bedside table, retrieved another pillow to help lift her head and shoulders higher for a drink. "Can you hold the glass, or do you want my help?"

"I can try." She took the glass in trembling fingers but got it to her lips. She sipped at the water, then began to drink greedily, downing the contents. She handed him the glass. "More?"

"You should wait a bit. You may not hold it down if you drink too much, too fast."

"Where am I? Who are you?"

"I am Doctor Roman Hayes, but you may call me 'Doc.' This is my office. I also live in this building and operate a trading post of sorts. I call this place the Triad and we are at the base of the Guadalupe Mountains."

"How did I get here?"

"I found you on the Triad veranda this morning. My dog Loafer announced your presence there. This is Loafer." He gestured toward the dog, which was watching with interest.

"I am very confused. I need time to think."

"There will be plenty of time to sort this all out later. If you will permit me, I would like to examine you more carefully and see if we can do something to make you feel better."

"I guess that would be okay. I just realized I don't have a stitch on. But you are a doctor, so I suppose that's alright." Her voice was noticeably stronger now.

He plucked the gown he had set aside for her from the wall peg near the bed. "Can you slip into this? I can step out of the room if you like."

She raised herself up on her elbows and dropped back down. "You had better help me. I am so weak."

He propped her up while she slipped her arms through the sleeves. Then he tugged it about her gaunt form and helped her lie back. He could see that the effort exhausted her.

"When was the last time you ate?"

"I don't remember. But right now, I am thirsty."

Doc retrieved another glass of water and assisted her with drinking this time. "Drink slowly," he admonished. "You must be in a lot of pain. Tell me about it."

"Well, my nose is the worst. I touched it and almost screamed. It hurts clear up into my eyes, but I could be dead. I can't complain."

"What hit you?"

"A man's fist."

"The same man who caused the bruising on your cheek and eye?"

"No."

"I see." But he did not. He decided it was best not to press for details just yet. It was irrelevant. For the present, she was a patient, nothing more. "Your name. What would you like to have me call you?"

She seemed to be pondering the question. Obviously, she was not ready to disclose her full name.

"Kat. You may call me Kat."

"Very well, Kat. I noticed the ribs on your left side are red and swollen. I am guessing you were kicked, and not by a horse."

"Yes. They hurt terribly when I move."

"I would like to examine them. Is that alright?"

"Yes."

He lifted the left side of her gown enough to expose the injured ribs and pressed his fingers against the swollen area. No flesh to cushion a blow. The ribs were perfectly defined, and he could feel no break or separation. They were likely cracked or badly bruised. Time was the only effective cure.

"I can wrap the ribs, but it could take several months for the pain to disappear. After a week, they will feel better each day. Your nose is what we should talk about. It is obviously broken. It will be quite twisted if I don't set it. The bone and cartilage must be realigned, and then I have some new tape that will help stabilize it, but like the ribs, healing will take some time. The pain should ease a lot in a few days' time. I can give you laudanum that will help the pain for both ribs and nose, but I don't like to use more than necessary or any longer than we absolutely must."

"So how long does this take?"

"Five minutes, but the manipulation is very painful. I should give you laudanum a few hours before. I could use chloroform to put you to sleep. That would eliminate the pain during the procedure, but in your weakened condition I would prefer not to do that."

"Do it now. Please."

"I told you it—"

"Now. I want it done."

Doc had done this many times without anesthesia during the war, often a nose smashed by a Yankee's rifle butt. There was no time for the niceties of anesthesia in those days. He shrugged. "Very well. You tell me to stop if you cannot handle the pain, and then we will try something else."

"That will not happen."

It was an awkward position to work from, but he bent over the bed, cupped the nose in both hands and began the manipulations with his fingers. She did not surrender a groan or whimper. When he had finished, he straightened up and saw that she had fainted. He hoped that had happened early on.

He left the room to find his tape and some cotton to stuff in her nose. When he returned, she was awake again.

As he applied the surgical tape, she said, "Thank you. It feels better already."

"I will prepare a dose of laudanum for you shortly."

"Not now. I don't have any money to pay you for this, but I will someday, I promise."

He chuckled, "Don't worry about it."

"Is there any way I could get something to eat?"

"Of course, I just thought you might not feel like it yet. I haven't had breakfast myself. I can offer eggs, bacon, and day-old biscuits. I've got butter and honey for the biscuits. Would you like coffee?"

"I usually don't drink coffee, but today it would be nice."

"Well, why don't you sleep a bit, and I'll bring breakfast in when it's ready. I will get the cookstove going, and then I should put the horses up and take care of some chores before I prepare breakfast. I will leave Loafer here to look after you. He's obviously quite interested in our visitor."

"You mentioned horses. What horses?"

"There were two left here when someone left you on the veranda last night."

"I don't remember that. Is one a red roan mare?"

"Yes, and a sorrel gelding."

"The roan is mine. Her name is Toughie."

Doc thought the name would fit well for the owner, too. He started for the door when she stopped him.

"And, Doc, there might be a loaded Winchester in the scabbard on the mare. Could you bring that in before you take her?"

Chapter 8

CONOR BYRNE RODE up to the Triad astride his gray gelding after Doc had finished chores and was returning to his patient. He waited on the veranda for Conor to hitch the horse and join him. "Thought I might not see you for a few days," Doc said.

"Checked out the cattle in the canyon at sunrise, scattered about in three or four small herd groups. I guess that's why they call them herd animals. They aren't inclined to wander off alone. I didn't see anything that needed my attention so figured I would make a trip over here to talk more about my moving the salt north to Roswell Smith's Trading Post. If I can hire on a man to help, I'm thinking I might go ahead and move the load in the next few days."

"That's fine with me. I'm betting you haven't had breakfast yet, and we're closing in on nine o'clock. Why don't you come in and have some breakfast. I am putting together some eggs and bacon anyhow—and some left-over biscuits. Last of my eggs, though. Maria's supposed to bring eggs by today. I don't suppose you have seen her yet?"

Conor joined him on the veranda. "Uh . . . as a matter of fact, I have. I had just as soon not run into her just now."

"I see." Doc did not pursue the topic. It was none of his business. "Well, I've got a patient to check on. I'll slip into my office and be over shortly if you want to make yourself at home in my quarters."

"I smell smoke. You must have the cookstove nearly ready. I'll get breakfast started if you like."

"That would be appreciated. You know your way around the kitchen."

The men parted, going through the separate entrances. When Doc walked into the patient's room to check on Kat, he found her asleep on her back, the rifle cradled in one arm. It concerned him that she might be expecting unwelcome company. Loafer sat next to the bed like a sentry. The dog seemed strangely infatuated by the uninvited visitor.

She would recover from her injuries and needed to be fattened up some, but if she stayed on for more than a few days, he would insist on knowing more about her dilemma and the risks assumed by those helping her. He decided to let her sleep till breakfast was ready. His bet was that a decent meal and mug of coffee would do better for Kat than any medicine he might offer.

When he entered the kitchen area at one end of a long, narrow room that also served as a parlor, Doc saw that Conor already had coffee brewing and had laid out strips of bacon in the big frying pan. "You don't waste time, do you, Irishman?"

"Try not to. How do want the eggs? Scrambled? Sunny side up?"

"I've got some of yesterday's biscuits in the covered dish under the cupboard. I'll get those warmed up. I'd say sunny side up. After I add a little honey, I like to dip my biscuit in the egg yolk. We'll need to make enough for my patient."

"I thought you were just seeing somebody. I didn't realize you had somebody in a hospital bed."

"Yeah, I'd just as well tell you the story about what happened before sunrise this morning. The Ghost left me some gifts."

"Gifts?"

"Yep. A young gal, two horses and two tongues."

Conor turned to him and said, "You've got my attention. I am listening."

As they finished preparing breakfast, Doc recited a short version of his morning awakening. "She will be fine in time, at least physically. Sometimes these things can mess up your head. I don't know what she's been through."

Conor said, "The tongue business gives me the chills."

"They are in a jar in the clinic surgery if you wish to examine them."

"I think I'll pass on that opportunity. Do you think it is like a scalp—that somebody removed tongues instead of hair from an enemy?"

"I have no idea. I am going to take a plate and cup of coffee to the young lady. You can ponder this while I'm gone. Go ahead and eat while everything is hot. Keep a tin plateful for me on top of the stove."

When he entered his patient's room, he was pleased to see that she was sitting up in bed with pillows propped against her back. She watched him silently as he set the plate and coffee mug on the side table.

"It appears you slept well during my absence," he said. "How is the pain? Do you need a dose of laudanum?"

"No, the pain is tolerable, and I did sleep very well. I think I woke up because I smelled the bacon."

"Can you handle the coffee cup if I leave it on the table? And feed yourself?"

"I think so. My fingers are shaky, but they will get the fork to my mouth. Could you put the plate on my lap?"

"Of course. I brought a towel I can place under the tin plate. Are you certain you don't need assistance?"

"I will be fine. Everything smells wonderful. There won't be any left. Is that butter and honey on the biscuits?"

"Yes. I hope that's alright."

"I will love it. Thank you." She hesitated. "I heard a voice coming from someplace. A man's voice. I think you were speaking with him. Who is it?"

She seemed worried about the voice. "His name is Conor Byrne, a friend, neighbor, and occasional business partner. He helped with breakfast. He stopped by to talk some business, but I told him I had a visitor and how I found you on the veranda outside the Triad."

"You have not told me much about it. I have no idea how I got here."

"We will talk after you eat and when you feel strong enough. I respect folks' privacy, but especially considering your concern about having a rifle at hand, I must know enough to decide if there are precautions I should be taking. I will not be throwing you to the wolves, I promise, but you must tell me how you came to be in this condition."

"I guess I can see that. I must think about this."

"Do you see that cowbell and rope behind you? Give that a few yanks if you need help. I will hear it. I won't be leaving the building until after we speak again."

When he returned to the kitchen, he took his plate off the stove and sat down. He forgot to grab the coffee pot and mug, but Conor got to his feet and tended to the oversight. As he placed the mug on the two-chaired table and poured the coffee, Conor said, "You are worried."

Doc said, "Yeah, I am. I'm concerned that the appearance of this young woman could get complicated and dangerous. I think life is going to change with her showing up here, but I won't be losing sleep over it. We will figure it out when we know what we are dealing with. I hope she will tell me more later this morning. She's struggling between truth and lie right now."

"How will you know whether she is lying or not?"

"No particular magic, but I suspect it won't be that hard to sort out."

"Aren't you curious about the owners of the tongues?"

"Yes, I am a mite."

"Do you think the Ghost killed some men?"

"It's possible, maybe worse if he did not. I would like to see if I can pick up a trail and find out where all this took place and locate any bodies."

"Why don't I ride over to Diego Munoz's place and see if I can hire him on for some tracking. He will do it for a bit of nothing just to get away from Lucia and that passel of kids for a spell. The woman's a taskmistress, I tell you. No siestas for the poor devil. If he tells her he's got paying work, she will tell him to go."

Diego's mother was Mescalero Apache, and he had lived with her mother's band for extended periods while growing up until the Mescalero started vacating their homelands and moving to the reservation. He was no more than thirty now but had scouted for the Army during the Comanche wars and that was when Conor first encountered the half-blood who spoke three languages—English, Spanish, and Apache, with different degrees of fluency.

Doc envied folks, and there were many in the Southwest, who were fluent in multiple languages. Of necessity, he had learned enough rudimentary Spanish to communicate passably with those friends and neighbors who could not speak English, but fluency evaded him. He knew that Conor had learned Spanish in college but had yet to master the conversational Mexican version. He often grumbled that the "Mexican folks speak too fast."

"Why don't you do that? I will pay him two dollars each day or part of one. Lucia will make him go for that. Both will be happy."

"I will head out now. I don't want to be here if Maria shows up. I will swing by Diego's on my way back to my place. I need to get my bedroll and put together a few supplies in case we are out more than a day. Maybe I will offer Diego the job helping me take the load to Roswell, too. He's a good man, and I enjoy his company."

"Okay by me. You're the one making the trip."

Conor headed for the door. "I'll grab a bite to eat at home and be back after lunch."

Chapter 9

KAT WAS SURPRISED to find herself hungry again when Doctor Hayes came into her room. "I have a beef stew on the stove and some fresh bread and apple pie a young neighbor lady left off this morning," he said. "I will bring you lunch shortly."

"Could I just get up and join you?"

"Do you feel strong enough?"

"I might need some help to the table. I would like to use the privy first, though."

"As I told you, there is a chamber pot under the bed. The walk to the privy might be a bit much."

"Please. I don't want you emptying the chamber pot."

She swung her legs off the bed and almost screamed when the pain ripped through her side but dug her teeth into her lower lip and vowed to endure it. The doctor extended his hand and helped pull her to her feet, then held her arm as they walked slowly to the privy some distance behind the building. Afterward, she washed her hands with a bar of lye soap at the kitchen sink while he pumped water.

When she was seated at the kitchen table, he ladled steaming stew into her bowl. "There is plenty of stew if you can eat more. Help yourself to the fresh bread and the butter bowl. Save room for pie."

He sat down and joined her. She took a bite of stew, and then another and another. "My goodness, this is delicious," she said.

"It has got a bit of everything in it. Taters, corn, a few tomatoes, lots of beans, whatever I could find."

"Cow hands call that 'son-of-a-bitch stew.'"

"Uh, yes, I guess they do."

"My name is Kathleen Ryan." She continued eating.

"Irish."

"Yes, my father was born in Ireland. He came to America as a small child. My mother was Mexican but born in what is now New Mexico Territory."

He gave her a tender smile that melted her. "So do I still call you Kat?"

"Yes, that is what my mother called me. My father insisted on Kathleen."

"Kat it shall be."

"You will not think much of me when I tell you my story. But you are entitled to the truth. You have been drawn into something that was none of your affair."

"I think it is in the book of Matthew that you will find the verse, 'Judge not, and ye be not judged.' Similar words appear in at least a half dozen places in the Bible and been repeated by many far wiser than I am. An Indian proverb says not to judge another man until you have walked two moons in his moccasins. I have needed this consideration more than once in my lifetime and have come to believe this."

"Are you a preacher, too?"

He chuckled, "Far from it."

"I am from Albuquerque. I escaped jail there."

"I see."

He did not seem surprised, but she decided he was a man not easily shocked and one who would not betray his cards in a poker game. She finished her stew. "I know I am being a pig, but could I have another bowl?"

He took her bowl and filled it from the pot on the stove. "You are not being a pig. You are doing just what the doctor ordered. This is how you get your strength back."

While she continued to eat, she said, "I tried to kill the man I lived with. He claimed I was his wife, but I was not."

She told Doctor Hayes about the circumstances that had placed her in her former home with Louie Gaynor, about the beatings he had inflicted, and the details of her escape from jail. She did not know why but she instinctively trusted this man and could not turn off the spigot that turned out her words. "So, you see, I am wanted for attempted murder, horse theft, breaking jail, maybe a dozen crimes. You are sharing a meal with a notorious, wanted outlaw. I could eat my pie now."

He smiled. "And a hungry outlaw, to boot." He scooped a piece of pie from its pan, put it on a dish, and slid it to her.

"Thank you." She took her fork and attacked the pie, stopping only to sip her coffee.

"May we talk about last night?"

"I don't see why not, but I don't remember a lot. As I told you, I rode for I don't know how many days, following a creek for most of that. Then, late yesterday afternoon I saw three riders behind me. I had seen the mountains in the distance for some time. I knew they could be the Guadalupe, but I was uncertain. I veered off the trail and headed for the mountains, figuring that the riders would not follow if they were not pursuing me, but if they did, I might find a hiding place there."

Doc said, "And they followed you?"

"Yes, as I feared. To make this short, I entered a canyon and found a place to make a stand. Two of the men found me—one rider had disappeared earlier. One of the men was Buford Walters, the deputy city marshal I had escaped from. He claimed that the other man—he had a red beard—was a deputy United States marshal. I think the name he gave was Joe Hadley. I didn't believe him, but I can't say for sure. I do know he is dead."

"You killed him?"

"No, but I am getting ahead of the story. We fired some shots back and forth, and I grazed Buford's cheek with a slug, but that ended when somebody took me from behind and choked me till I passed out. When I woke up, there were three men around a fire, but I closed my eyes right away and just listened. Buford and the so-called U.S. Marshal were quarreling. Hadley did not want any part of Buford's plans for me and was demanding his money. I think Buford gave it to him and then shot him in the back as he was walking away. I can't say exactly how it happened, but I am certain Buford killed the man and took his money."

"And what about the other man?" Doc asked.

"It turns out he was an Apache. I think Chiricahua was mentioned. Buford called him Cold Eyes, and when he came over to look at me, I understood why. His glare froze my blood. Anyway, he and Buford quarreled some because the Indian wanted me, too. They finally agreed that the Indian would go elsewhere for the night and take Hadley's body. The Indian got to keep Hadley's horse and tack and apparently could have me when Buford was done with me. There was talk about selling me in Mexico."

"So that finally left you alone with the city marshal?"

"Yes, deputy, actually. During their quarrel, I heard Hadley say something about Buford being demoted to deputy and probably on his way to being fired, I suppose because of me. Anyhow, that's when I got kicked in the ribs and my nose smashed. I wasn't giving in to him without a fight. I don't remember much after that. I know something pulled Buford off me, and I heard him screaming and gurgling and making awful sounds."

"You didn't see who came to your assistance then?"

"No. I vaguely recall someone picking me up in their arms. I opened my eyes once, sensing strong arms cradling me and the movement of a horse as we rode. My face seemed to be covered by a cascade of filmy, white hair. I decided I must be dead and closed my eyes and dropped off again. That's the last I remember before waking up in the hospital bed."

"Wait here a moment," Doc said. He got up and left the room while she finished her pie and coffee.

When he returned, he laid a deputy city marshal's badge and a bear claw on a rawhide string on the table in front of her. "These were among the contents of a little bag left on the veranda with you."

"I suppose the badge was Buford's. I couldn't say, but I would guess the bear claw belonged to the Indian."

"There were also two gold Spanish doubloons."

"That means nothing to me."

"That's what the Ghost of the Guadalupe leaves when he visits my place. I will explain later."

"Ghost? You aren't serious."

"You will hear more about this legend if you stay here, but the Ghost was without a doubt in my mind your rescuer last night."

"This is getting creepy."

"Do you have a strong stomach?" Doc asked.

"Full, but my stomach hasn't felt this good for days."

"That's not exactly what I meant. But I am not going to hide anything from you. Two human tongues were in that little bag, also. I will spare you the sight, but they are in a jar in a cupboard temporarily."

She grimaced and felt the slightest queasiness in her stomach. "I can't imagine what that means. I suppose Buford's tongue is one. Does that tell us he is dead?"

"It doesn't really do that. We don't even know for certain whose tongues they are. Conor Byrne is taking a tracker with him this afternoon to see if they can find where the struggle took place, hopefully locate any bodies or make some guesses as to what happened."

"And if they find bodies?"

"They will bury them, after attempting to identify them, which should not be difficult if the scavengers have not already done too much damage."

"I am tired. Could I return to my bed?"

"Certainly. I will help you. You must be having a lot of pain. Would you let me give you some laudanum?"

Her hunger satisfied, the pain, especially in her nose and face, was on the edge of unbearable. "Yes, could we try a light dose?"

"Of course. We want to relieve the pain, but I do not wish for you to become dependent on it. I doubt if that is a risk in your case the way I have had to coax you to take anything. And, Kat, if it will ease your mind any, you may stay here for as long as you wish. You may occupy the patient space for now, but if it is needed for others, there is a spare bedroom in the residence area—with a bolt lock on the sleeper's side."

She found the latter reassurance funny. She could not think of another man she trusted these days, but for some unexplainable reason, she had absolutely no fear of Doctor Roman Hayes.

Chapter 10

CONOR MET DOC on the Triad veranda, where the owner was waiting in his favorite rocker. "Diego will be along soon," he told Doc. "I decided to bring along a packhorse for the supplies. It's a light load, but I didn't know what I might be hauling back."

"No bodies. I see you've got two shovels. Bury any bodies right there. Get their descriptions in your head as best you can, but I don't want anybody buried on my place if we can avoid it, and the distance to tote a rotting corpse someplace else is too great. Besides, I think we want to put as much distance between ourselves and this incident as we can."

"That gal, whoever she is, appears to be mighty close if you are looking for distance."

Doc surrendered a sheepish grin. "You got me on that one."

"You aren't going to tell me anymore about her, are you?"

"Not now. Let's just take this one day at a time. You will likely know more sooner than you want. I can say this, though. You should find at least one body. There could be two more, absent tongues, of course. If you don't find their corpses, I would welcome any clues about what became of them."

"How is she doing? What's her name?"

"She will be okay in time. Broken nose and bruised ribs can be dang painful, but the injuries won't kill her. Her name? She goes by Kat."

"Cat. Like the animal?"

"Like in Kathleen."

"Irish girl?"

"Sort of."

"You know you are building up a mystery girl here. I hope I get to meet her soon."

"Soon enough, I would guess. But I need to know more about what happened out there. She was unconscious during most of it."

Conor nodded toward the east. "I see Diego's dust moving this way. We should be on our way in fifteen minutes."

"Did you tell him about the tongues?"

"Yep. He said that would be Chiricahua doings. Of course, he's got Mescalero blood and might not be inclined to name his people."

"I never even thought about Apache. You don't suppose the Ghost is Apache?"

Conor shrugged. "I guess the footprints he leaves are always moccasins."

"Which he could have purchased from the Triad trading post on one of his night visits or made himself. Boots might not be the best rock-climbing mountain footwear. I guess I am not ready to tag him as an Indian just yet, although I can't say that I care. He has never done me any harm, and I think the Ghost's presence discouraged the Apache from raiding my place in the early years, fool that I was for setting up out here during the Apache and Comanche wars. On the other hand, bands from both tribes were good customers during those years."

Diego Munoz rode into the yard astride a bay gelding, a big, muscular beast that dwarfed the rider who was a slim, wiry man standing no more than five and a half feet. Diego was a handsome rascal, though, with an easy smile and neatly trimmed, narrow mustache. Conor knew that Diego was smart as a whip but often played dumb to put another person off guard. His wife, Lucia, was an eye-turner and no mental slouch either, and Conor knew that the couple tended to live a game of dueling wits. Their six-year marriage had produced three children so far, two boys and a girl.

When Diego reined in at the hitching post, he doffed his Stetson and waved it, offering a big smile. "Buenas tardes. I hope I not keep my friends waiting long time."

Conor said, "No. I needed to chat with Doc a bit. I was worried Lucia would not let you go," he teased.

Diego laughed, "She say stay away but send money. She need no more babies now, she say." He shrugged, "What do I do? She must have me in the bed when I am there. It is my curse to be wanted for such skills."

Conor shook his head and stepped off the veranda and grabbed the lead rope of the sorrel packhorse before swinging into his gray's saddle. "Let's ride. Hope to be back in a few days, Doc." He reined his gray west.

"Adios," Diego said, as he gave Doc a salute and nudged his mount ahead to join Conor.

Fifty yards from the Triad, Diego said, "Hold back. I go ahead and pick up trail. Two horses, right?"

"I think so." He slowed Stoic to a walk, while Diego rode some distance ahead before he dismounted, dropped his bay's reins, and began to weave back and forth across the desert land that edged the Guadalupe Mountains.

Conor reined in when he reached Diego's abandoned horse, noting that the critter gnawed at a patch of brown grass while it waited patiently for its owner. Of course, the horse was well-trained. Diego's skills with horses were unparalleled in Conor's experience. On the other hand, he had not found much that Diego could not do when there was a difficult task to complete.

Shortly, Diego trotted back toward Conor and the horses. "I find it," he said. "Easy trail for now. I bet they come from One Horse Pass."

"Never heard of it."

"They call One Horse because so skinny only one horse go through many places. Take you to west side of mountain. Like big crack in rock wall."

"How far?"

"About two hours. Two more to pass through. Come out in canyon. Mountains on west side be very rough, chopped up with canyons."

"Yeah," Conor said, "I have been through the mountain to the southwest side with the salt wagon and mules, but we always had to take the wagon pass. And I've never even skirted the foothills to the north along the west side."

"We can get through pass before dark but best camp then. I know places where we find water and some grass for horses. I scout here for Army many times."

"That sounds good. Lead the way."

The pass was more difficult than Diego had made it sound. His time estimate to the entrance had been on target, but Conor's timepiece told him they had been three hours in the so-called pass now with no end in sight. For the last hour, Diego had been saying, "Soon, soon."

The trail led through what appeared to be a giant fissure in the stone walls of the mountain. At places the trail was flat, but at other times there would be steep, shale rises that would force them to dismount and lead the animals. The fissure widened occasionally to the extent that they could move two abreast for a spell before it abruptly turned into the eye of a needle. It made him nervous to look skyward and see the craggy ledges that nearly shut off the sunlight, and he tried not to think about the chances of a rockslide that would bury them here.

And what if they encountered a stone cork ahead that closed the trail, leaving them without room to turn around? Conor had an aversion to enclosed places generally, one reason he had not explored the countless caves that were like pock scars on the cliffs and walls of the Guadalupe. He had been invited by a friend once to head to the northeastern edge of the mountains to venture into the enormous network of caverns there. He had found a reason to be too busy. He preferred warring with the Comanche. After undergoing this trek, however, the prospect did not seem so formidable.

"Hey, Conor," Diego called back to him, "the light shine ahead. See, I say 'soon.'"

"That was two hours ago." As Diego told him, they shortly emerged into a small canyon. It was nearly sundown, and it made no sense to search out the trail tonight. "Can we camp here?" he asked his guide.

"Si, this good as any, and I not know the other canyons good. We follow canyon wall and will find water for us and horses. Grass there, too. Wood for fire."

"Lead on. Let's get settled in."

A half hour later, they had the horses unsaddled, watered, and staked out on grass that was lush in comparison to what they had passed through earlier in the day. Diego gathered firewood from dead ash scattered about, a rarity in a land notoriously lacking in hardwoods for burning, while Conor laid out the fire and readied to cook some beans and bacon in a small kettle he had anchored to the packhorse. They would have to settle for day-old biscuits that were in a bag Doc had handed him, but that was better than nothing. There would be ample biscuits for several more meals, so they should not starve.

Conor started the fire, counting on Diego to show up with an armful of wood to feed it soon. A few minutes later, Diego stepped out of the brush with an ample supply clutched in his arms. Soon, Conor was dishing beans and bacon into their tin plates.

"Gracias," Diego said. "I like this. Lucia is good cook but wants the Mexican all time. I scout with Army and drive the cattle and horses and like other things sometimes." He grinned. "I learn quickly that I do not complain, though. Lucia make you wish you did not."

"Lucia is a good woman for you, and she works hard. I saw that enormous garden she has started behind your house. She is irrigating it from the stream that goes by your place. Did you dig the ditches?"

"We both do. She going to sell corn and beans and such to Doc for the trading post. Make good money if grows. I help harvest. Lucia, she know about money—too much sometimes. But I love her. Si, Lucia good woman for me. I am lucky man."

They sat silently while they ate, and Conor found his thoughts turning to Maria. By his count, he had five days remaining to comply with her ultimatum. He supposed life might be good with her. It would be nice to have a woman to share his bed at night, to come home to after a journey with the wagon. She also knew about money, but he had a feeling that her husband would be expected to be the sole source and that she would expect plenty of it. Still, he liked Maria, enjoyed her company, and felt an overwhelming physical attraction to her.

Certainly, he could not fault her for demanding a commitment. He even gave her grudging respect for asserting herself and felt she was entitled to a decision from him face to face. Love? Maybe. Was not respect and desire at least part of that? Perhaps any missing ingredients would come later. Finally, he had been enjoying the conjugal benefits of marriage with this woman for a year now. What kind of man was he who would do that and shrug off any sense of obligation? Maria, so far as he knew, was not a promiscuous woman, and she had every reason to expect him to do the honorable thing. When he returned from this mission, he would ride over to the Sanchez homestead, make his peace with Maria, and propose marriage.

He was abruptly yanked from his thoughts by Diego's soft voice. "Somebody watches us, Conor—from high on the canyon wall behind us. Do not look over your shoulder. You will not see him."

"But you can see him?"

"No, I feel him. It is my Apache blood telling me."

"Is he Apache?"

"No. It is Ghost of the Guadalupe. He means us no harm, I think. Maybe he watches over us or is just curious."

"So you believe in the Ghost?"

"All in shadow of Guadalupe believe. Some think he is angel from God come to protect the people here."

Conor had trouble seeing an angel cutting out men's tongues, but he had no evidence to argue to the contrary. Regardless, the Ghost had never been known to harm those settling in the foothills and desert below the mountains. He had been known to help himself to produce of one sort or another, always leaving a doubloon or two in its place, far exceeding value in gold over the worth of the merchandise.

Conor said, "Well, if he is here to watch over us, I am going to clean up and lay out my bedroll and call it a night. I would like to get an early start and try to get home before nightfall tomorrow if we can."

"Doc pay me more if we take another night. Lucia like that."

"I will suggest he pay you a bonus, and you can put that in your hideaway place."

Diego furrowed his brow. "How you know I have hide-away place?"

"Lucky guess, but you just confirmed it."

Diego grinned. "Lucky guess. Cannot be a man without dinero. Lucia not be happy if she find out."

"Your secret is safe with me."

The next morning, they built a small fire for coffee and ate a cold breakfast of beef jerky and more stale biscuits before saddling up and heading out of the canyon. Diego quickly picked up the trail. The ground was soft and sandy here, and there had been no rain to obliterate the tracks. The feathered-out hoofprints led them past other small canyons until they reached an entryway that opened to a larger canyon with steeper, towering stone walls.

Diego led him into the depths, but circling black vultures removed the need for trail sign. Odds were that human bodies were the attraction. In less than fifteen minutes they came across the mutilated corpse of a red-haired man. The garments that had covered him were now shredded and stripped away and his left arm was missing, likely dragged off by a four-footed scavenger. The men dismounted and only then did the bravest of the black harbingers of death flap their broad wings and lift themselves skyward.

"This must be the man who the Albuquerque deputy claimed was a deputy U.S. marshal. I'll see if I can find a badge or papers anyplace. Then I will find a spot to bury him if you want to scout the area and see if you can uncover any sign of the other two men."

"Why bury? Another day, and he be gone."

"I just can't do that. He is a man. What's left of him should be buried. Somebody out there loves him or did once."

Diego shrugged. "Will see what I can find of these others."

Conor retrieved the shovel from the packhorse while Diego commenced pacing the area with his head down and eyes to the ground like a birddog tracking wild game. He searched out a spot nearby that promised easy digging for a grave, but soon learned that there was no such place. The easy digging ended a foot deep before the digger struck limestone. He decided the man's remains would have to settle for a shallow grave. He worked several hours, chopping away at the brittle rock before he abandoned the task at a bit over two feet. He figured that would hold what was left of the man, and they could pile some stones over the burial place to help discourage the scavengers.

After searching the shredded clothing for any signs of identification, he dragged the grisly corpse to the grave. He completed the burial, and Diego appeared when the last stone was hoisted onto the mound of the grave.

"Excellent timing," Conor told his friend.

Diego grinned and shrugged. "Remember, I say leave him for animal food."

"Yeah, I guess you did. I hope you learned more than I have. I found no deputy U.S. marshal's badge and nothing that would tell me anything about the man."

"Yes. I can tell you things. I find two places with much blood—dry and brown now. You see where men build fire here. Another a half mile to south on far side of canyon. Apache, I think Chiricahua, go there from here. Blood there, but he ride away on unshod horse. Follow tracks to canyon opening. He turn south. Go without tongue, I think. Other man leave, too. He go north."

"Probably toward Albuquerque if he can make it in that shape."

"Lots of blood. Apache will survive. White man—maybe not."

"Well, Doc mostly wanted to know what became of the other men. He knew about the fellow I just buried. I think he was hoping we would be burying two more when we got here. I think our business is done. Let's saddle up and head home." He paused a moment. "By the way, do you think the Ghost is still watching us?"

"Si, he watches."

Chapter 11

KAT FOUND HERSELF restless now after a few days of sitting or lying in bed. She had awakened from a midmorning nap when she heard Doc speaking from the examination room in clumsy Spanish, repeating himself when he could not make the woman understand. The room branched off the small reception area on the opposite side from Kat's present quarters. The voices were muffled, but she gathered that the woman was with child and that Doc was attempting to convey instructions of some sort. She wished she could step in to interpret, but it was not her place.

She tossed her sheet and blanket back and swung her legs out of bed. She was thinking of getting dressed and exploring the building and her surroundings. She would like to visit the roan mare she had named Toughie. Doc had assured her the mare was fine, as was the gelding that had accompanied her. She knew nothing about the gelding or about what happened after Buford Walters commenced his assault on her. She remembered screams and had a vague recollection of being cradled in the arms of someone who held her as they rocked in the saddle of a trotting horse.

Doc talked about the Ghost bringing her to this place. She did not believe in ghosts, and Doc had been evasive during her inquiries about this spirit that possibly saved her life. And the Triad fit the strangeness of her situation, set at the base of the mountain in semi-desert functioning as a trading post, residence, and hospital, of sorts. A man made a living from this? He was seeing a patient now, though, so there must be some folks hereabouts. Doc assured her she could remain for as long as she wished, but a person could not spend a lifetime in a place like this. Sooner or later, she would need to move on.

She stood and paused a bit, waiting for the dizziness to pass. Doc had told her it was likely the effects of the laudanum. He said that the dose she was taking was minimal and that she could have more for up to a week if she required it for the pain. She was determined to abandon the stuff tomorrow. She wanted to remove the fog from her head, pain be damned. She needed something to do.

It occurred to her then that she did not have a stitch of clothing to wear. She supposed her things had been laundered and put away someplace or were at least still available. She walked about her room, cold and spartan, no paintings or other decorations on the white walls. Two beds with side tables and kerosene lamps, not much else.

She turned at a soft rapping on the door frame. "Oh, hello, Doc. I've got to get out of this bed and move around, do something, but I can't find my clothes."

Doc smiled. She loved the twinkling of his pale, blue eyes. His smile, though usually close-mouthed, seemed to come often and easily, and she had yet to hear him raise his voice.

"I have a lady who picks up my laundry once a week, and she took them to do with my wash. If you come into my store, we will pick out a few things. I recommend some britches, maybe moccasins or boots and a few cotton shirts—underthings, of course. You will probably need boys' sizes in most of your garments if you don't want to swim in them. Think about whether you would allow me to shear your beautiful hair off for now, so it maybe falls over your ears a mite and doesn't drop below the neck. Pick a hat, maybe a wide-brimmed Plainsman to top your head and cast a shadow on your face when you are out and about. I think you might want more of a boy-look for strangers who pass by. Locals will know, but they will keep quiet if I pass the word."

"You are thinking the law might be looking for me."

"From what you have told me, it seems possible. It wouldn't hurt to change your look a bit in case there are posters out on you, or somebody comes by asking questions."

"You are willing to harbor a criminal, even lie to the law?"

Doc chuckled, "Need a little excitement in my life anyhow."

"You could go to jail, too."

"I've been worse places, I promise, but I won't be losing sleep over the possibility."

"Can I take a bath someplace?"

"I've got high class accommodations in the hospital's back room. A big old clawfoot tub that drains through a pipe and into a gully. I can boil some water in the kitchen, get several buckets of water from the pump, and fill it to your liking. Can you get in and out without a problem? We might have to wait until I can get one of the neighbor ladies over to help."

"I will be fine if I move slow-like. My ribs are sore, but the rest of me is working. How about that haircut first?

Then we can find me something to wear. Maybe you want to wait till after lunch for the bath."

"Lunch around here is whatever time we eat. I am betting you would like to get yourself all cleaned up first. I can be working on lunch while you do the bath."

"You make me feel like I am in a fancy hotel."

"Young lady, after what you have been through, I think you are entitled. I am honored to be your host."

Again, this man almost cracked the hard shell she had formed over the years and tears burned her eyes before she stopped the flow. No man had ever treated her with such kindness and understanding, not even her father, who was a good man but tended to be reserved and distant, not inclined to verbal assurances or praise.

Several hours later, Kat felt alive again, a new person in appearance and confidence. After a lunch of fried potatoes and roasted beef sandwiches topped by apple cobbler from Doc's Dutch oven, she was stuffed and content sitting across the table from Doc, who had just placed two cups of steaming coffee on the table and sat down across from her.

"Thank you, Doc. It was a perfect meal, but I ate too much."

"We have got to keep you eating for a spell and get some meat on your bones."

She shrugged. "Papa always said I was so skinny I couldn't cast a shadow. Other times he would claim I was skinny and strong like a razorback hog. I never knew quite how to take that. Mama said I would just be lucky if I stayed that way my whole life. I am down some, though, these past months, and I'm sure I left a few pounds out there on the desert."

"Well, your doctor thinks you are making excellent progress on your recovery. You're going to be fine. The nose will feel much better and most of the swelling will be gone in a week's time. The ribs will improve day by day, but you will receive little reminders for a long spell. Just pay attention when they are hurting."

"What can I do here?"

"What do you mean?"

"Well, if the offer is still good, I would like to stay on a spell. But I don't want you waiting on me all the time. I would like to earn my keep. I can cook halfway decent. Louie Gaynor let me know if I wasn't feeding him well enough. I love working with horses and had my own when Papa was alive, a buckskin gelding, but Louie sold him off. Afraid I was a big baby about it when I found out. I am awfully attached to the mare I rustled from Buford, but I don't know if it is good to keep her on your place in case the law comes snooping."

"Toughie will stay, but we will run her with the small grazing herd, so she is likely to be out to pasture if strangers stop by. I have rented Diego Munoz's blood bay stallion to run with my eight mares for a time if you don't mind your roan getting with foal."

"That would be wonderful. I didn't know you raised horses."

"Not much of a herd. Conor talked me into it, said between us we could raise enough horses to drive a bunch to one of the Army posts for sale every year. Conor's an ambitious young man, and he has got me working harder in my old age than I planned."

"And you love it."

"Can't say that I mind it, but I'm moving a lot slower than I did a few years back. How are you with numbers?"

"I finished eighth grade in Albuquerque. I was always good with numbers, but I haven't used them a lot the past few years. My mother was Mexican, and I speak and write Spanish—she insisted, told me it would be valuable in New Mexico and the borderlands."

"Your mother was very wise. My Spanish consists of words and phrases. I can't read or write the language. I could use an interpreter sometimes. I especially need help inventorying and ordering supplies for the trading post. Maybe you could clerk in the store if you stay around, but for now we ought to keep you out of sight as much as possible."

"You just figure out what I can do. Tomorrow, I would like to start making myself useful."

"I will ponder this and have work for tomorrow. We will start with a half day's work and hold off on your handling the livestock for now."

"And Doc?"

"Yes?"

"You said I could move into your spare room when I was ready."

"Of course."

"I am ready. I don't like the feel of a hospital room, and you might need it for somebody else. If you like, I could help with your patients who need care, bathing, feeding and the like."

Doc said, "I had not thought of that, but you could be a lot of help there. I go for days without patients sometimes, but they tend to turn up the same day when I can't take care of everyone fast enough. I could use an assistant on those days. We just might be able to do business, Kathleen Ryan. Now, why don't I show you your new room, and we'll see if it suits you. If you like it, there is no reason you cannot move right in—just in time for an afternoon nap. The nap is doctor's orders."

Chapter 12

CONOR GAVE DIEGO a gold eagle for two days' work. The second in his pocket would be returned to Doc, who had advanced the extra in case the mission took longer than anticipated.

Before they parted, Conor said, "I would like to take the salt loads up to Roswell a week from today, if that suits you."

"I be ready. Three days to get there. Maybe two back, you think?"

"Yeah. We will need to leave early in the morning, but I will stop by your place and talk to you about it a day or two ahead of time."

"And this time, you give me money for Lucia and other money for Diego, okay?"

"How about I give Diego one dollar out of every five. You can give Lucia four dollars."

"That be good. You good friend, Conor. You under-stand."

"Diego, when it comes to women, I fear I shall never know enough, but I am trying to learn."

Conor rode on to the Triad to give Doc a report before heading back to his place. It was late afternoon, and he would not mind a supper invite. He was tired, and the trail food had been subsistence fare. When he approached the Triad, the only life he saw on the veranda was a snoozing Loafer. The dog lifted his head when Conor dismounted at the hitching rail, and then went back to sleep.

He decided to try the trading post first. His was the only horse hitched at the rail, so it did not appear Doc had any patients, and stable chores would already be completed. Doctor Roman Hayes was a creature of habit notwithstanding his easy-going demeanor.

When he walked into the trading post door, he passed the counter near the entrance and cast his eyes about a large room with nary a vacant space on the walls and back-to-back shelves stretched through the center with just enough room for single file walking space. The sign above the exterior door read "Hayes Trading Post," but it was organized more like a city general store. Folks within forty miles distance came here to purchase their essen-tials. Doc's problem was that there were not that many people living within the radius, although he still did business with Apache or other native tribes' people who passed through the Guadalupe.

Early on, Doc had told him, word passed among the Indians that they were welcome there for any merchandise except guns, and he was more than glad to trade for furs, silver or anything he might market elsewhere. Moves to the reservation had depleted that trade in recent years, but resistors still stopped from time to time. Rumors persisted that the Triad was under the protection of the Ghost, and Doc, of course, did nothing to discourage it.

He caught sight of Doc at the far end of the room stacking canned goods on shelves. "Hey, Doc," he called. "I'm back."

Doc turned and gave him a wave before making his way down the aisle. "I didn't hear you come in. You move like a danged Indian."

"Or your hearing is slipping some."

"I wouldn't deny it. Stay for supper? Baked beans with chopped beef and leftover cobbler. Fresh biscuits. I have a young lady helping in the kitchen right now. It's time you meet her."

"You talked me into it. Do I hold the report till then?"

"I think so. She should hear it firsthand. Maybe she can fill in some gaps."

"She knows about the tongues and all?"

"She does, and I don't think you could say much that would upset her. She has been through some trials in her life. Wait here a minute, though, so I can ask her to set another plate and alert her to a guest."

Doc disappeared through the doorway that connected to the residence and returned shortly. "Kat—her full name is Kathleen Ryan—did not seem pleased, but don't take it personally. She has good reason to be suspicious of men. Just tell the story, and we will see how it goes."

"Well, her name sounds Irish. We ought to get along."

"It might be more complicated than that."

"You are making me feel as welcome as a rabid skunk."

"Don't concern yourself. You will get along fine once we settle in for supper."

Conor was surprised when he entered the kitchen and saw someone who at first glance appeared to be a skinny young Mexican boy who had got the worst end of a barroom fight. The glare from her unswollen eye and the firm set of her lips indicated he was not a welcome guest. Doc introduced them, and Conor responded with a friendly, "Pleased to meet you, ma'am."

She offered a neutral, "Hello."

One end of the kitchen table was pushed against the wall, and Doc took a chair opposite, which left Conor and Kat facing each other across the table. The biscuits and baked bean-beef mix were on the table with a pot of coffee and pitcher of water. Doc passed the food to Kat first, and Conor noticed that she dished out healthy helpings of the bean concoction and started with two biscuits.

There was an awkward silence before Doc spoke. "Conor, I think you could just go ahead and tell us what you and Diego learned on your little trip."

Conor offered a summary of the visit to the canyon and his burial of the man who was identified by Buford Walters as a deputy United States marshal.

Kat said, "Buford lied like he always does. The man was not a killer, though, or he wouldn't have decided to leave when Buford announced his plans for me. A deputy U.S marshal would have pulled rank. He would have taken charge and ordered me taken prisoner and delivered back to Albuquerque."

Conor thought Kat's conclusion made sense. "And we did not turn up a badge, although scavengers had pretty much shredded the man's clothes."

Doc said, "I think the Ghost would have recovered it and left it with his other, uh . . . trophies. But you found no other bodies?"

"No. Diego found signs indicating that two riders, one mounted on an unshod horse, departed the canyon, one heading north and the other south, both leaving blood trails. Quite obviously they embarked on their journeys minus their tongues. My guess is that the Apache survived. I am not so certain about the other man. He could be lying along a trail somewhere."

Kat said, "I hope he is dead and that he suffered." Her voice was ice cold. She was a bit of a scary little creature, he thought. Best not to cross her.

Kat got up to retrieve the cobbler warming on the woodstove and he watched as she walked. The snug denims revealed that she was indeed a woman, not big hipped, but there was female in there and the orange cotton shirt suggested small, firm breasts beneath the fabric. With her nose and face healed, a man might find her attractive enough. Her figure would certainly not be considered voluptuous, though, like Maria's, the woman who would soon be his wife.

She plucked the cobbler pan from the stove and turned, biting her lower lip and shooting angry fire with her good eye when she caught him perusing her form. He cast his eyes downward, embarrassed at her discovery of his scrutiny.

Kat stepped over to the table and dropped the pan in front of the men. "I am very tired. I am going to bed." She kept her glare fastened on Conor. "I wish I could say it was a pleasure meeting you, Mister Byrne." She wheeled and left the room.

Doc looked at Conor quizzically. "I missed something."

"Let's say I was studying her a bit, and she caught me. She obviously does not welcome a man's eyes."

Doc lifted his eyebrows and surrendered a small smile. "You will need to be wary of her sharp tongue. For that matter, you might just keep your distance for a spell. A man in Albuquerque who mistreated her got his head bashed in with an axe."

"She killed him?"

"He was alive when she last saw him. That's all she knows."

"Is it safe to have her living here with you?"

"Oh, I'm not worried about that. We are getting along well enough. I tell you this because you will hear about it sooner or later. I have already pulled you in on this more than I should have. You are entitled to know that Kat may be wanted by the law on various charges including jail escape. I am not comfortable discussing all the details. I would prefer that someday you hear it from her."

"I think I would prefer not to hear anything from her anytime soon."

"I intend to help her all I can. I will not turn her over to the law. I don't want to implicate you any further, so I won't ask you for any assistance beyond not contacting the authorities."

"Doc, there is no way I would do anything to bring the law down on you, but it appears you may be harboring a criminal. Do you want to end up in jail over this?"

"If I do, I will sell this place to you cheap."

Conor sighed. "Well, count me in for whatever you need. Maybe we can share a cell in the new prison they are wanting to build in Santa Fe. I've got a hunch the Ghost will be keeping an eye on things, too. Diego said he was watching us during our visit to the canyon."

Chapter 13

I T WAS THE day before Maria's deadline, and Conor entered the Hayes Trading Post to see if Doc had a necklace, ring, or other jewelry that might be acceptable for presentation when he proposed to his bride-to-be. He had convinced himself that he should marry Maria, who had shared his bed with some frequency the past year with marriage as her obvious goal. He had never hinted that his intentions were less than honorable and had not given it any thought when caught up in the passion of their lovemaking. His brain was dormant at such moments.

He walked to the counter and picked up the cowbell that customers were to use when needing service. He shook the big bell, knowing that Doc would hear the clanging if he was anywhere within the Triad or nearby. The door between the store and the residence opened, and Kathleen Ryan stepped into the big room. When she saw him, she stopped for a moment. The look on her face was not welcoming. He could see that the swelling about her eye and nose had gone down some, promising something more flattering beneath. He wondered what a smile might do for that face.

"Doc is with a patient. May I help you with something?"

She wore her jeans and calf-high Apache-style moccasins today with a bright blue shirt. A wide-brimmed Plainsman hat held by a rawhide thong around her neck was suspended on her back between her shoulders. She looked like she should be herding cattle instead of clerking in a general store. "Are you working here now?"

"I asked if I could help you, didn't I? But, yes, I step in if Doc's not available and try to pick up slack where I can. Can I find something for you?"

This was not going to be easy, but he hated to show up at Maria's empty handed. "I am looking for a piece of jewelry for a lady, uh, something that might be taken as a token of love."

She gave him a look of suspicion, both green eyes revealed now, beautiful, expressive eyes, he thought, even if he did not like their message.

"I can show you some Navajo pieces that are quite nice. They have just started serious marketing of their work, according to Doc. Follow me."

She turned down one of the aisles toward the end of the room, and he could not keep his eyes from watching her graceful movement and the gentle swing of her backside. At first glance, she might be taken for a boy but not at the second. He wondered how old she was. Should a man on the brink of marriage be undressing other women in his head?

She stopped at a drawered cabinet and pulled out a drawer. Spread out on black cloth were silver bracelets, rings, and necklaces, many decorated with polished turquoise. "This is all we have. I don't suppose there is much demand for such things here. They would be luxuries that few could afford."

He was baffled by the display. He had no idea what a woman would like, especially Maria. It occurred to him that he did not know all that much about Maria beyond her naked body. He certainly liked that, but he had been unaware of her pursuit of a man with the potential of acquiring wealth until the night of her ultimatum. Certainly, he had that ambition, but it was somehow the pursuit and not the acquisition that interested him. He thought of himself as a happy man even if he was presently poor as a desert grasshopper. He was not so sure about Maria. Would he ever be enough?

"Do you have any suggestions?"

"I have never had much jewelry and few occasions to wear it. I don't know that I am a good judge."

"Just tell me what strikes your fancy."

She studied the pieces. "I would be wary of a ring. Chances aren't good it would fit the lady and she would have to find someone to adjust it. I doubt if Doc can do that. I wouldn't know if there are silversmiths in the area." She picked up a necklace and draped the thread-like silver chain over her slender fingers. The pendant was a small, oval-shaped silver piece embedded with a tiny, turquoise flying eagle. "I love this one. Simple, symbolic."

"Symbolic?"

"Of freedom."

He was uncertain how Maria would view it, but he rather liked the thought. "I will take it. Do you know the cost?"

"I will need to check Doc's price listing under the front counter." She took the necklace and headed back to the front, Conor following and enjoying the view, pervert that he had conceded he was.

Kat checked the price. "Five dollars. Quite expensive, I fear."

"I have an account with Doc. Can you add this to it? Tell him I will bring everything up to date when we sell the salt in Roswell in about ten days. I know it won't be a problem."

"I don't know. He hasn't explained how these things work."

"Kat, I assure you it is not a problem."

"Miss Ryan, please." She had warmed up for a few minutes, but the ice storm had returned.

"Miss Ryan. I need the piece this morning. Doc and I are business partners in several ventures. He would not take kindly to my having difficulty with this purchase."

"I guess he knows where to find you." She handed him the necklace and took a pencil and began writing down the transaction.

He decided to make one more effort to negotiate a truce. "Look, Miss Ryan. I am terribly sorry we got off to a bad start the other night. We have some things in common. I'm Irish, and you apparently have Irish heritage. Your name—"

"My father was Irish. A good man. But I have known a lot of no-good Irishmen. I don't give a damn about anybody's bloodline."

"Well, I apologize if I offended you in some way that evening."

"I don't like men looking at me the way you were. I know what was on your mind."

"As a matter of fact, you do not, Miss Ryan. You seem to fancy yourself as the goddess Aphrodite." He took the necklace and stomped out of the store.

It was late morning when Conor approached the Sanchez farmstead astride Stoic. He had ridden the horse at a near walk while he cooled down from his unpleasantness with Miss Kathleen Ryan and then pondered the challenge ahead where he would make a lifetime commitment to Maria Sanchez. He planned to ask her to stroll with him a short distance from the house, so they might enjoy a few moments of privacy. After that, he had scripted a dozen scenarios where he might profess his love, present the necklace, and ask her hand in marriage.

He was uncertain of the custom among the local Mexican families, and he thought it a bit of silliness, but he was prepared to ask Felipe Sanchez for his daughter's hand in marriage if Maria wished. He supposed they should set a date, but he would leave that to her. Tomorrow, if she wished. A year from now would be better so long as they could resume conjugal relations forthwith. Of course, if she found herself with child, marriage would be immediate. He was prepared to comply with her wishes—to a point.

He rode into the yard and found Maria outside hanging wet laundry on a rope line. Her father and two younger brothers were in the goat pen where they appeared to be working with the goat herd, probably castrating the male kids. Felipe maintained a herd of about fifty nanny goats and three or four billies that were his family's main source of income.

He dismounted and hitched Stoic onto a rail in front of the small adobe house and strolled around the house where Maria waited. She had obviously seen him arrive. "Good morning, Maria."

"Good morning, Conor. This is a surprise. I did not expect you."

"I don't know why not. Tomorrow was the day. I would like to talk. Could we walk away from the house a bit?" He offered his arm, and she took it.

They strolled silently onto the near-barren surrounding prairie before stopping. Then he turned to her and embraced her, lowering his face to kiss her before she stiffened and stepped back.

"Not now," she said. "Tell me what you came to tell me."

"I have been thinking these past days, Maria. It is time."

"Time for what?"

He did not like the hostility in her voice. He had experienced enough of that from women today. "It is time we married. I came to tell you I love you and want you to be my wife. I am asking you now, Maria. Will you marry me? You name the date. It is in your hands."

She showed a bit of softness in her eyes and demeanor now. He thought there may have been a few tears glistening in those dark eyes. "I did not expect this, Conor. I am surprised. I am sorry, but I will not marry you. I have been thinking, too. You are a good man, a kind man, and I could ask for no more considerate lover, but I have decided you do not offer great prospects. A person cannot make a decent living in this godforsaken land, and you are already married to it. You will not leave, will you?"

He did not need to think. "No."

"You are crazy, like Doc Hayes and my padre. I want more, and I am sick of this land. Padre has agreed to help me get to Santa Fe before the summer is out, and I will make a place for myself there, find a man who can provide for me in the way I desire. I am sorry, I truly am. I should not have set the deadline, but in a way, I set one for myself and thought about what I really wanted. She stepped forward and kissed his cheek. I will miss you, my dear Conor, and I will remember always the moments we shared together. And I do love you, but not enough."

"I understand," he said. He offered his arm. "Let me walk you back to the house."

When he rode away from the Sanchez property, he felt a mix of disappointment and relief. He suspected, though, that the outcome was for the best. Maria may have saved him from a life he would have regretted. He hoped she found the man and the future she dreamed of. Perhaps he would hang the eagle necklace on his shack wall. A symbol of freedom.

Chapter 14

URING HER TWO weeks helping Doc Hayes at the Triad, Kat had felt something of a rebirth in her life. Sometimes it felt like some of the horrors of the past few years were just nightmares, visions that disappeared with the light of day. Other times, however, they returned and haunted her, soured her mood and sent her into a withdrawal from others. Those days, she asked Doc if she could work outdoors or in the garden.

She sat now in one of the rockers on the veranda, watching the sun send a red glow above the mountaintops, signaling that its full light would be arriving soon. She loved the quiet of the mountains and the nearly barren lands that surrounded much of the Guadalupe. She had fallen in love with this country that many deemed worthless, and she itched to explore every inch of it, climb into the mountains and seek a breathtaking over-view.

The bandages had been removed from her nose yes-terday and the bruises about her nose and eye were fad-ing as the swollen flesh shrank. She had dared to look in the mirror this morning and had not been horrified. She did not consider herself a beauty, but others, espe-cially men, did not seem to find her ugly. She had come to suspect, however, that they were more interested in the private place between her thighs than the features of her face. Regardless, she had never been obsessed about her appearance.

Doc had told her that the small bump on the bridge of her nose would likely get smaller yet, but she should not expect it to disappear. She did not care. What she cared about was what she was to do next. As much as she had come to love this country, she did not see how she could remain much longer. Each day posed a risk to Doc that she would be discovered and that the law would learn he had been protecting a dangerous criminal. She felt strong as ever now and figured she had even gained a few pounds from all the food Doc had been putting on her plate.

Her only excuse for staying now was that she did not know where to go. Well, that and the fact that she did not want to leave Doc and this land. In a short time, she had formed a type of bond with a man and place she never enjoyed before. Doc had become the father that hapless Flinn Ryan simply had been unable to be. That was not to say she had not loved her father despite the reality that the bottle always ended up first in his life.

The residence door opened, and she turned to see Doc carrying out a little square table, which he placed between her rocker and the empty one that he always claimed. The first thing she noticed was that embedded on the top was a checkerboard made of individual alternating dark and tan colored squares. She guessed the dark pieces to be walnut, because she had seen such craftsmanship by her father on several occasions. She looked up at Doc questioningly.

"Just stay put. I am serving breakfast today."

He left and returned with Loafer at his heels. He put a heaping plate of biscuits and fried eggs beside her on the table and a smaller one for himself. "I will be back with coffee and jam," he said.

She started to get up from the rocker. "I can help."

"Nope. I am serving breakfast this morning. You have beat me to it three days in a row. Makes me feel like I'm not much of a host."

When they were seated, they ate silently while Loafer sat between them, successfully begging bites from each.

Doc said, "Loafer likes this. He's stealing double off the table lately."

After downing the last of three biscuits, Kat said, "Speaking of tables. This one is too nice to eat off of."

"Haven't used it for over eight years. Made it with my son. At ten years of age, he was a better craftsman than his old pop. We played a lot of checkers and chess on this table, his little sister, too."

"I didn't know you had children."

"Joseph and Mariah. Good Jewish names. Their mother's doings. Her name was Ruth."

"You are Jewish? Not that it means much to me."

"I'm not. I'm still working on what I am. Ruth hadn't been to synagogue since she was a small child, but her parents had been devout when the family moved to Austin, Texas and her father commenced doctoring there. No Jewish meeting places at the time, which wouldn't have made much sense, because all the Jews lived in a single house. I met him during the war, where we both served as surgeons for the Confederate Army."

"And Ruth?" She assumed Ruth had died, but he had not said so.

"She's buried on a rise at the mountain base within a ten-minute walk from here. I will show you in a bit, if you like."

"Yes, I would like that. And where are your children?"

"They are with Ruth."

Oh, my God. She wished she had not asked. "I'm so sorry. I don't know what to say."

"As a doctor, I have seen a lot of family losses. A couple with ten children can expect to lose half before they are grown, maybe one or both parents, too. I never know what to say. I guess 'I'm sorry' is about it. In the end folks must come to terms with these things in their own ways. Some don't and live out their lives in private hells."

"And you are not living in a private hell?"

"No, this place is my heaven. I have a sense of purpose here and enjoy dealing with the challenges of each day. Oh, the sadness and melancholy sneak in now and then, and I think about what might have been. At first, I thought 'Why me, why the ones I love?' I was angry and bitter. Strangely, it was Ruth's father, almost speaking from his own grave, who gave me the words that lifted me up. He spoke them during the war when we were lamenting all the needless pain people were suffering because of the death and destruction. He said, 'Remember, always, don't be bitter about the wrongs against you or the tragedies that life may throw at you. Be better.' You must lift yourself above these things, be the best that you can be at what you choose. Do not give in to whatever forces that have turned against you. Be better, not bitter."

Kat said, "Be better, not bitter. Are you sending me a message?"

Doc smiled. "Could be. Let's take a walk."

They strolled to the mountain's base beyond the stable and climbed a half dozen stone steps to a flat, plateau-like outcropping. The area was longer and wider than it appeared at ground level, and she estimated that twenty-five or more could be buried here. He led her to an area near the mountain's sheer wall, where four limestone rocks sat in a row, backed by a large stone with "Hayes" engraved on the face. The smaller stones bore the names of Roman Hayes, Ruth Hayes, Joseph Hayes, and Mariah Hayes.

They stood there silently for a spell as Kat studied the marker stones. Roman's date of death, of course, was blank. The others had all died on June 30 almost eight years earlier. The anniversary was approaching. Ruth had been almost forty years old, Joseph, ten, and Mariah, five.

Doc said, "I was wounded during the war, a nasty shoulder wound but Ruth's father, Isaac Rosen, patched me up fine. I was given a two-month medical furlough and, since I had no living family, he insisted I go to Austin and stay with his family for a spell. That's when I met Ruth. She was a striking woman, a schoolteacher, and, amazingly, unmarried in her late twenties. I think her Jewishness might have had something to do with that. Anyway, before I returned from furlough, we were married. It was a year before mail reached me informing me that I had left her with child and that I had a son."

She hesitated to ask but had to know. "What happened?"

"Comanchero. Fool that I was, I left them here a week with two trusted Mexican workers to keep an eye out. They died, too, that day but were buried on family plots at their own farmsteads. By this time, we were under the protection of the Apache, so I did not worry about their bands. The Comanchero bands were made up of a mix of Anglos, Mexicans, half-blood Indians—a few full—and even a few Negroes. They attacked, and Ruth and the kids must have fought them off to the end or they would have been captured and sold as slaves in Mexico—the children possibly to bordellos. Ruth and Joe could handle rifles. The place was looted and burned out. It sounds awful, but I am glad they died here."

As they went down the steps and walked away, Kat said, "I feel like I belong. I want to stay here if it is not a problem."

"I want you to stay here. This is your home for as long as you want it to be."

Chapter 15

LATER, THE MORNING of the cemetery visit, Kat was in the trading post compiling a list of the store's inventory. She had remarked casually that it appeared to her that there were too many items on the shelves that would never sell, and a shortage of others that could not keep up with demand, such as flour, salt, sugar and the like.

Doc had declared, "You are now in charge of inventory. Make a list of what you think we need and what we have a surplus of. We will go over it together. Juan Torres is making a journey to El Paso next week. I have been planning to have him purchase a big Studebaker wagon for me and bring back a load of merchandise. I do business with a bank there and will be sending a letter of instructions with him. Hauling costs won't be any more for a full load than a half load."

"You go to El Paso to get your merchandise?"

"They have rail service there now. We can pick up about anything we need."

"But you rely upon going that far to stock the store?"

"We have wholesalers come by when it suits them, mostly to unload items they could not sell at the Roswell post. We are lucky to have a wagon stop by every few months, and then we only get what Roswell did not want."

She thought the merchandise displays needed rearranging. There was no logical order. Some canned goods were at one end of the store, others were at the opposite end. Some clothes might be found with flour and others with horse tack, and, of course, no separation between male and female garments. She had to remind herself that she was not boss, but she sensed that Doc might welcome dropping such details in someone else's hands.

She peered out the window as Doc had warned her to do frequently. He was glad to have her tending to the store, but if she saw anyone coming that she did not recognize, she had been instructed to vacate and summon him. She saw a dust cloud moving in the direction of the Triad and waited at the window. Soon, three riders emerged from the cloud. As they neared, she confirmed that she recognized neither horses nor riders. One was official-looking, wearing a vest and jacket and string tie. The other two had the look of hired guns. Her thoughts: the law or bounty hunters.

She left her pencil and paper on the counter and rushed through the door to the residence, shutting and putting the bolt lock in place behind her. Then she went into the medical offices where Doc sat at a desk, sharpening surgical scalpels and knives. "Doc, strangers coming. I don't like their looks."

Doc got up, walked to his office door, and locked it. "I will lock the residence door and then go into the trading post. You put your ear to the door and listen. Like we planned if I learn they are looking for you, I will say 'You are at the wrong place gentlemen' and then you head out the back for your hideout in the stable loft. Your rifle ready?"

"Dang right it is."

He locked the outer residence door and entered the trading post instructing her to lock the door behind him again.

She obeyed and waited with her ear to the door. It was a lightweight door, and it was not difficult to hear voices in the store area when sitting in the residential parlor. This was by design, since ordinarily Doc had been the only person to tend to business off both sides of the residence.

When the men entered, Doc offered a polite welcome. "Good afternoon, gentlemen. I am Roman Hayes, the owner of this establishment. Can I help you with something?"

"I know who you are, Doctor Roman Hayes, and as a matter of fact, you can help," responded a voice that had a bit of a Mexican accent. "My name is Emilio Ortiz, and I am an attorney and counselor from Santa Fe representing the heirs of the late Rodrigo Mendoza, who are the rightful owners of the property you occupy and upon which you are trespassing. My friends here are assisting with service of notices to all who are residing on the Mendoza land grant, which, I might add, covers in excess of 100,000 acres, well beyond the land you have unlawfully taken. Every person who has acquired a parcel from you will also be required to vacate."

"Let me see the written notice," Doc said.

There was a long silence. Finally, Doc spoke. "You are giving me two months to vacate. Interesting."

"Your property is part of the Mendoza land grant. The person you purchased it from owned nothing, so you bought nothing."

"I am not a lawyer, but I do know that this notice is not a court order." Kat thought Doc's voice sounded amazingly calm.

"We hope the occupants will cooperate and save everyone legal expense and other unpleasantness."

"Unpleasantness?"

"Calhoun and Marx here will be in command of enforcers. If you and others do not comply with the notice, let us say that they and their associates will see to compliance. They have vast experience from range wars in cattle country to the north. They work very efficiently. Folks can get hurt or die. To avoid this, I am authorized to offer twenty-five cents per acre to folks to sign off any claim and move out. Since you have more useful buildings than most on your tract, you would be paid an additional one hundred dollars above the per acre price."

"Your generosity is overwhelming. Now, I would take it kindly if you and your enforcers would be on your way. You have given me something to think about."

The other man's voice sounded ice-cold. "You had damn well better think, Doctor Hayes. You will be hearing from me again soon, and I hope you come up with the right answer."

Kat heard booted feet stomping across the floor, and then the door slammed.

She released the door bolt, opened the door and walked into the trading post. She found Doc leaning back against the counter, stroking his beard thoughtfully and his eyes fixed on the recent visitors who were mounting their horses outside. His voice had been calm, but now he appeared red-faced and short of breath.

He turned his head toward Kat when he was aware of her presence. "They were not looking for you."

"I know. I heard. It sounded like they brought trouble, though."

"Yep, it seems as much."

"You don't look well, perhaps you should sit down."

He swiped a handkerchief over his sweaty brow. "I'll be fine. It was all I could do not to punch that arrogant ass in the mouth."

"What are you going to do?" She walked over to him and rested her hand on his forearm.

"Well, I must talk to Conor, get his advice."

Why in blazes was he always consulting with Conor Byrne? "I don't understand why you need to talk to Conor. What does he have to do with it?"

"You don't like Conor, do you?"

"No, I don't."

"Why not?"

"I don't like the way he looks at me sometimes—what I see in his eyes. And I have thought about how I feel, and I suppose I am a little jealous of your friendship. I can't explain why."

Doc shook his head from side to side. "Most women that see Conor are wishing he would look at them the way he looks at you."

"Well, I don't like it."

"I stay out of business between young men and women. You will have to figure it all out for yourself. Conor is seeing a young woman anyhow. He will keep his distance if that's what you want."

"I know he is seeing someone. I sold him a necklace, remember?"

"That's right. I wonder how Maria liked it. I haven't seen her lately."

She hated Maria now, too, whoever she was, but could not explain why. She guessed because the woman wore the necklace with the pendant she liked. "She should like it, but I guess everybody's got different tastes about such things. I have never worn much jewelry in my life, which is fine with me."

"What do you know about Conor?"

"Enough."

"No, I don't think so. I purchased about twenty thousand acres when I got this place. I sold five thousand of that to Conor and a few thousand to the ten or so Mexican families that live out here. I have promised to sell Conor the rest of my land except the Triad and the three thousand acres that extend into the canyon when he is ready. My point is that he has a huge stake in what happens here. I must discuss this with him."

"I guess I can see that."

"Furthermore," Doc said, "I value his judgment and opinion. Conor is a graduate of West Point. Do you know what that is?"

"Yes, I have heard of it. It is the Army military academy."

"It is, and he is an educated man."

"You are an educated man."

"I guess it depends on the definition of education. You said you finished eighth grade?"

"Yes."

"Well, I finished seventh by the skin of my teeth."

"But you are a doctor."

"Some might dispute that. I will tell the story of my education another time, if you remind me. Anyway, Conor fought the Comanche during the Red River War and was a first lieutenant in line for promotion to captain when he decided not to reenlist. I never asked him why he did not, but he passed through this place during his service. That was the first and last time I saw him till he showed up again in civilian garb and said he wanted to make a life here. I still can't figure out why. You have got to have a little defect in your brain to see this land as paradise."

"Very well. I don't have a stake in this anyhow. And I do see why Conor Byrne has got to be involved."

"Kat, you do have a stake in this, and you will be with me when I speak with Conor. You do not have to like him, but I hope you can understand why there must be a truce between the two of you."

"Yes, I guess so. I feel like I just found home, and I sure don't want to lose it. When will he be back from the Roswell Trading Post?"

"If they are on schedule, I am looking for him in about two days, not more than three."

Chapter 16

CONOR RELIEVED DIEGO of handling the mule teams for the Studebaker wagon when they were within a mile of the Munoz rancho. He paid his friend three dollars paper money for each of the seven days out, a generous wage which Lucia would expect accounted for and gave him a ten dollar-gold eagle which Diego secreted in his saddle bags. The conspiracy was unspoken but understood.

"Will be a good night when Lucia see the money. It make her happy, and she want to make me happy. Know what I mean?"

Conor smiled. "I know what you mean." He headed his wagon with the mule string and Stoic trailing behind toward the Triad. Diego's remarks about Lucia turned Conor's mind to Maria. Had he been a fool not to propose marriage to her when the relationship was fresh? It would be nice to have her waiting for him tonight. Or had he experienced a narrow escape from a life in hell? He guessed he would never know.

When he turned the mules toward the warehouse building where he would leave the wagon, he was pleasantly surprised to find the warehouse door open and Kat Ryan standing beside it waving him through. When he reined in the teams and braked the wagon and climbed down, he saw that Kat was already unhitching the mule string and Stoic from the rear of the wagon.

Kat said, "Doc saw your wagon dust fifteen minutes ago. He has been watching for you—thought you would show up today. He is seeing a patient right now. I told him I could help. I have never hitched or unhitched teams from a wagon, but I can get these tag-along critters to the stream for a drink and get your horse unsaddled while you unhitch the wagon teams."

"My thanks for whatever you can do. It would be nice to get that started. It's not necessary to unsaddle my horse, though. It's only a bit past two o'clock. I'll head home when we've got the mules cared for and turned out to graze."

"No. Doc wants to talk. It's important. You can stay for supper, Mister Byrne."

Kat's tone was matter of fact, not friendly but not hostile. He did not want to fuss with this young woman . . .

or girl. He still was not certain how old she might be. She looked like a kid, but her manner somehow suggested she was beyond childhood, and according to Doc she had some time with a man who claimed to be her husband. Of course, he had just turned twenty-six and perspective was starting to change.

"I guess I can do that. I hired somebody for chores for tonight and tomorrow yet."

Later, Doc, Conor, and Kat sat in the small parlor area of the residence, Doc and Kat sharing the settee and Conor seated in the rocking chair facing them. These pieces and two lamp tables constituted the furnishings near the fireplace in the long room that extended to the kitchen. A dining table that was pulled out when more guests were present was pressed against one wall near the kitchen end of the room.

Doc spoke to Conor. "Kat has a chicken and assortment of vegetables on a slow bake in the Dutch oven in the fire pit outback. She baked rancher's bread in the oven yesterday, and you won't be satisfied with one slice. And there is the left-over apple cake. I took me on a Dutch oven wizard here. You will enjoy your supper a few hours from now."

Kat said, "I never had the option of cooking on anything but open fire. I haven't figured out what to do with your woodstove yet, and we sure don't want a fire burning in the fireplace this time of year. You are getting the chicken, by the way, because one of Doc's patients left one as a payment on account this morning. Do you ever receive cash money, Doc?"

"Oh, that happens on occasion. Frankly, I generally come out better with the bartered goods. Not much cash in these parts."

Conor judged that Kat still seemed uneasy in his presence but working with him in getting the mules stripped down and watered seemed to dull her fangs some. He had yet to see her smile, but the perpetual scowl had abandoned her face, which was far prettier than it was at their first meeting.

Doc said, "I guess it is time to get down to business. Conor, I asked for this little meeting because a problem has been laid at my feet—it is your problem, too, unfortunately. I have had a visit from a Santa Fe lawyer and a few men he calls 'enforcers.' He presented me with this notice." He handed Conor the notice.

Conor read the official-looking document. "He is claiming that you don't own the Triad land. I heard someone was snooping around, asking questions of the folks around here about how they acquired their properties, how long they had been here, that sort of thing."

Doc related the story of his confrontation with attorney Emilio Ortiz. "This doesn't just affect me, of course. All of you who have purchased parcels from me are affected. If my ownership is invalid, so is yours. You may have a notice posted at your residence when you get home, or they may be testing me first. The man said that the Mendoza grant included 100,000 acres, so we are not the only ones affected, but there aren't many settlors in this part of the territory, so I have no idea who claims that land."

"We need to do a lot of research, and we must have our own lawyer soon."

"I can buy back the tracts I have sold off, including yours. I will make it right with folks."

"But where does that leave you?"

"I am not leaving here. I will stake Kat to a fresh start someplace, but I am not leaving. I will die first and hope somebody buries me with Ruth and the kids."

"Forget about buying me out. I am not going anyplace, and to hell with the sixty days."

Kat said, "Forget about the stake. I am not leaving, either."

Doc said, "There will be violence if we don't find a way to head this off." As always, he spoke matter-of-factly without a hint of excitement in his voice.

"The territorial land records are in Santa Fe," Conor said. "We must build a legal case to back us eventually, and I have mentioned before that when I completed my purchases from you that I wanted to have a legal metes and bounds survey made of the property and filed in the public records. As near as I know the measured footage on the parcel boundaries is very vague with corners marked off by movable stones or trees that could disappear in ten years. Much of my training at West Point was engineering, and, as you know, this has always troubled me."

Doc nodded. "And you are right, of course. I barely know enough about doctoring. I am moving into a foreign land on the matters we are dealing with here. This is going to take money. I have hundreds of gold doubloons the Ghost has deposited here over the years. They are buried in a steel box at the northeast corner of the stable. It is time to turn some of them into spendable money."

"It will take some money. As you know, I still owe you money on my land. I am not much help on that part."

"This is my responsibility, but I must ask you to take command of this battle, soldier. I am at a loss, and I am just too danged worn out to deal with all this."

Conor said, "This is my suggestion. Let me go to Santa Fe and find us a lawyer. We must obtain good legal advice first. If the lawyer agrees, I would like to contact a friend of mine in El Paso. He is an engineer and planning to do surveying work in Mexico and Texas. I can send him a telegram from Santa Fe and find out if he is available to take on our job here. He is just getting started in the business, and I might be able to lure him here. If not, perhaps he can recommend somebody else, or the lawyer can identify someone."

"Yes, do this. How soon do you wish to leave?"

"I will need tomorrow to get ready, so I will try for the next morning. I think it will take at least five days to get there if I take two horses, so I can switch. I will take a packhorse or mule, too. I will likely be gone for two weeks. It could be a bit longer."

"You will need to take the gold to an assay office. I have no idea how much gold is in a doubloon. You can probably sell them there. You can easily carry half of what I've got if you are taking a pack animal. I'm sure that would get us started with a lawyer. I will arrange for Diego to check your livestock mornings and evenings, and I will check also from time to time myself. Now there is one other item to discuss." He turned to Kat, "Are you still willing to do this, Kat?"

She looked at Conor warily. "Yes, I guess so."

Doc said, "Kat may require a lawyer also. I have told you bits and pieces of her story, but I did not feel at liberty to tell you everything. You know that she has some unsettled matters with the law, but you should know the details. I want you to present her story hypothetically to a lawyer. Do not reveal her name unless you receive assurance of confidentiality. I don't know if a lawyer would have some ethical or legal obligation to reveal her whereabouts."

Conor thought his mission was becoming unduly complicated, but he understood that the vast distance to travel for legal assistance dictated that as many objectives as possible be resolved in a single trip. "I am listening."

Kat spoke hesitantly at first, fastening her eyes on his. "Some details I am not comfortable repeating, but I will tell you my story. I want you to have some idea of how I came to be in this predicament. Understand that I blame no person but myself. I accept responsibility for the bad choices I have made in my life. At Doc's suggestion, I am working at putting aside any bitterness about my past and working on bettering myself and my life."

"A good lesson for all of us," Conor said. "Sometimes, blaming others is just an excuse for our own shortcomings. I have done that."

Kat continued, "The problems you are concerned about commenced when my father died." She was obviously uncomfortable telling her story, but she met his gaze unflinchingly as she recited the tale of how she came to be at the Triad. Conor assumed that her memory was selective about more sensitive matters, but he did not feel she was withholding anything of significance.

When Kat reached the confrontation with her pursuers in one of the Guadalupe canyons, she told of Buford Walters's attack and her blackout just before someone or something took him away. She stopped abruptly. "That is my story, all you are going to hear anyway."

Conor nodded. "You have lived a long nightmare. I want to return to your arrest and escape from jail. You are certain that up to that point no charges had been formally filed against you?"

"I am positive. There likely would have been none. Buford was probably going to turn me over to Louie. That would have been worse than hanging as far as I am concerned. I was not going to wait, and I have no second thoughts about that decision."

Conor thought about her story for several minutes before he spoke. "We don't even know if charges have been filed against you or if you are a fugitive as far as the law is concerned." He looked at Doc, who had remained silent and somber as Kat spoke. "It will add a few more days to my travels, but I think I should swing over to Albuquerque on the way and see what I can learn. It is getting to be a big city I am told, maybe as many as three thousand people now, but still small enough that there is plenty of local gossip in the taverns and liveries."

"Try the Welcome Inn," Kat said. "It's the big social center there. That's where Louie and Buford spent a lot of evenings. Food, liquor, and women, in whatever order a man chooses." Conor detected more than a little sarcasm in her remark.

Doc said, "You are right, Conor. A lawyer cannot be much help without the facts. Maybe we are worrying about nothing as far as Kat's legal problems are concerned."

Conor did not suggest that they might not be worrying enough.

Chapter 17

DOC ENTERED THE trading post early morning several days after Conor had departed for Santa Fe. Three gold doubloons on the counter told him that the Ghost had visited the night before. It never ceased to puzzle him how the Ghost entered the store, which was locked with the keyed lock at night, but not with the bolt lock that was available. He had no desire to keep the Ghost out. The keyed lock would keep out most intruders, he figured, and he and the Ghost had been friends for many years now without ever having a face-to-face meeting.

He reached for the doubloons when he saw they were resting on top of a parchment sheet that was penciled with a sketch of some kind. He picked up the coins and then studied the sketch. It was of the northeasterly mountain face that ran across the southerly edge of Doc's invisible, jagged border that ended some hundred yards into the mountain's bluffs and slopes and included a half dozen canyons. He had never walked the boundaries, portions were inaccessible, but he had been to the corner markers, one of which was an enormous, immovable boulder and the other an ancient pine.

He thought the simple sketch quite good, showing the location of the Triad and surrounding buildings and the canyon where his animals grazed. It was not drawn to scale, which was unnecessary. A stick figure holding a rifle stood near a boulder at one end, and another stick figure was next to a pine at the other. A third was posted on a ledge within rifle range of the Triad as near as he could judge. The Ghost was obviously warning him that men were watching his land and that one was near enough to take him down with a rifle shot.

Several concerns raced through his mind. Kat had left for an early morning ride on Toughie an hour earlier. He did not like the idea of strangers lurking on the property with a young woman riding about, however, with her short hair and Plainsman hat, he hoped they might not recognize her as female. The devils likely carried telescopes for this duty, however, and they would get a close-up view.

It also worried him that someone might be following Conor. If they were watching the place, they would have known of his earlier visit. Emilio Ortiz would be concerned about any emissary to Santa Fe, and a man with two horses and a pack mule would be suspected of commencing a long journey. Ortiz would want to keep other lawyers away from the dispute. Doc also had to consider that while it would simplify the lawyer's task if Doc would just transfer his interest in the land, the occupant's death would be more convenient than battling in the courts. Once the Mendoza claimants took possession, who would challenge them? The legal process would become a mere formality.

He stepped out onto the veranda and found Loafer basking in the morning sunlight. "I suppose you welcomed the Ghost last night and told him to go right on in," Doc told the dog.

Loafer appeared disinterested in anything Doc had to say. Doc cast his eyes about, hoping to see some sign of Kat returning but found only an empty horizon. He remembered now that she had planned to ride over to Conor's to check the place. It was only two miles distant, though, and that should not take long. Diego was taking care of any chores, so there was nothing for her to do. She had never been to Conor's homestead, and he suspected she was more curious than anything else.

He decided to see what he could do about breakfast. He had been spoiled since Kat's arrival. At her insistence, she had been preparing breakfast most days. Sometimes they shared cooking and domestic chores, but he admitted that he was not resisting seriously her efforts to take over primary responsibility. The little gal was increasingly a working fool as her health improved and there was no slowing her down. His pace was more like a turtle's, slow and steady, and a tired turtle at that.

He had just taken the biscuits out of the woodstove oven when Kat walked in. "Doc, you didn't have to do this. I had planned to do breakfast." She walked to the stove to confirm coffee was brewing and lifted the lid on the frying pan. "I thought I smelled bacon clear from the stable."

"I like to keep in practice," Doc said.

"And I like to earn my keep."

"You more than earn your keep. You are like having a housekeeper and a hired man in a single package, not to mention a clerk and bookkeeper. I've got to start paying you a wage."

"You feed me, clothe me, provide everything I need. I don't want pay," she said as she filled her plate and sat down at the table. "Good Lord, Doc, I eat twice as much as you."

"Just the same, we are going to agree on a wage. You should be setting aside some money for the future."

"Doc, until you send me away, this is my future."

"You are not going to be sent away, but I am not a young man. I won't be here forever."

"I don't even want to think about that."

Doc sipped at his coffee and said, "The Ghost visited last night."

"He did? How do you know?"

He told her about the doubloons and sketch.

"We are being watched?"

"Yes. I don't want you riding out on your own in the mornings until this land fuss is settled."

"It sounds like this is more than a fuss. Anyway, I will stay close to home. I don't want to ride over to Conor's place anymore, that's for sure."

"What do you mean?"

"It's depressing. How does a man live like that? I know I shouldn't have, but the door to his cabin—if you want to call it that—was unlocked and I peeked in. A pig wouldn't set forth in that mess. A good north wind is going to blow it away one of these days. And the stable is cleaner—but three horses and no workspace? And if the wind takes that shack, the stable goes with it, I fear."

"Conor is a bachelor. His folks were small farmers, and he never had much growing up. A very interesting young man. He will have more someday, but he is very patient and a hard worker. He studies Stoicism. His gray gelding is named Stoic for his calmness. He says I am a natural Stoic, but I have never read a word of the stuff and don't plan to."

"I never heard of it. What is it? Some kind of religion?"

"No. I guess you would call it a philosophy that goes back to the ancient Greeks and Romans. He often quotes a man named Marcus Aurelius, who was emperor of Rome. I guess he wrote about the philosophy."

"Conor is a strange man, isn't he?"

"Some might say so, but lots of folks think I'm strange. And a few might think you are."

"You think I am strange, don't you?"

He finished a biscuit and thought about her question for a moment. Then he said, "Yes, I think you qualify. Fortunately, I like strange."

Chapter 18

CONOR DECIDED TO stay over at the Roswell Trading Post his second night out. There was a room available there for a half dollar, and it would be his last opportunity for a bed till he reached Albuquerque, not that he cared that much. He especially wanted to grab the chance to put his critters up in a stable and pamper them a bit before starting the longest leg of their journey.

And he also wanted to see if the man who had been following him showed up here. It would be difficult for a rider to resist the opportunity to resupply and have a drink or two at the little tavern attached to the post. The trader informed him that the tavern also served meals. The other choice was to prepare his own in a fire ring out back.

As to the rider who had been trailing him, Conor would not recognize the man if he appeared, but he rode a white-stockinged, black horse that would be easy enough to identify. He dropped his gear in the rented room, which was barely wide enough for a bed and lamp table. A single, straight-back chair sat just off the foot of the bed, and that was the extent of the furnishings. He checked the bedsheets, pleasantly surprised that they appeared to be freshly laundered.

He tossed the saddlebags containing the doubloons over his shoulder and headed for the tavern. He was not about to separate himself from the treasury, and he figured it would not be all that unusual for a rider to carry his saddlebags with him. As he stepped out onto the boardwalk that connected the rented room, trading post, and tavern, he saw a slim rider, astride a white-stockinged black gelding, dismount and hitch the mount to the rail in front of the tavern. A cigarette dangled from the corner of the man's lips, and his pale complexion contrasted sharply to the bushy black mustache that encroached upon his upper lip. He tossed a glance at Conor and paused briefly as if uncertain what he should do. He decided to continue to the tavern and pushed his way through the batwing doors.

Conor followed and walked up to the bar and edged in beside the man, deliberately invading his space. The bartender, a chunky round-faced man with whisker-bristled cheeks, stepped over. "What will it be gents?"

"A whiskey," Conor said. "I am buying for my friend here, too. And I would like a supper menu."

The other man turned and glared at Conor. "Make mine whiskey, too. But I don't need no stranger buying my drinks."

The bartender's eyes darted back and forth between the two customers. "Roasted beef and beans. Fried taters if the cook's got some. Apple pie if he's got a piece left. That's the menu tonight and every night. Costs a dollar. Think on it. I'll get your drinks."

Conor spoke to his hostile drinking companion. "I'm not a stranger, mister. I am guessing you know my name, but for the record, it's Conor Byrne. What's your handle?"

"None of your damn business, and we ain't never met."

The bartender appeared and poured two drinks. The follower tossed a half dollar on the bar. "Will that cover mine?"

"Yep."

The man walked away and took a seat at a table in the corner of the tavern which would seat no more than twenty people. Conor paid for his drink and told the bartender, "I will have the beef and beans with any extras the cook will add on."

"I'll tell him. Be maybe a half hour to warm things up. Will you be needing another drink?"

"Only coffee, if you've got it."

"Cook has got some brewing. Tends to be on the muddy side."

"That will do. Sounds like the stuff I make."

Conor picked up his whiskey glass and strolled over to his new acquaintance's table and sat down across from him.

The man looked at him with astonishment. "What the hell? I didn't invite you over here."

"We need to have a chat."

"I don't feel like no chat."

Conner said, "You have been following me for two days now. I am guessing you are a part of the so-called enforcers outfit hired by the Santa Fe lawyer, Ortiz. I can save you a lot of time and trouble if you are concerned about my destination."

"I got nothing to say to you."

"My first stop will be Albuquerque. After that, I will be riding on to Santa Fe to speak with a lawyer there. See, I have saved you a lot of time. The question I have is, what are you supposed to do when you determine where I am headed? Are you to kill me before I get to the lawyer or

160

just let someone know that I contacted one? I am thinking that I am not supposed to arrive in Santa Fe."

"You must be crazy, Byrne. I ain't been following you, and I don't give a shit where you are going or what you are going to do when you get there."

"Well, if you are telling the truth, we won't have a problem, but I am giving you fair warning that if you crowd me within rifle range, I will be testing my marksmanship."

The nameless man slurped the remaining contents of his glass down, stood, and walked out of the tavern. The bartender yelled at Conor, "Hey, cowboy. Chow's ready. No table service in this place. Pick up your plates at the bar. Coffee will be a bit yet."

Conor went to the bar to retrieve his meal and settle with the bartender. He was pleased to find he had been granted both the fried potatoes and apple pie. He returned to his table, chose a chair that faced the door, and ate his supper, which turned out to be decent fare.

When Conor walked back to his room, he moved quickly and was watchful for any unexpected movement. He thought it unlikely the man would attempt a killing in the tiny settlement but would be more inclined to wait for opportunities away from potential witnesses. Still, he had laid down the gauntlet, and he could tell the man was seething with anger and could not be counted upon to use good sense. He would not have the patience to wait many days out, though, and more than likely one of them would be dead within a few days. When he entered his room, he placed his Colt on the table adjacent to the bed and propped the chair against the door and then pulled off his boots and stretched out on the bed. Sleep snatched him up almost instantly.

Chapter 19

BEFORE HE LEFT the Roswell Trading Post, Conor discussed with the trader the demand for more salt there. The Cahill ranch had snatched up every ounce delivered by Conor and would buy two or three times that much as soon as it was available. The trader was willing to take delivery and handle marketing of the salt for a small commission. This set Conor to thinking about other opportunities in the salt business again. He would have a serious talk with Doc upon return to the Triad.

Conor rode Stoic this morning, heading a few miles east before swinging north to follow the course of the Pecos River. He figured he might save a day or two by cutting northwesterly, but he did not know that country and worried about the availability of water. He planned to stay with the river till he reached the now abandoned Fort Sumner and then would angle west toward Albuquerque. Time was important but that should not surrender to prudence.

He had seen no sign of the enforcer so far but had not expected to. His trail with two horses and a mule could be followed by a ten-year-old. The man would not risk Winchester slugs being fired his way. Odds were that he would make his move at night. He would be anxious to do the job he was sent to do. Conor wanted to get the game over, so he could get some sleep nights.

That night, Conor set up camp where the narrow ribbon of a sandy stream and the Pecos River intersected. The Pecos's steep banks sometimes made accessing the water a challenge. The shallow stream's water could be reached easily, and the critters could drink directly from the clear water without negotiating the often-treacherous footing downslope to the river channel.

The grass was lush here, unlike the near desert he had settled further south, and the horses and mule would have good grazing during the cool night, he thought. He laid out his bedroll near a thick cluster of desert willow that offered cover from the south and east, blocking the view of any would-be killer who might approach from those directions. The river would prevent any attack from the east.

He made a cold camp, settling on beef jerky and a few slices of bread for supper. As the sun dropped over the western horizon, he picked up his rifle, abandoned his bedroll and slipped deeper into the mass of willows beyond his blankets. He sat down on the ground and leaned against the multiple trunks of one of the taller, sturdier trees that formed a canopy over the area.

The night was so still, he could not even hear rustling of leaves in the breeze. A near two-thirds moon furnished some light outside his hideout. He waited several hours and had almost decided that this was not to be the night when he heard soft footsteps from the south. His visitor.

Soon, he saw a shadowy figure clutching a pistol skirting the trees and turning toward his empty bedroll. Suddenly, the man froze, obviously discovering that there was no occupant in the sleeping place. Conor was no more than twenty feet distant, and his target was outlined nicely in the moonlight. He left his Winchester leaning against a tree, slipped his Colt from its holster, and lifted himself up on one knee. "Good evening," he said. "I have been expecting company."

The visitor started and then swung his pistol toward the trees.

Conor said, "Please don't make me shoot you. I hate killing folks."

The man lowered his gun.

"That's better. Now just drop it on the ground. If you follow instructions, you have got a fair chance to live."

The enforcer obeyed.

"Now, you just wait while I make my way out there." He grabbed his rifle in his free hand and worked his way through the trees and back into the clearing where the man waited.

When he stepped out, the other man spoke. "Calhoun told me you was a greenhorn. I'm thinking you been around some."

"Army. Comanche wars."

"What now?"

"I am going to ask you some questions. If you give the right answers, you will probably live."

"You're serious? You ain't going to kill me? You know I wasn't coming up here just to say howdy?"

"I figured as much. There will be some conditions if I let you go. Now, first question. What is your name?"

He shrugged. "I go by Link Tatum these days."

Conor decided not to pursue the topic. The man had likely used a half dozen names. "Why were you planning to kill me?"

"Well, that's what I'm paid to do. Kill folks if it is necessary. Usually, it's gunfights, and the other feller is shooting at me, too. But I'm what some folks call a hired gun, I guess. They told me to follow you and stop you if you was headed to Santa Fe. Only one way to stop you."

"Who is your employer—your boss?"

"I've worked for Calhoun and Marx for five years now."

"And just who are Calhoun and Marx?"

"They're the boss men. They get the jobs. Mostly range wars, sometimes vigilante work, catching and stringing up horse and cattle thieves and the like. They deal with whoever hired us, get paid and then pay us what we have agreed to. Beats cowhand work for thirty dollars a month."

It crossed Conor's mind that turning this man loose would likely free him to kill others in the future. But shoot him down in cold blood? "I understand you call yourselves enforcers. How many men are riding with you?"

"I suppose near twenty in all. Maybe a few more. Sometimes Calhoun or Marx have men posted someplace that we don't even know about."

"Who are you working for now?"

"Well, I seen this Emilio Ortiz talking to Calhoun a couple of times, and he's rode out with Calhoun and Marx for maybe two to three weeks now to tell folks to get off the land. Them that don't will get burned out and kicked off by the enforcers. That's when we start our real work."

"But you know that Ortiz is not really who you are working for, don't you?"

"Not for a fact. But there's rumors Ortiz works for some outfit called the Santa Fe Ring."

Conor judged that the man was not lying. He was not divulging any information that had not already been elicited by Doc or guessed. The confirmation could be useful, though, when he met with the lawyer. Keeping his gun leveled at his prisoner, he stepped a few paces to where he had left his saddle and the mule's load. He found some rawhide strips in one of the mule's bags and walked over to Link Tatum.

"What you doing?" Tatum asked.

"I'm not going to stay up with you all night. I need some shuteye. Turn around and put your hands behind your back." He quickly cinched the man's wrists together. "Sit down and stretch your legs out in front of you."

Tatum obeyed but, losing his balance, half fell to the earth. Conor hitched the man's ankles together.

The man protested. "I can't sleep like this."

"But I can. Where is your horse?"

"Got him hitched to a tree maybe quarter mile back along the river."

Conor left for less than fifteen minutes and returned with the horse. He unsaddled the animal and staked the white-stockinged gelding out with the others. He spread out Tatum's bedroll a good ten feet from his own and helped the man scoot on top of it.

"Now, I am going to grab some sleep," Conor said.

"What about me? I can't sleep hog-tied like this."

"Sleep or don't. I am not fool enough to cut you loose. I am tired after waiting up for you to visit." He slipped out of his boots and removed his gun belt, placing the Colt within easy reach and covering it with his hat. In a few minutes his eyes closed, and he dropped into a deep slumber.

Conor opened his eyes with the sun's appearance. He sat up and looked over at his guest and was met by a pair of dark eyes glaring at him. Tatum said, "I got to piss bad."

Conor crawled out of his blankets and pulled on his boots before rising and buckling the gun belt about his waist. "I guess that's allowed. I'm going to untie you and let you go in a few minutes anyhow." Conor stepped over and began releasing the rawhide bindings. "Don't try to leave my sight. I'm a fair shot with this Colt."

Tatum stepped away several paces and relieved himself with a big sigh, then buttoning his britches, he turned and faced Conor again. "You're letting me go?"

"I can't be taking you with me, and this morning I am not in the mood to shoot an unarmed man. If I see you again, though, you will earn a slug between your eyes. I want you out of here now."

"How about giving me my guns back? Then I'll take my saddle and get my horse and be on my way."

"It doesn't work that way. You are not taking your guns or saddle or horse."

"I don't understand. You can't do that."

"I just did. Take your bedroll if you want."

"You expect me to walk?"

"I would say you are getting off easy for a man who was aiming to kill me. You follow the Pecos south. In two days that should take you within an easy hop of the Roswell Trading Post."

"I got ten dollars in my pocket. That won't buy me a horse and saddle."

"You can purchase a fair amount of foodstuffs with that. You will be hungry by the time you get there. I suspect Cahill's always hurting for hands. Maybe you can find some honest work for a change. I think I am giving you an opportunity. Now, I am going to be moving on. You get yourself headed in the opposite direction."

Tatum scowled but knelt and began rolling up his blankets. "Damned horse thief," he grumbled.

Conor watched as Tatum started his journey down the river trail, making certain he was a good distance away before breaking camp and packing the mule and saddling the horses. He decided he would ride the stocking-footed gelding first today. He liked the looks of the critter, and he had never rustled a horse before.

Chapter 20

FELIPE SANCHEZ AND Diego and Lucia Munoz sat with Doc and Kat in the Triad hospital waiting area. Doc had informed the two men that they should meet to discuss the Mendoza land grant claim. Lucia was not about to be excluded from any discussion and had accompanied her husband. Felipe's daughter, Maria, opened the door and entered the office, claiming the last chair. "Madre said I should find out what is happening," she said, and claimed the last chair.

Kat had not seen the young woman before, but Doc had mentioned that Maria and Conor had mutual romantic attractions of some sort. She wondered if Maria was the woman for whom he had purchased the necklace. If so, it did not appear above the generous bosom she displayed beyond good taste. Maria was incredibly beautiful, though, and would turn any man's eye her way. Kat did not like her.

Doc said, "Both of your families have received notices to vacate your properties, and I am informed others have, also. You acquired your tracts from me. First, I want to assure you that if you lose your land that I will refund what you paid. If you decide you do not want to fight the Mendoza claim, you may collect whatever payment you can from the lawyer, Ortiz, and I will still return the amount you paid me."

Lucia said, "But we do not wish to leave. Our children were born here. We have worked very hard to improve the land. Now that I have water, I grow things in my garden that no one thought possible. We must fight this."

"Conor Byrne is on his way to Santa Fe now to speak with a lawyer. I will pay for the costs of legal help, but we must prepare to defend our properties if these men try to move us from the land." He looked at Lucia. "I would like for you and Diego to contact all the other owners and find out what they intend to do. Those who plan to resist must agree to form a relay to notify neighbors of any attack on their property, so the remainder of us can come to their assistance. When Conor returns, I will ask him to set up a plan of resistance. His military background best qualifies him to do this."

"Doctor Hayes?" It was Felipe Sanchez.

"Yes, Felipe."

Sanchez was a bony figure with a starved look, likely quick and wiry in his youth, but the years had taken a toll, and the man could have passed for a beat-up seventy years. Kat suspected, however, that given the young ages of his wife and children who had visited the store on several occasions, he was likely nearer fifty. "I have many goats but very little money. I have never owned my own land before. I stay, and I die here if I must, even if I must send my family away for their safety." He tossed a wary glance at his daughter.

"And you are a fool, Padre. You are all fools. These men will kill you without a second thought. And die for this land that can barely support a rabbit? I am leaving this place. It is like living in hell. I intend to seek opportunities in Santa Fe. I refuse to remain and wither up and die like so many of the flowers that struggle to survive. And as for Emilio Ortiz, I have met him, and I found him to be a kind and helpful man. He just has a job to do. Perhaps you should have been more thorough in seeking out the history of the land you purchased, Doctor."

When Doc did not respond, Kat fought off the urge to rise to his defense. She worried also that that the woman's mention of knowing Ortiz indicated they might have a spy in their midst. If Maria had been lured by Ortiz to Santa Fe, it was not likely for noble purposes. Kat suspected Maria might just be moving to another kind of hell. She wondered if the Mexican beauty had told Conor of her plans. Of course, she did not know for certain that Maria was the woman for whom he had purchased the pendant.

After an awkward silence, Felipe Sanchez addressed his daughter. "Maria, please go now. I did not invite you to this meeting, and until this moment I was not aware of your acquaintance with Mister Ortiz."

"Padre, he was with the men who visited a month ago asking questions about the rancho. He spoke with me after you were so unfriendly and walked away. He means us no harm. You should take whatever money he offers and accept Doctor Hayes's refund and go with me to Santa Fe. You can sell your goat herd and buy a house there. You would have money left over and could easily find work."

"But I am where I want to be, doing what I want to do. Now, go. We will talk when I get home."

Maria got up, stomped to the door and departed.

"I apologize, Doctor. I do not blame you for the problem. Maria has become very difficult lately."

"You are not responsible for her words, and I fear there is a certain truth to them. I did not take the care I should have with purchase of the land. We must stay in contact, all of us. If you see anything of a suspicious nature, let me know immediately."

They talked a bit longer about Diego and Lucia contacting the other farmstead owners, nine in all, and agreed to invite all to a meeting as soon as Conor returned.

Felipe remained behind when the Munoz couple departed, and he stepped over to Doc before leaving. "I do not know what to say. Maria has changed so much in a few weeks. She was such a loving, helpful daughter. Now she and her mama fight over everything. She treats her brothers and sisters like slaves. The men who visited that first time did not give their names. Until today, I did not know that the lawyer was one of them."

Doc said, "You will want to take care about what you tell her now. You do realize that?"

"Yes, of course. I just don't understand. She had her heart set on marrying Conor Byrne, and then when he asked her, she turned him down. Conor is a good man. She will never find better. It saddened her mama and me that she did this."

"Well, the only certain thing about life is change. Perhaps she will yet come to see things differently."

Felipe nodded, "We can only hope."

After Felipe rode away, Doc and Kat stood on the veranda. Doc said, "I feel badly for Felipe and Sofia, such good, hard-working folks."

"It would be hard to have your own child turn against you the way Maria has. She has obviously been influenced by Ortiz."

"Appears that way. I am thinking these folks are not going to wait for the law to sort this all out, which makes me wonder if their legal claim is as strong as they make it out to be."

Kat said, "Those men posted on the mountain walls make me nervous. One of them could have a spyglass focused on us right now. Why are they doing this?"

"They aren't hiding. Maybe they are wanting to scare folks into leaving, but it's hard to say. They could have other mischief in mind. We must keep an eye out and not stray far alone."

"I am not straying anyplace."

Chapter 21

KAT HAD ARGUED with Doc about his suggestion that she accompany him with Pablo Torres to the young blacksmith's home more than a half hour distant to assist his wife, Martina, with the delivery of her first child. The residence, Doc had explained, lay in a cluster of four homes of craftsmen bordering Doc's land to the east.

The families there were among the trading post's regular customers who often showed up monthly in a little caravan with at least two buckboards. Customers like this and occasional passers-by who crossed the Guadalupe pass were what allowed the business to subsist. Pablo's brother, Juan, a carpenter, stone mason, and master of anything to do with building, and his young family also lived in the little community. The brothers could be counted on as Doc's allies, although they did not reside within the area of the land grant claim.

Kat had insisted she should remain to mind the store and look after the place in case Doc's visit turned out to be an extended one. Besides, she told him that Loafer would be there to protect her. Doc laughed but had conceded that birthing time of first babies were especially difficult to predict and had finally relented, riding out with Pablo late morning. It was midafternoon now as she worked on inventory in the store with Loafer dozing just outside the entry door, which was propped open to pull in some air. The two windows were open, too, but the scorching sun's heat was winning.

She had been working off and on inventorying the store's contents since her arrival and saw early on that inventory management was not Doc's forte. They had a single bag of flour in stock and ten frying pans. She would give odds that a pan had not been sold in a year or more. Most folks would have such items before they ever settled nearby. The store was overstocked on so many things and understocked on necessities. He had already surrendered inventory decisions to her, and she found herself enjoying the challenges of merchandising.

But it was obvious they needed more customers. The Indian trade was the business mainstay in the early days, Doc had told her. He had made a nice living then. The reservation had nearly eliminated those customers, although occasionally Comanche or Apache resistors stopped by.

Loafer growled out on the veranda, and she looked up and got a glimpse through the near window of a sorrel horse hitched outside. Then she heard boots on the veranda before a big man nearly filled the door space and paused. He stared at her for several minutes, obviously giving her a serious appraisal, and it made her uneasy. She inched her hand under the counter to confirm that the pistol grip was within reach. Loafer continued to growl.

"May I help you," she said.

"Maybe." He stepped into the room, menacing, dark eyes still fixed on her. She saw now that he was a good foot taller, broad-chested and easily more than twice her weight. Shaggy, brown hair dropped to the man's shoulders, and a razor had not touched his face for a week, but he might clean up well. "What do you need?" she asked.

"I bet the fellers you was female. Others said you was a boy. Damned if you ain't a pretty thing at that."

She ignored his remark. Her experience told her that many crude men were harmless, just ill mannered. "I said, what do you need?"

"What are you selling?"

"Anything that's in the store. I can help you find something, or you are free to walk about and choose what you need."

"I would like what's behind the counter."

She turned and looked at the floor to ceiling shelves behind her. "Which item?"

A hand closed like a vice on her wrist and whipped her around to face him. "You, little lady. I'm talking about you. How much for a poke?"

"Let go of me. You couldn't pay me enough."

"Then, I'll have one for free."

He yanked her forward, halfway pulling her over the counter, then he screamed and released her, stumbling backwards and crashing to the floor. She landed on her buttocks behind the counter but leaped to her feet when she heard Loafer roaring like an attacking wolf and the man thrashing and cursing on the floor. "You're dead, cur," the stranger yelled.

Kat grabbed her Colt and moved around the counter just as the man unholstered his own pistol and aimed it at the snarling dog that held fast to his other arm. "Stop," Kat yelled. "Drop your gun, and I will call the dog off." She had no idea if Loafer would respond to such a command. She had never seen this side of the dog.

The man instead turned his weapon toward her, and she squeezed the Colt's trigger, flinching with the weapon's roar when the jolt of the weapon's kickback hit her shoulder. The intruder's pistol clattered to the floor and a splotch of blood began to widen on his chest. Loafer released his arm and backed away, and Kat stepped over, set the pistol barrel within a foot of the man's head, and placed another shot between the eyes. She had not finished the job with Louie Gaynor. She was taking no such chance here.

Loafer came over and looked up at her with worried eyes. She knelt and hugged him and scratched his ears. "Good dog. Brave dog."

Now what? She was not strong enough to move this man. Besides, the others would likely be watching the place from their mountainside sentry posts. They likely would have heard the gunfire, but it would depend upon which post this man had been responsible for. The distance from east to west would be at least several miles, and the others would not have necessarily known that this visit was being made. She hoped that the dead man had covered the nearest watch post more directly above the Triad. If so, he possibly could just disappear.

She went into the living area, retrieved Doc's spyglass, and stepped out onto the edge of the veranda, gambling that she would not be seen by an observer. As she scanned the cliffs that towered above the foothills and desert lands below, she saw no sign of an observer. The men who kept watch from each end of Doc's land would not likely be able to see her.

She spoke to Loafer, who stood beside her, sticking with her like glue now. "Well, fella, I think we will put up that sorry son-of-a-bitch's horse and get the critter out of sight. I guess the store's out of business for the day. Doc's not going to like the chore facing him when he gets back. I just hope it will be soon."

Chapter 22

I T WAS NEARLY dark when Doc approached the Triad. He was tired, but a good tired. He had just delivered a healthy baby boy to the Torres home, and baby and mother were doing fine. There was something about new life, human or animal, that lifted a man's spirits. So much of his medical experience, especially, during the war, had involved helplessly watching men die or merely being the powerless sympathizer when disease struck and wiped out half a family. Yes, there was satisfaction in ministering to folks' medical needs, but the failures weighed heavily on his mind, haunted him from time to time.

He saw a lamplight in the residence, but the remainder of the building was dark. He had no doubt that Kat had already tended to the barn chores. She never stopped moving. She would finish one project and then move on to another, attacking each task like she was killing snakes. He had given up suggesting that she relax a bit more. She was an odd one, but he thought the world of her and was grateful for the day she entered his life. They needed each other.

He reined his mount toward the stable, and when he dismounted and led the horse through the wide door, he was surprised to find a guest in one of the stalls, a sorrel gelding. A saddle and tack lay next to the stall gate. Was Kat entertaining a visitor in the residence?

After getting his mare unsaddled and brushed down, he picked up his medical satchel and headed for the house. He was greeted by Kat and Loafer when he stepped onto the veranda, and the young woman stepped up and hugged him tightly, almost toppling him and totally surprising him by their first such physical contact. Not that he minded one bit.

"I didn't see you two hidden in the shadows," Doc said. "You startled me. But the welcome was nice."

"I've got supper waiting. Biscuits and stew. Apple cake is leftover, but I've got your black coffee."

"I'm starving. I'm still not used to having supper ready when I come home from visits like this. I might be on my way to getting spoiled."

"You deserve some spoiling. Let's go in."

Doc was hungry and figured he might have eaten more than Kat for a change. She put a mug of steaming coffee on the table along with a saucer and a thick slice of apple cake. Only then did Doc remember the strange horse in the stable. "We haven't spoken much. There is a sorrel gelding and saddle in the stable. Are we taking on boarders?"

"I was going to talk to you about that after you finished eating. A man. He is in the trading post."

"And you didn't invite him to supper?"

"He's not hungry. He's dead."

Doc put his fork down. "You've got a dead man in there? What in blazes?"

"He was too big for me to move. Once we get him out, I will clean up the blood. It looks like a slaughterhouse in front of the counter."

Doc pushed his chair back. "I should look. Maybe he is not dead."

"He's dead. I guarantee it. You eat your cake and enjoy your coffee while I tell you about it."

"I am listening."

"It all started when this rider showed up. Loafer did not like him from the start." Kat might have been delivering a school lecture as she calmly related the story of her encounter with the stranger while Doc ate his cake between sips of coffee. She made it sound like the entire event was all in a day's work.

When she finished her story, Doc asked, "You are certain he is with this enforcers bunch?"

"One of the watchers. I am certain he was the one set up to keep an eye on goings on at the Triad."

"We should bury the man yet tonight. We will plant him in the horse corral. There won't be any sign of it in a few days' time. Between us, we should be able to drag him out on the veranda. We will get a rope under his arms and have a horse drag him from there. We should turn his horse out in the canyon pasture where it would take some work to sort it out and identify the critter."

"It doesn't take you long to decide what to do."

"Let's say, I have had a life before the Guadalupe."

Loafer was sitting by his chair, and he reached down to scratch the dog's ears. "I can't believe Loafer attacked that man. I hear him growl about once a year. I always considered him about as ferocious as a cotton tail bunny. Maybe he is more watchdog than I gave him credit for."

"Maybe he just knows who to be worried about."

Doc shrugged. "Could be, but today he earned his keep, that's for darned sure. Pop's proud of you, Loafer." He downed the remaining contents of his mug and rose from the chair. "We have got work to do. I had better see just what you've got in the post room."

Doc led the way and Kat followed him to the entry door. He opened it and stepped inside the room. "Where is the body?"

Kat came up beside him. "It's gone." She pointed to the spot where she had left the dead man. "I left him right where he went down. Look, you can see the blood."

"You are absolutely certain he died? We may need to get a lantern and look around outside."

"Doc, I shot him twice. The second time, I placed a slug between his eyes. He is dead."

Doc walked over to the counter and found the answer to his question. Two Spanish doubloons lay on top. He picked them up and showed Kat. "Your friend the Ghost was here."

Chapter 23

AFTER DISCOVERING THAT the outlaw's body had disappeared, Doc and Kat cleaned the blood from the store's oak floor. Kat found that no amount of rubbing with soapy water would remove some of the stains. Dark splotches would remain as a reminder of the day, not that it worried her any. Following the example of the man who had taken her in, she was beginning to shed deeds past. Doc had said many times when she lamented her past life, "What's done is done." He never encouraged self-pity much. Today would be done in several hours.

While she finished the task, Doc went out to the stable to release the bay gelding into the canyon pasture. Later, as bedtime approached, they sat in the parlor drinking coffee, discussing the fate of Kate's visitor and speculating about what trouble the man's disappearance might trigger and what responses they should be prepared to make.

"If somebody comes by and asks about him," Doc said, "we have never seen the man or have any idea who they are talking about. Can you tell a good lie?"

"I have a lot of experience at that. Why do you think the Ghost took the body—and when?"

"I think the Ghost knew you were here alone and saw the man coming here. By the time he came down from the slopes, the shooting had already taken place. He knew the body needed to be removed and waited till you locked the entrance and took the horse to the stable. That would have given him at least a half hour, maybe twice that. You would have discovered it earlier if you had gone back into the room."

"That I had no desire to do. I guess Loafer followed me to the stable, so he would not have alerted me."

"Loafer lets the Ghost come and go as he pleases. I guess they are friends."

"Well, however it happened, we were saved a lot of trouble."

"Yes. We should be paying him instead of the other way around. Of course, he left the doubloons just to let us know he had been here."

"I cannot imagine where he gets those things."

"He has left a lot of them over the years. He way over-pays, but he has helped me stay in business. It's only a guess, but I am wondering if he did not find a treasure of gold and valuables hidden by early Spaniards in one of the caves on the mountain. There are hundreds of caves up there. He likely lives in one."

"I wonder if we will ever meet him?"

"Hard to say. Only if he wants us to, I suspect."

"I almost forgot. I am embarrassed I never asked. The call you were out on—the baby. Did everything go alright?"

Doc smiled, "Yep. At least something went alright to-day. No serious problems. First time baby, so sometimes that's a little trickier. But the family is doing fine. Good family. Pablo is a very skilled blacksmith, a skilled car-penter, too, and works with his brother when Juan needs help. I fear he will not be able to earn enough of a liv-ing here to support a family, though, unless we can get more people to live in the area or get more folks to pass through."

"It appears to me that you could use more patients or customers, too."

"I get by. I've got a little money banked in El Paso that Ruth's parents left me when she died. They are gone now, too, and had no other children. I don't need much."

"But you've got me here now feeding at your trough."

"You, my dear, have been a godsend. Fate smiled on me when you came here. You are not a burden, and you more than pay your way. But you give me incentive to look more to the future and to gain more ambition again. Conor did that, too." He gestured upward. "It's like somebody up there said, 'No, you cannot have your son and daughter back, but maybe this will help some.' You are six or seven years younger than Conor, about the same age difference as Joseph and Mariah."

She saw tears glistening in his eyes and moved quickly to change the subject. "You never told me how you became a doctor. You said you never had special schooling."

"Only experience. I was raised on a small farm in Tennessee. My pa was handy with cow and horse injuries and ailments and helped with a lot of animal births, especially cattle. He took me with him from the time I was five years old. As I got bigger, I helped him pull a lot of calves into this world. He died when I was seventeen, and folks started asking me to help, and soon I took over where Pa left off. There were no vet schools anyplace, and a man became a veterinary surgeon by experience and self-declaration."

"So you started out as a veterinary surgeon?"

"That's what I did till the war came along. I had a good practice, liked what I did, and made a decent living. Supported my first wife and son quite well."

"You were married before?"

"Diphtheria took them both. I was the closest thing to a physician within fifty miles. I did what I could, but mostly I just watched them die. That was almost eight years before the war came along."

And he picked himself up and went on, she thought. How many have had to do such things? It made a person inclined to savor each day. "I am so sorry. You make my life's journey look like a path through a flower garden."

He was silent for a few moments. "And then came the war. I enlisted with most of the neighboring young men, although in my mid-thirties I was older than most. It was not about slavery to me or most of my friends. My family never owned slaves. Few in our wooded, small farm country ever had. It was about our homeland, duty, that sort of thing. I doubt if most soldiers ever give that much thought to the political motives or purposes of wars. Anyhow, I ended up as an aide in a battlefield hospital."

"That is where you met your father-in-law, Isaac Rosen."

"Yep. I assisted him, and he was surprised at my know-how. Not that much difference between animals and people, you know. Stopping the bleeding takes the same care. There was a severe shortage of medical staff, especially as the war turned bad for the South. One thing led to another, and in a year's time I was operating at my own station, treating every kind of wound, performing amputations and the like. Shortly before I was wounded, Isaac started referring to me as 'Doctor Hayes' and even showed up one day with silver double shoulder bars and a piece of paper declaring that I was commissioned a captain in the Confederate Army medical corps—a big jump from sergeant. Isaac Rosen was a colonel. Anyhow, in a short time I went from country vet to medical doctor, about the only good thing, besides Ruth and the kids, that came out of the war, as far as I was concerned. There were no physician licensing requirements in the territories and most western states, so I came out of the war a medical doctor."

"And how did you end up here?"

"I wanted no more of wars, and I knew that the peace at Appomattox was just the beginning of a new kind of war. I started looking for an escape. I saw this place with twenty thousand acres advertised in Austin, and I met up with the man who owned it—or thought he did. I took off a month to come out here and look at it with him. We made a bargain, and I became a big landowner of acres that grew nothing and was overrun by Apache and Comanche."

"And your wife agreed to it?"

"It took some talking, but she loved me and sort of took to the idea of a great adventure. She was not a timid, fearful woman. Reminds me of somebody in this room. I only pick up bits and pieces here of what is going on in this country and the world. A life of ignorance about some things is not all that bad."

Chapter 24

CONOR HAD NEVER visited Albuquerque. It seemed to be a thriving town, growing in a helter-skelter fashion without noticeable separation of professional establishments or general stores from taverns or liveries as a man might see in other small towns. He supposed it would eventually sort itself out. He rode Stoic at a walk, his train of two horses and mule following.

He reined in at the first livery he came to and dismounted. Stepping inside, he found a young man with a pitchfork cleaning a stall. The stable hand sensed his presence and turned to face him, setting the pitchfork aside. He was a towheaded youngster no more than sixteen, Conor thought, and he offered a friendly smile.

"Howdy, mister," he said, "I'm Dave. What can I do for you?"

"Can you put up three horses and a mule overnight?"

"We sure can. No problem on Tuesdays. Now if you had showed up on a Friday, that would likely be a problem. Fridays and Saturdays, there ain't much room."

"I will be staying over tonight. I'm not sure yet about tomorrow night, but I won't be around on Friday."

Dave cited the rates, and Conor paid him and surrendered his critters. "I will stop by after lunch tomorrow and pay for another day if I decide to stay on."

"That's plenty good."

"Any ideas where I might want to stay—also need a shave and bath. I've been on the trail a spell."

"You seem a respectable sort. You might try The Castle. It's the only lodging house in town that's got a barber shop attached, hot baths, and even a decent eating place. Costs a bit more, though. Lots cheaper than Santa Fe, they say."

Dave told him where to find the hotel, and Conor pressed two bits in the boy's palm in appreciation. He headed out the door with heavy saddlebags slung over each shoulder, then stopped and turned back, "Oh, Dave," he hollered down the stable aisle where the boy was leading the horses and mule. "Where is a tavern called the Welcome Inn?"

"I don't recommend it, but it's just two buildings west of your hotel."

Conor checked into the hotel and found the second-floor room clean and quite nice. He felt out of place, dirty and stinking from all the days on the trail. It was midafternoon, and he decided to claim a bath at the rear of the main floor. After that, he would get a barber's shave, although he did not need a haircut. Every few months, Maria had kept his hair cut to suit him—or herself. Of course, that routine would be changing. Barbers tended to be a treasure trove of gossip and information.

He searched out a place to hide the gold doubloons. They were becoming a nuisance, and he was anxious to get them to Santa Fe, negotiate a sale, and deposit the proceeds in a bank. He located some loose floorboards beneath the carpet under the bed, pushed the bed aside, and used his skinning knife from the saddlebags to pry the boards up. Finally, he lifted the ends of two of the wide planks and was able to spread out the entire saddlebag between the floor joists before pushing the planks back into place and restoring the carpet and bed to their original places.

The bath refreshed him, and his next stop was the hotel barbershop. When he entered, he saw that a grizzled man with white hair falling to his shoulders was in the barber chair, but no others were waiting. Satisfied there were no customers ahead of him, Conor claimed a spot on one of the benches that lined the wall. The barber, a bald, skinny man with a black handlebar mustache that arched like the horns of a longhorn steer, was bent over the customer with a large clipper, working the blades like he was sheering a sheep. Enough hair to stuff a pillow was piling up on the floor, and from the man's clean-shaven face, Conor suspected much of that came from a beard that had been shorn off earlier.

"Likely be another twenty minutes with George here," the barber said. "Looks like you will just be needing a shave."

"Yes. That will do me today."

"Doing my yearly today," George said with a gravelly voice. "Fixing myself up some before I visit the ladies at the Welcome Inn tonight."

"I'll be over there later myself," Conor said. "I will buy you a drink or two if we meet up."

"Ain't likely to turn it down," George said. "Don't mind spending a dollar for a fifteen-minute poke, but I got my own still in the foothills northwest of here, and I hate paying tavern prices for rotgut that ain't as good as my own."

"How far is your place from here?"

"Three wagon days. I come down to the big city once a year. Trading post a day from my place for my in between needs. Got me a cozy one-room cabin, and I trap and hunt. Not many of us left now. I deal some furs and skins at the trading post but bring a wagon load of the best here every year. Get twice the money."

"Sounds like a lonely life to some, but I understand it."

"Yep. Sometimes a man is his own best company. Got me a dog and two mules. That's enough most of the time. No Apaches up that way these days, and the Navajos and me get along good enough. Now, you know all about me. It would be a fair trade if you tell me what you're up to in this place. You don't live hereabouts, I'm guessing."

"Nope. Just passing through unless an opportunity comes up. My name is Conor Byrne. I did some soldiering during the last few years of the Red River War. I've done some scouting for the Army since, but I'm done with that. I figured I would rest up for a day or two and then head up to Santa Fe and see what kind of work I might find there."

The barber paused from his shearing. "Irishman, huh? Thought you had that look."

Conor was not going to ask about "that look," but he wondered if the man was hostile toward the Irish. Such animosity was not that uncommon. "Yeah, my folks were both Irish, born and raised in Pennsylvania, though. Their folks came from the old country. Indentured servants, all of them." He saw no reason to lie about his background, fewer chances of entrapping himself with an unnecessary lie. That did not mean he was not prepared to tell a tale or two to learn what he wanted.

"You can call me Sam," the barber said. "What kind of work are you looking for? Maybe I can help some. I got a fair handle on what might be available here."

"Well, I was thinking about looking for a law job. My pop was a county sheriff back home, and I sort of grew up with that. Of course, I would have to start out as the lowest deputy. I doubt if Albuquerque would have any need for that."

George said, "The lawmen here are crooked as snakes in a cactus patch."

The barber said, "Now, George, that ain't fair."

"Well, I heard that your town marshal Yarberry is being held in the county jail for killing some feller. Shot him in the back, I heard."

"Well, he is being held for trial, but he ain't been proved guilty. And I'm told by some it was a fair gunfight."

"Do they need a deputy?" Conor asked.

The barber said, "They need a good one, that's for sure. We got old Buford Walters hanging onto the job by his fingertips till the town council decides what to do.

Betwixt you and me, the man's a halfwit, and now he can't talk."

"Best for us all," George said. "Never spoke a word that made sense."

"I don't understand," Conor said. "What do you mean he can't talk?"

The barber said, "He lost his tongue. To make a long story short, he had a girl locked up in jail. She tricked him somehow, and Buford got locked up in her place. She steals his horse, and a few days later he takes off after her with some cowhand he hired on and an Apache scout named 'Cold Eyes.' Most thought he would bring the girl back slung across a horse's back. He came back alone and without his tongue. Somebody cut it out."

"Sounds ghastly. What happened?"

"Nobody knows for sure. He sort of gobbles like a turkey when he tries to talk. He reads just enough to get by, but when it comes to writing he don't make much sense. Can't spell out but a few words on paper. But him and that girl's man, Louie Gaynor, ain't giving up on finding that girl when they're both well enough to ride. Buford is blaming her for his lot and Louie is after payback."

"What did she do to end up in jail?"

George chuckled, "I heard she near hammered his brains out with the butt end of an axe while he was sleeping. Son-of-a bitch likely earned it. They say he beat the hell out of her, and she was always walking around with a bruised-up face. I'd give her a medal for the deed. I know Louie. One mean bastard, sober or drunk."

"Were they married?"

"No," the barber said. "Louie claims they were common law, whatever that is. Her name is Kathleen Ryan. Half your kind, the other half Mexican. Father was a fine carpenter when sober, which was not often enough. Mother was a sweet lady, did cleaning and cooking for folks about town. Somehow, after the folks died, Louie ended up with their little ranch and the girl."

"Is there a reward out for her capture?"

"None that I've heard about. They say the county sheriff isn't butting in, even though he thinks any crime against Louie took place in his jurisdiction, not the town's. He was in the shop the other day and said, since nobody got killed, he didn't see it as any different than a tavern brawl. He's got enough concerns dealing with the killings and rustlings in the county. He said, 'The town marshal's office bit off the problem, so they can eat it.'"

Later, after the barber was finished with him, Conor gave Sam a dollar for the fifty-cent shave. The stop had been a good investment. By the time they had finished talking, Conor had elicited more information than he had hoped to dig up. He would still visit the Welcome Inn this evening for a spell, but tomorrow he would be following the wagon road to Santa Fe.

Chapter 25

CONOR ATE DINNER in the hotel dining room and indulged himself in a rare nap in his room before walking the short distance to the Welcome Inn. When he entered, he was struck by the fact that he had visited this place before in countless western towns starting with his Army stopover at Fort Riley, Kansas and a visit to nearby Junction City. Smoke-filled, a lingering sweat smell that battled with the odor of kerosene lanterns for dominance. Dark and dingy. There was a long bar off to the left, ending at a staircase to a second floor, where two women in seductive poses, one quite pretty, the other not so much, waited to escort those interested to a few moments of heaven.

Tables were scattered in front of the bar for sit-down drinkers, and to the rear of the room men gathered around tables dealing cards, the lucky ones identified by stacks of poker chips at their places. Several intense games appeared in progress. He walked up to the bar, and as if on cue, George from the barber shop came down the stairway and limped over to him.

"You still good for that drink or two?" George said.

"I sure am. What will it be?"

"Whiskey."

"I'll join you."

"Make it three then. I'll take my two upfront, if it's all the same to you."

The old devil ought to give him more information for that, Conner figured. A sleepy-eyed bartender about Conor's own height and thin as a toothpick moved in behind the bar and asked, "What will it be gents?"

"Three whiskeys," Conor said.

He returned with the drinks. Conor paid him, and they moved to a table. Although he was not expecting trouble, Conor claimed a chair facing the batwing doors. He looked at George, who did not seem quite so ancient with his hair shorn and long beard shaved off.

George said, "I thank you for the drinks, Conor. You seem like a good man. A man with some education, I think. And you ain't looking for a lawman's job. You didn't fool Sam the barber none, neither. You need to hone your lying skills some. I doubt you've had much experience."

Conor sighed. "No, I wasn't looking for a lawman's job. I came to town to get some information. I am not free to say why."

"Don't matter none. I've had my poke, and I'm free to talk a spell. I need to whittle away some time in case I decide to go back for seconds. Ask me what you want to know. I'd wager it's about Buford Walters. Might cost you one more drink. That will be all I'll be drinking tonight."

What did he have to lose? Somehow, he trusted George not to say anything to the men he was interested in. And did he care?

'You guessed right. I'm interested in Walters and Louie Gaynor. I'm just collecting information for a friend."

"Well, I know both fellers but only good enough to say howdy when I can't escape it. They wouldn't waste a minute talking to an old buzzard like me. Now Buford, he ain't the dumbest guy in the county, but he better hope the other guy don't die."

"Any rumors on Buford's plans?"

"Well, he will hang on to that deputy's job until they take his jail keys away, which will likely be at the town council's meeting a few weeks from now, I hear. I guess I got a little sympathy for the feller not being able to talk and all. Doubt he's done any real work since he growed up, and I don't think he will be calling auctions. Maybe he could sweep out taverns and that sort of thing, clean barn stalls maybe. He won't take that up anyhow till him and Louie track down Kat Ryan and give her what they think is her due. Buford blames that little Kat for him losing his tongue." He chuckled, "Buford thinks Kat's got his tongue."

George looked at him for approval of the pun, and Conor smiled and nodded. "You sound like you might have known Kat."

"Yep. Her pa, poor feller, was a good man if it wasn't for the demon that had him by the balls. I'd see Kat when I stopped by their place from time to time. Turned into a damn pretty girl with the sweetest smile. She would talk your head off and could charm a man out of his mule if she took a notion. Never saw her after that Louie Gaynor took her in. Damn shame. When you see Kat, you tell her that George Underhill sends her his best."

She had the sweetest smile? Well, he certainly had not seen a trace of it. This old trapper was reading him like a book. Conor abandoned any thought of a career as a detective. "So you think Buford and this Gaynor will be going after her?"

"Yep. And if they catch her, they will hold her a few days and have some fun, and then they will kill her. They won't be bringing her back here alive. I guarantee it. I hope you will look after her. I take it you don't know that Louie and Buford are both here tonight?"

"They are? Where?"

"Poker tables. Just turn your head a mite. The one closest to the wall. Buford's the feller what looks like a big apple and is waving his hands about, Louie's the big galoot built like a grizzly and his forehead and face on this side caved in like a mashed tomato. He might just be the meanest man in the county, especially now, with second place far behind."

Conor thought it would simplify things if he just killed both men while he was still here, but he was not inclined to risk his own hanging, and deep down he knew that cold-blooded killing wasn't in him. And there was a good chance they would never find Kat anyhow. "George," he said, "you have been very helpful. I will give Kat your best." He reached his hand across the table and shook George's firmly. "I had best be moving on. I'd like to grab a good night's shuteye before I head to Santa Fe in the morning. I will pay that bartender for that third drink on my way out, and I hope you can get that second poke."

George laughed. "Won't be for lack of trying. Good luck, my friend."

Chapter 26

DANNA SINCLAIR WAS a person who inspired confidence, Conor thought—calm, deliberate in her speech, and a striking, strawberry-blonde woman with sapphire-blue eyes and Nordic features. He figured she must stand ten or eleven inches over five feet, because when she stood to shake his hand and greet him upon entering her private office, she nearly matched his height in her heeled shoes.

He was seated in front of her desk now, and her face was framed in the window behind her desk, the sunlight giving the hair that fell over her shoulders a coppery tint. She looked at him with searching eyes. He knew she was reading him, evaluating this man who had talked his way past her Mexican clerk and into her private office without an appointment.

Bypassing small talk, the lawyer moved immediately to business. "Well, Mister Byrne, you hooked me when you told Linda de la Cruz you wanted to see me about a land grant case." She paused. "May I call you Conor?"

"Yes, of course. I would prefer that."

"And I am Danna. I am curious, how did you find your way to our office and me in particular?"

"You were recommended by Rylee O'Brian, the vice-president of the Second National Bank. I met her when I was setting up a new bank account there. She is a delightful young woman and went out of her way to be helpful. She said that land grant issues were your specialty."

"I work with many real estate matters, but I am the only one in our firm who handles land grant disputes—and there are enough of those to take up most of my time. Why don't you just tell me your story, so I can decide if I might be the lawyer to help you."

"Well, your client would be Doctor Roman Hayes." Conor removed an envelope from the inner pocket of the new doeskin jacket he had purchased for the different visits he needed to make in Santa Fe. He slid the envelope across the desk. "Doctor Hayes wrote a letter granting me authority to retain a lawyer and to speak on his behalf. I gave the bank a similar letter, because I am dealing with his money. They are sending other papers for his signature back with me, and I can do the same for you if you take the case."

She opened the envelope and scanned the letter. "You have not seen the contents?"

"No. I took it that he did not intend me to."

"He must truly trust you." She put the letter aside.

"I hope so. Anyhow, you wanted the story. Here it is." He started with Doc's original acquisition of the twenty thousand acres at the base of the Guadalupe Mountains and showed her a pencil-sketched map showing approximate locations of tracts that had been sold off and the notice delivered to Doc by Emilio Ortiz. He also gave her the deed that transferred the property to Doc. "I checked at the courthouse. The deed has been registered in the territory land records. There are no deeds for the parcels sold to me and the Mexican families. He needed to make a trip to Santa Fe to do that and kept putting it off. We have letters describing the parcels by physical locations and declaring that the purchase was made and the price."

Danna said, "There is no surveyed description of anything, including the doctor's original purchase, but that is not unusual. Much of the land out here is not legally surveyed."

"I have wired a friend of mine in El Paso. He is a West Point graduate just starting in the surveying business. I will stay in town a few days on the chance he can be located and responds quickly. I will authorize the telegraph office to deliver the message to you if it does not come in before I must go. I don't like leaving Doc alone with those so-called enforcers about."

"For good reason, I assure you. Emilio Ortiz represents an informal group called the Santa Fe Ring. These men acquire property and money more by intimidation and violence than by law. He would not be pleased with my involvement."

"It sounds like you are the lawyer we are looking for."

She was silent for a bit, looking upward like an answer was floating above her somewhere. Based upon her supposed expertise, Conor had thought she might be an older woman, but female attorneys were so few, it stood to reason that he would be dealing with a younger woman. He guessed Danna Sinclair as a year or two on either side of thirty.

Finally, Danna spoke. "I don't know if you can afford me. A case like this will be a huge demand on my time. It could be months before we get before a judge with evidence. At some point, I may find it necessary to visit the property. I would prefer to wait for the legal survey and that will take a lot of time, I am guessing. I cannot handle this for a set fee. I would bill you three dollars an hour for my time and would require a retainer fee of five hundred dollars which would be applied to the hourly fees as

earned. Additional deposits would be required when services exceed that amount. Notice that I say 'when' not 'if.'"

"I can write a draft today, if you like."

"Wait till you are ready to leave town. I wish to check
out a few things in the territorial records and do a bit of
research. I can give you my initial thoughts about strategy then. Also, Doctor Hayes had a separate letter in the
envelope that lists some unrelated legal work he requires.
I wish to turn this over to Josh Rivers, our senior partner,
and I hope to be able to send that back with you."

"Do you handle criminal matters?"

"I do not personally and neither does Josh. The three
other lawyers in the firm take a greater variety of cases.
Marty Locke is at our Fort Sill office right now. Harper
Conrad or Jael Rivers could probably advise you. You
could make an appointment with either of them on your
way out." She stood, and he understood he had used up
his time.

He made an appointment with Jael Rivers for the next
day, learning that she was the wife of Josh Rivers and re-
calling a newspaper story about a novel he had read not
more than a year ago, "The Last Hunt" by Tabitha Rivers,
Josh's sister, who was quoted as saying that the book was
roughly based on the story of Josh and Jael Rivers. Now it
was coming back to him. Jael Rivers had been abducted

by the Comanche as a twelve or thirteen-year-old, as he recalled, eventually claimed as wife of a Comanche warrior.

Because of her affinity for languages, speaking at least five fluently, she had become an interpreter for the great Comanche chief, Quanah Parker. Josh Rivers's baby son had also been abducted and his first wife killed by Comanche, and Jael, by then known as She Who Speaks, had adopted him. He was piecing the Rivers family together now. It would be interesting to meet this law wrangler.

Conor strolled south along the boardwalk edging the Plaza where the Rivers & Sinclair offices were located in one of the many two-story structures, most apparently new, frame buildings replacing old adobe business places like the scattering of crumbling stores that were still occupied. At the north end of the Plaza was the recently remodeled Palace of the Governors, center of government originally for the early Spanish claimants, then the Mexican governors, and finally the United States. It was a beautiful building, he thought, but certainly not a castle. It was one of the few single-story structures remaining on the Plaza.

He crossed the street headed for his lodging place, the Exchange Hotel, located in the southeast corner of the Plaza, passing the bandstand in the center of the Plaza, enclosed by what appeared to be a new picket fence. There seemed to be a lot of new in this ancient city. He decided to have lunch at the Exchange and afterward possibly grab a quick siesta in his room, which was reasonably cool with its thick adobe walls. He figured that once he departed Santa Fe, he would not be indulging in a midday nap for months.

Later, the siesta turned out to be a brief one. He had just stretched out on the bed top, closed his eyes, and started to escape into a welcoming sleep, when a rapping on his room door yanked him back. Reflexively, he reached for his Colt, holstered and lying on the bedside lamp table. Clutching the Colt, he stumbled to the door, but prior to releasing the bolt lock, said, "Who is it?"

A boy's voice replied, "Tomas, senor. Telegram."

It had to be Henry Flipper's reply. Unbelievably fast. He was either hungry or overloaded with other work. He dug in his pocket and dug out a quarter. Usually, a ten-cent piece was ample, but he was in a generous mood today since his mission was falling into place so far—if Flipper did not ruin it. He opened the door and found a boy of ten or eleven years standing there with a grin on his face. The smile was worth a quarter. The boy handed him the message, and Conor gave him the quarter, eliciting wide eyes and a bigger smile.

"Gracias, senor." He wheeled and headed down the hall.

"And gracias to you, Tomas," Conor called after him.

He sat down on the bed, tearing open the envelope that contained the message. He unfolded the telegram and read: "Triad one week. Find starting point. Old surveys. Texas border. River. Henry."

He was elated to learn that his old friend would take on the survey job. Selfishly, he wanted to see Henry Flipper again, but he also knew him to be a man of keen intelligence, who would not be intimidated by the enforcers should they intervene. Another piece to solving the puzzle should arrive about the time of his own return.

Chapter 27

CONOR SPENT MOST of the afternoon that he received Flipper's telegram, as well as a large part of the next morning, at the territorial recorder's office. He had reached a dead end by the time of his afternoon appointment with Jael Rivers, and he waited now in the law firm's reception area.

Precisely at the scheduled time, the attorney stepped into the room and said, "Conor Byrne?"

He stood, "Yes, ma'am."

She extended her hand, offering a firm grip. "I am Jael."

She was not as tall as her female partner, but he guessed she would reach nearly five and one-half feet. Jael quickly put him at ease with a smile that revealed a dimple in her right cheek. With black hair tied back in a ponytail and light tawny-skin, she could have passed for Comanche or at least a half-blood, but he had read that her slaughtered parents had both been Jewish. He guessed her age at a few years short of thirty, but it did not matter for she was not short of life experience, and by all accounts she was whip smart.

She led him to her office, and they both sat down at her desk.

"Now, Conor, I understand you have another legal matter to discuss with me, but Danna asked me to convey a message, and I would like to take that up first."

"Certainly."

"She was needed in Taos to view another land grant property with a man who is facing a similar challenge from the same folks. The judge had the U.S. marshal deliver an order setting the case for trial next week. Danna thought the trial would be at least a month away, so she is forced to give the case priority."

"I understand that, but I do need to get back to my ranch near the Guadalupe Mountains. When does she expect to return?"

"It could be several days, but she says it is unnecessary to wait for her. She would like to visit you and Doctor Hayes at the site and view the land and interview the doctor."

At three dollars an hour, Conor was not certain Doc could afford the lawyer's journey.

The lawyer must have read his mind. She assured him, "Travel time would be charged against the retainer at twenty dollars per day. Time spent in conference with you and Doctor Hayes and personally inspecting the property would revert to the hourly rate. We assume you would provide lodging and meals while on site."

"I am sure we can arrange for everything. She might need to sleep in a hospital room."

"That sounds luxurious. You will need to sketch some directions with landmarks, that sort of thing."

"That's easy enough, but surely she won't travel alone."

Jael smiled. "I assure you she is capable, but that is our worry. I might accompany her—at no additional cost. I was on the Texas side of the Guadalupe with our Comanche band some years back, but Quanah was headed to Mexico at the time. I loved those mountains. I know I would enjoy seeing the New Mexico side. I would consider it a vacation, so to speak. Any other party would be included in the travel allowance."

Conor wondered if the lawyer was sane. "So when might we expect her? I have a surveyor coming to start a survey within a week, and Danna will want to know that. It could take him a month. It would be nice if she could speak with him."

"Of course. She will have the trial next week, which should take three or four days, and she will have other business to get in order, as well as research to do. Expect her within three to four weeks from now. In the meantime, she intends to inform Emilio Ortiz that she is representing Doctor Hayes—assuming the retainer is acceptable."

"I will write the draft before I leave the office."

She smiled again. "You picked up that hint nicely. Danna said to tell you that she would like you to be aware that the doctor's case would probably be based upon a theory of law called adverse possession to back up his deed to the grant land. Its application to territories governed by federal law is ambiguous, but it has a history in the common law—court cases—that goes back centuries. In essence, if a person occupies and exercises exclusive, unchallenged control over property for a specified number of years—ten is often the standard—he may establish title by court order notwithstanding any outstanding deed. Lawyers call the lawsuit a quiet title action."

"I have heard of such things."

"It is not uncommon in the states, where properties often lack recorded deeds to establish ownership. Doctor Hayes should be thinking about all the things he has done to show that he assumed he owned the entire property, not just this structure you call the Triad. She will discuss this with him. Understand that Ortiz still has the burden of proving the property was even part of a land grant. You should be very concerned that his employers might decide not to wait for the courts to handle this and begin physically removing people from the land. Doctor Hayes's death would be very convenient."

"Do you really believe they would resort to murder?"

"Yes."

"I need to get back to the Guadalupe."

"Tell me about the other legal matter."

"I am a bit concerned. I am speaking for another person. How much can I say in confidence?"

"This person would be my client, not you?"

"Yes."

"I could speak in total confidence with my client regarding a crime he or she may or may not have committed, so long as I was not informed of a crime the client intended to commit in the future. Only then would I need to inform legal authorities or testify about a conversation."

"Let me speak hypothetically, so we bypass some of the issues you speak of. Would that work?"

"An excellent idea."

"Suppose a woman did physical harm to a man and was placed in jail and subsequently the woman escaped leaving a deputy town marshal locked up in her place?"

"This is getting very interesting. A fictional story, of course."

"Suppose then that she takes the deputy's horse and is now hiding out many miles away. It is possible that the deputy might have tracked her down and tried to rape and kill her but that a ghost intervened and cut out the deputy's tongue."

"You are not a fiction writer?"

"What is the saying? 'Truth is stranger than fiction.' That should be enough of the story for our purposes, I think."

Jael said, "I have lived a life of bizarre and tragic incidents, but I must say this is an interesting outline of a story that needs considerable fleshing out."

"And assume that no charges of any kind have been filed against such a woman."

"I say that the woman should stay put. If she learns that charges have been filed, she should immediately speak to her lawyer. If arrested, she should not say a word without consulting with her lawyer. If she speaks to her lawyer before her arrest, the lawyer has no obligation to report her whereabouts to the authorities. All conversations, again, are confidential—unless the woman tells her lawyer she is going to commit a future crime or asks the lawyer to participate in some criminal act."

"I think you have told me what I need to know for now. If you choose to visit the Triad, it is not impossible you might meet a person like this."

"What are my chances of encountering a ghost?"

"Let us say that stranger things have happened."

"You are an ornery cuss, Conor. You have certainly piqued my curiosity. Are you trying to lure me to the Triad?"

"Could be."

Jael took a bulky sealed envelope from the top of her desk and handed it to Conor. "These are some documents prepared by my husband, Josh Rivers, at the request of Doctor Hayes. They include signing instructions. I trust you will deliver them to the good doctor."

"Of course. I will be going directly to his residence."

"You may leave your retainer draft with Linda on your way out. Don't forget to drop your route map off before you depart Santa Fe."

Chapter 28

EMILIO ORTIZ SAT on a bench in the park adjacent to the bandstand near the Plaza's center. Beside him was his young law clerk, a sincere, eager to please Anglo named Herman Bales, who had been surreptitiously watching a man who identified himself as "Conor Byrne" in the territory recorder's office. Ortiz had been alerted earlier by an assistant in the recorder's office that a man was spending a great deal of time searching the public records in the office pertaining to the Hayes land. Ortiz had promptly dispatched Bales to keep an eye on the stranger.

From their vantage point on the bench, they had an unobstructed view of the entrance to the Rivers & Sinclair office. The door opened, and a tall man wearing a doeskin jacket stepped out onto the boardwalk and placed a low-crowned hat on his head.

"That's the man," Bales said. "He has been at the recorder's all morning, and he knows a lot more about land records than an ordinary cowboy. When he asked questions of the staff, he sounded like a man with some education. He talked a lot about surveys and legal descriptions."

"He is obviously working with the Rivers firm, no doubt that Sinclair woman. You can go back to the office. I need to call on someone."

Ortiz sat on the bench until Bales disappeared around a corner on his way to his own law office a block off the Plaza. He preferred an out-of-the-way office, since having a single client, he was not seeking business from the public. He got up and walked across the street on the side of the Plaza opposite the Rivers office and entered a building bearing a modest, black-on-white sign that read "Paxton Land Management."

He was greeted by a young Mexican woman seated at the sole desk in the front office. He liked Zoe Castillo well enough but resented her authority. She was essentially Morton Paxton's guard dog and decided who got a personal audience with the arrogant walrus. Paxton was his contact with the Santa Fe Ring, but he was only a front man for the Ring with no more authority than himself.

"Good afternoon, Zoe. I must see Mort. Now." She was a petite, pretty thing but tough as nails, and he knew a loaded derringer sat inside her desk drawer. She had used it once on an angry man who tried to bypass her station, shooting him only in the fleshy buttocks but accomplishing her mission.

"He is very busy this afternoon. May I tell him the nature of your business?"

"Tell him 'Mendoza.' I think he will wish to see me."

She got up and disappeared down a short hall behind her desk. In a few minutes, she returned. "He will make time to see you. Go on back."

He walked down the hallway, stopped at the only door, and stepped in. Morton Paxton sat behind his desk in a high-backed swivel chair, hands folded across his enormous belly, his chin nearly hidden by bloated jowls, his heavy eyelids giving his narrowed eyes a porcine look. He nodded toward the door, signaling that Ortiz should close it. Ortiz complied and took one of the straight-back chairs in front of the massive desk, which was the only object displaying the slightest elegance within an otherwise drab room.

"Well, what's the problem?" Paxton said, swiping his perspiring, bald pate, his high-pitched voice seeming peculiar for such a large man.

"Sinclair is going to be representing the people defending the Mendoza land grant claim."

"So?"

"She's the best when it comes to land titles, and we both know Angel Mendoza's history will not stand scrutiny."

"You found the drunken no-good."

"I was misled. It doesn't matter now. Anybody we found would have been a problem. You know, I always had doubts about this case."

"We both just do what we're told. For some reason this fits the plan for owning everything in the southeast part of the territory that is within forty to fifty miles on each side of the Pecos River. They want to work their way up to Chisum's land and even take him out. They want to own everything that adjoins the Pecos—both sides, as I say. My contact says that time is running out, whatever the hell that means."

"Congress is talking about some kind of land grant commission to investigate claims. If that happens, the days of claiming lands by bringing in hired guns are over."

"Well, they ain't over yet. If you can't beat that woman in a courtroom, you had better put those enforcers to work."

"It might require killing Roman Hayes and others who get in the way."

"If you want to keep your job, you had damn well better do what it takes. And if you prefer to depart your job, I recommend buying yourself a cemetery plot and making arrangements with the undertaker. We both know there is only one way out of what we are doing."

Chapter 29

K AT SAT ON the veranda, gazing out on the silent, moonlit desert. The sun had just dropped behind the mountains to the west, and she was waiting for Doc to return from another baby delivery. He had been concerned about leaving her alone at the Triad at night again, but she had a loaded Winchester lying across her lap and the faithful Loafer sleeping on a rug at her side.

She worried more about Doc. It seemed to her that he was more likely to be the target of an attack. She knew nothing about the fine points of legal matters, but Doc's demise certainly would appear to be a great convenience for the land grant claimants.

Since her arrival at the Triad, she had met members of most of the Mexican families who resided within a half day's ride of the Triad. The land might be barren, but the women were obviously fertile. The babies were welcomed into obviously happy families, though, where everyone learned to work hard and appreciated what little they had. There was much to be learned from these good people, she thought. People could work for a better tomorrow but still be happy with what they had.

Her eyes fastened on shadows dancing on the flatlands to the west. She watched as they moved in the Triad's direction. She could not make out the forms yet, but the bouncing shadows suggested more than a single horse. Her grip tightened on the rifle. It could not be Doc. He would be returning from the northeast. Loafer had not stirred, so he obviously sensed nothing. He had saved her once, but Doc had warned her not to rely on the dog.

She got up and stepped back into the shadow of the overhang. She could make out a man's form now, a lone rider leading two critters. She thought one might be a mule, a pack animal probably. She wondered if it could be Conor Byrne because he was due back by now, having been gone for over two weeks.

Minutes later, her suspicion was confirmed when Conor rode into the yard astride his gelding, Stoic. Kat lowered her Winchester and stepped out to greet their neighbor. When he dismounted and started to hitch the horses and mule to the rail, he looked up and saw her standing there. "Good evening, Miss Ryan," he said. "I hope you weren't intending to shoot me with that rifle."

"It depended on who you turned out to be, Mister Byrne." It occurred to her that the "mister" and "miss" business was getting a little silly. She was still not totally trusting of this man, but Doc had made him an important part of their team and she should try to get along with him so long as he kept his distance. "I don't have any objection if you wish to call me Kat . . . or Kathleen, if you prefer."

"Kathleen. I rather like that. It sounds more Irish. And you know I prefer 'Conor.' Mister has always been your choice."

"Alright. That's settled. It is not eight o'clock yet. Have you had some supper?"

"As a matter of fact, I have not. I had some jerky and stale biscuits a bit before high noon. I was hoping I might beg some scraps off Doc."

"Well, Doc isn't here. He is at the Serrano place bringing a new baby into this wicked world. I was holding three times the roasted beef Doc would eat for his supper along with a kettle of beans and fresh baked bread. Blueberry pie, too. If you want to put the critters up in the stable, I'll have it ready along with a pot of coffee by the time you get back here."

"That adds up to more than I have eaten since leaving Santa Fe. I will tend to the animals, maybe stay around till Doc gets home, if you don't object."

"I guess that would be okay, but it might be late."

"I'll lay out my bedroll on the porch if it gets too late."

She shrugged. She wondered if he was trying to be her protector but reminded herself not to resent the gesture. Was she becoming a more conciliatory Kat Ryan?

When Conor returned from the stable and sat down at the kitchen table, she put a plate of vittles in front of him and poured water fresh from the well in the glass. "Coffee later?"

"With the pie would be nice."

She sat down across the table and watched him eat like a starving man. She liked his eyes, hazel she guessed they would be called, seemingly changing colors with the light from green to brown or even a grayish tint sometimes. She had not noticed before but thought they were kind eyes, seductive in a way. A woman had to take care with men like that, she supposed.

Conor paused. "Kathleen, have you eaten? I don't want to be taking your share of supper."

"I ate earlier. I am not good at waiting to eat." She did not mention that she had likely matched him bite for bite. She had probably added more than a few pounds since arriving at the Triad, but Doc still insisted she was still too skinny.

After Conor took his first bite of the pie, he said, "Kathleen, everything has been delicious. You are an excellent cook. Thank you."

She was grateful for the bronze tint of her skin now because she could feel the heat of her flushing cheeks. "You are welcome. I like to cook where it is appreciated— a new experience since I came here. Can you share any news from your journey?"

"Of course. After achieving a full stomach, that was next on my agenda." He slid his chair back from the table, hoisted one leg over the other knee and sipped his coffee. "First, I will tell about what I learned in Albuquerque."

"You did visit Albuquerque then?"

"Yep. I met a friend of yours there who sent his best, an older gentleman by the name of George Underhill."

She smiled. "I would love to see Uncle George again. He was a character, and I adored him. I never saw him again after Papa died." She noticed that Conor's eyes were fixed on her face, and she wondered for a moment if she had a stain on her teeth.

"George was a well of information. I stumbled onto him in a barber shop, and he was an enormous help. First, the good news. It appears you are not a wanted criminal.

There are no warrants out for your arrest. Public opinion seems to be that Louie Gaynor got what was coming to him, and there's not much sympathy for Deputy Buford Walters, either, even though he lost his tongue."

"I thought Buford might be dead."

"Nope. George and I met up at the Welcome Inn, and he pointed out Louie and Buford sitting at one of the poker tables. Rumor is that when Louie has recovered, the two plan to try to track you down again. That was the bad news."

"Well, I'm not surprised at that. But do you think I am free of the law?"

"For now. I spoke with a lawyer hypothetically about your situation. She says not to do anything for now. Charges could be filed yet but hope for the best. This lawyer—her name is Jael Rivers—will represent you if need be. You may be able to talk to her yourself if she joins the land grant lawyer on her visit here. I'll save that story for Doc. I gather you haven't had a surveyor show up here yet?"

"No. I didn't know we were expecting one."

"I hired him by telegram from Santa Fe. He is coming from El Paso. He is an old West Point friend of mine. I plan to put him up at my place."

She was horrified that a young surveyor would be forced to nest in that mess. "Maybe you would like to have me tidy up the place some before you have a guest."

"Oh, Henry has slept worse places, I promise you."

"I would love to do it, Conor. Please. I could come over tomorrow morning. I would bring the buckboard with the extra mattress Doc has stowed away in the storeroom, some sheets and blankets, too. I know he won't care. You don't want your friend sleeping on the hard floor, do you?"

"I guess not. I hadn't thought about it."

"Will you be helping him?"

"Yeah, I said I would. It usually takes two."

"You can take breakfast and supper over here if you like."

"Don't you need to check with Doc about this?"

"And what do you think Doc would say?"

"Okay, I guess we can plan on that, but I feel like I am putting you to a lot of work and trouble."

"Not at all, and I want to see this work done."

"Well, you need to be thinking about where you are going to lodge guests if you have a few law wranglers show up here in a few weeks."

"I'll figure it out."

"There is something you should know. I am told that we are up against a group called the Santa Fe Ring. They do not hesitate to resort to violence to get what they want. They may be willing to direct their enforcers to do some killing to gain the grant property. Doc is in special danger. We have got to keep an eye out for strangers. The next time he has a night call, I would like for you or Doc to let me know, so I can go with him."

"He won't like that idea."

"I know it, and maybe he won't have any more night calls for a spell. It's not like we have a thousand people here at the base of the Guadalupe."

She decided that Conor should be told about the killing that took place while he was gone. He was probably going to think she had the temperament of a notorious outlaw when she told him about it.

"We did have an incident while you were gone. It should be cooling outside now. Perhaps we could take our coffee and go out on the veranda for that story."

"Now, you have for darn sure got me curious."

They claimed side by side rockers on the veranda where Loafer still slept.

Kat said, "Loafer proved himself a hero that night."

"Loafer?"

"Yes." She related her story of the attack by the enforcer, as Conor listened in a spellbound silence. When she finished, she said, "I guess that's about it. No body to prove it, but there are blood stains on the trading post floor."

"And you shot this man?"

"Twice. A bad habit of mine. I can't seem to stop with one strike."

"I am not sure what to make of you, Kathleen, but you seem to be able to look after yourself right well."

"No man will treat me like Louie did ever again. I guarantee that."

"Nobody has been by to ask questions about this guy?"

"It happened right after you left, so it has been almost two weeks, and we have not heard anything. I have no idea whether they suspect that we did something or think the man deserted."

"Or maybe they are waiting for word from higher ups on how to deal with their missing enforcer. I have a bad feeling we haven't seen the end of bloodshed. The Triad is built like a fortress, so if you don't get caught by surprise, you should be able to hold off an attack. I worry about the Mexican families. There are a few adobe houses that could help defenders. Most are not more than wood shacks, though. They would be tinder boxes if somebody chose to burn them out. I want to clear it with Doc, but I think they should be encouraged to come here if that type of war starts. I have been thinking about this."

She caught sight of a dark rider moving in from the east. "Doc's coming now. I can tell by the easy lope."

"Good. I can give him a report on the Santa Fe lawyer while he eats, and we can kick around a few strategies before grabbing some sleep. I think I will just settle here on the veranda for the night and ride on to my place in the morning."

"Good. You can help me get the buckboard hitched and loaded and ride along with me. Remember? I've got a cleaning job, and you can help."

"You just don't let things go once you sink your teeth in, do you?"

Chapter 30

BLUE JEANS AND booted Kat drove the two mules and buckboard on the dusty trail to Conor's cabin. It was a light load consisting of a straw mattress, blankets, and Conor's saddle and tack. A single mule would have sufficed, but Doc liked to keep the teams working together. Conor had hitched Stoic at the rear of the wagon and joined Kat on the seat.

She clearly had no intention of surrendering the reins, and that was fine with him. He had sensed neither welcome nor hostility when he climbed onto the seat. Her mouth was set firm this morning, but he had enjoyed a glimpse of a smile the night before and found it charming. He would bet that Kathleen Ryan had no idea that men might find her more than pretty, even with that raven hair cut almost as short as his own.

Doc had been dead wrong if he held the illusion that he could make her look like a boy. While her modest bosom seemed easily enough contained, every movement of her body was graceful as a leaping doe antelope. She could not hide her femininity with shorn hair. While he was undeniably attracted to Kathleen Ryan, he vowed to have the good sense to dodge any temptation to attempt kindling of a romance with her, especially if she had an axe nearby.

"There is really not that much to do at my place," Conor said. "You can just drop off the mattress and head back if you like. You can for certain get back to the Triad before noon."

"I have seen your cabin."

"No, you haven't."

"The door was unlocked, so I went in for a few minutes just to look around."

"You had no right." He fought to stay calm, but it annoyed him that she would enter his home without his permission.

"I suppose not."

"There is no supposing about it. You had no right. Rein the mules to a halt."

She did, and he vacated the wagon seat, saddled Stoic and mounted his gelding. "Now, go ahead. You obviously know the way." He could swear he could see a triumphant smile struggling to break out on her lips.

When she pulled ahead with the mule team, Conor followed the wagon two-horse lengths behind. A few miles later when they approached his property, he nudged Stoic ahead, swinging up on the driver's side of the wagon and signaling a halt.

As she slowed the buckboard to a stop, he pointed to the eastern horizon. "Smoke."

"Your cabin?"

"It appears so. Wait here, I'm going to ride ahead and see what's going on. If you hear gunfire, turn this wagon around and head for the Triad at a run." She reached under the wagon seat and pulled out her Winchester, quickly levering a cartridge into the chamber before setting the rifle on the seat beside her.

Conor gave Stoic a gentle nudge with his boot heels urging the horse ahead at a fast gallop toward the smoke that was spiraling skyward. Then he suddenly saw a second plume. As he approached, he saw that both the cabin and stable were in flames and that three men, one mounted and holding the reins of horses for two hurrying about the yard carrying torches. They obviously had not noticed him yet.

He reined in his horse, pulled his rifle from its scabbard and dismounted, knowing that mounted riders rarely took down their targets by shooting from a moving horse. He aimed at the mounted rider and squeezed the trigger. The rifle cracked, and he saw the rider slump forward in his saddle, releasing his hold on the reins of the other horses. The arsonists dropped their torches and raced to grab the reins of their horses. Conor snapped off a wild shot that raised dust at one man's feet before he stepped into a stirrup and swung into the saddle of a sorrel gelding. His partner, already saddled, fired several shots at Conor, and before he could get off another shot, a rifle cracked from behind him, and the shooter plunged from his mount.

Conor whirled, rifle ready, relaxing when he saw Kat some ten paces behind him with her Winchester in her hands. The buckboard and other critters were farther back on the trail. He turned his attention back to the raiders, watching the wounded rider race his mount from the yard with his companion following in the dust, leaving their friend sprawled out in the dirt. The down man's horse trailed the others.

He turned back to Kathleen. "Damn it, Kathleen. I told you to head back to the Triad if you heard gunfire."

"I was right behind you, so it was a little late to turn around by the time the shooting started."

"But I told you to wait."

She was walking up to him now, fire in her eyes. "You didn't say 'please.' I take better to asking than ordering."

"Would it have made a difference?"

"It might have."

Conor doubted that. He said, "Well, I guess I should thank you for the help. Thanks." He did not speak the words with a smile. He turned and snatched Stoic's reins and started leading the horse toward the downed rider and the crumbling buildings. There was no rush now. The walls had collapsed, the roofs had caved into the two infernos, and there were no other structures to be rescued or protected.

He walked over to the man that Kat had shot and knelt beside the still form. He was a younger man with a thick mustache and whiskery face. Eyes frozen open in fear like he knew he had taken his last breath. Dead center chest wound, probably right where she aimed. She seemed to have a 'take no prisoners' attitude about life. She was a tiny thing, but the little rattlers carried enough venom to kill you, too.

Kat drove the wagon into the yard and leaped off the seat. "Is he dead?"

"Yeah, I'm afraid so."

"Afraid so? You don't shoot a gun at somebody with the notion of scaring them."

"I know. I just don't like killing folks. He had a mother and father someplace, maybe brothers and sisters. He could have had a wife and children for all I know."

"And he would have put a slug in your head if he got the chance. I don't understand you. I thought you were a soldier."

"That is why I left soldiering as soon as my time was served. I'll kill if I am forced to, but it gives me no pleasure as it seems to do to some."

"Well, I can't argue with that. What now?"

"You can head back if you want, or you can stay as it suits you. The cabin is starting to burn out, the corner with the bedroom is still standing. I had almost a hundred dollars in gold eagles and other odds and ends squirreled away under floorboards there. I have an Army Colt with the money, too. I would like to dig around and see if there is anything useful I can salvage. Later, I will go back to Doc's and see if he can put me up in his stable loft for a spell. Henry and I can bunk there for now, I guess."

"I brought some lunch. I figured to be here the whole day. I'll stay around a spell. Maybe there is something you will want to take back in the buckboard."

"I doubt it, but your company is welcome. I will try to be more congenial."

"And maybe I can be less snappish. With what happened here, I guess I should cut some slack. If you haven't noticed, my tongue can be sharp and quick sometimes."

He offered a half smile and nodded. "I've noticed. Truth is I sort of like your spunk."

"Spunk?"

He turned away and walked over to a pile of cedar limbs he had left in the yard, scraps from posts he had carved with his axe from stout trees he had dragged down with mules from the Guadalupe foothills. He rummaged through the stack till he found a solid stick a bit longer than four feet that he thought would work. Kat moved in beside him and ferreted out her own.

"We can use these to probe and scrape the hot coals in the building ruins," he said.

"I figured that's what you had in mind. Mine's got sort of a kettle hook on the end from a sawed-off branch. Maybe I can catch something."

They walked over to the smoldering remains of the little cabin. "I am going to see if I can find my money. You can look for whatever treasures you want."

He went to the corner of the ruins where his life's savings should be hidden and began kicking away half-burnt timbers and clearing a path to the corner. Many of the floorboards had been burned through to the dirt a few inches below. And when he reached the hideaway, he found that the board cover had been eaten away there, also. Fire had devoured the leather bag that held the coins, but the gold eagles were only singed slightly. He bent over and plucked out the coins as well as the Army Colt and the silver, flying eagle pendant and chain he had purchased for Maria. He also retrieved a small, pearl-handled skinning knife his grandfather had brought with him from Ireland, his lone family heirloom.

He slipped the knife in his belt and stuffed the coins and pendant in his pocket and scratched around in the rubble a bit longer before deciding there was nothing else that interested him. He saw Kat working intently at the opposite end of the cabin and stepped out of the mess and walked around the perimeter to join her.

"Did you find what you were looking for?" Kat asked, when he walked up to her.

"Yep. The cabin wasn't much, and anything else can be replaced. Doc's got clothes and other necessities at the trading post. I will need to do some serious thinking before I decide about rebuilding. I'm wondering if I shouldn't move everything back in the canyon a short distance, nearer the livestock and a water supply. I wouldn't even think about it till this land grant fuss is finished, though."

"I would say it has grown beyond a fuss now."

"Yeah, I am afraid so. I see you have fished out the Dutch oven and some cooking things."

"Yes. We should take these with us. The oven could come in handy if we are going to be feeding you and your friend and possibly a few others for a spell. We could use your cookstove, too, and set it up outside. But it won't be going anyplace, and it would burn our flesh to the bone if we tried to handle it today."

Conor said, "If you are about done, I suggest we get the critters to the stream to drink, and we can eat that lunch early and head on back to Doc's."

They enjoyed a lunch of roasted beef sandwiches and ginger cookies along the stream near the canyon opening where a few cottonwood trees provided shade. They sat cross-legged facing each other with a half dozen feet separating them while they ate.

"I love this spot," Kat said, "and the canyon is lush with grasses and has a fair scattering of trees. It's like the Triad in a way. It seems surrounded by desert, but it is an easy walk to the canyon where you enter a different world."

"Yeah, and higher up, you enter still another. You will find oak, maple, juniper, and other trees there. We try to harvest enough oak and hardwoods for firewood several times a year to see us through, and Doc has a good source of wood at the far end of his canyon. Most of the time we try to preserve it for cooking, but a few months we need it for heat. A lot of nights, a fire would be nice, but I generally count on the carryover coals in the stove from supper and a pile of blankets."

"So you do go up in the mountains?"

"Oh, yes. I love it up there."

"But you have never encountered the Ghost?"

He chuckled. "No. I wouldn't mind his help cutting wood, though. He seems choosy about what he helps with."

"Why do you stay in this lonely place?"

"I like the isolation. I don't think of it as lonely. There is life all around us if we pay attention, just not much of the human kind. Off to your right, see that doe and fawn on the knoll watching us? Raccoons and possums come around at night, and you will hear the mountain lions scream from the hills in the darkness, see one on occasion. You can catch sight of a mama bear and her cubs now and then. Every darned kind of reptile. Birds of all sorts. We've got company here."

"Alright. You don't need to convince me, and I don't find it lonely, either. Doc says I can stay on here as long as I want, and I cannot imagine leaving as long as he owns the place. If I don't die first, I will be at the foot of the Guadalupe to help him when he is old and feeble. If something happens to Doc, only then will I think about moving on. I am free here, and with Doc I found family."

"Speaking of free." He dug into his pocket, pulled out the chain and pendant and tossed it to her.

It fell into her lap. She picked it up and looked at it, and he could see her eyes widen in surprise. "The beautiful pendant I sold you. I don't understand."

"It was with my gold coins and a knife that my grandfather brought over from Ireland. I remember you mentioned that to you the eagle was a symbol of freedom. I would like you to have it."

"But you were buying it for a lady friend."

"Maria. I never gave it to her, and we had a parting of the ways, as I suspect you know. I didn't know what to do with it. I think you should have it."

"I can't. I don't want to feel obligated. Sometimes, I don't even like you much."

Conor laughed. "On occasion, the feeling is mutual. It is a gift. There is no obligation that goes with it. Nothing. It is not a gift if someone is expected to give something in return. You don't have to wear it if you don't want, or you can wait till it feels right. Maybe you don't wear jewelry. I have never seen you wear any."

"I have never owned a piece of jewelry." She stood up. "Can you fasten the chain for me?"

He got up and stepped behind her as she put the pendant in place, and he took the two ends of the chain from her slim fingers. When it was fastened, he moved in front of her and examined the chain. She was wearing a collared green shirt, but the short chain lifted the eagle pendant high on her bosom, so it was framed by the green vee of the neckline. He knew next to nothing about jewelry, but against the background of her dark skin, the pendant looked stunning.

"The pendant is where it belongs, Kathleen," he said.

"Thank you," she said. Her eyes glistened and a tear rolled down one cheek. She turned away and began folding the cloth on which their lunch had set. "We need to get back to the Triad. Doc should be told about what happened here."

"I don't have a shovel. I can't leave the dead man for the scavengers. I'll wrap the body in one of the blankets, and we will take him with us. I guess we can plant him in the horse lot if Doc is alright with that."

"It ought to be soft digging anyhow."

Chapter 31

DOC HAYES WAS on his way back to the Triad after releasing the pack mule and Conor's spare mount into the canyon pasture when he saw a rider and a packhorse riding in from the west. His first instinct was to rush for the Triad, but if the man meant him harm, he could be easily intercepted. Besides, he found himself short of breath from the work he had already done.

He looked down at the dog that had been staying closer to him than usual since morning. Loafer seemed unconcerned about the appearance of a stranger, which meant absolutely nothing. Chiding himself for not carrying a pistol during these potentially dangerous days, he continued his sauntering pace toward the veranda.

As the visitor neared, Doc judged the man former Army from the erect way he carried himself in the saddle, much like Conor Byrne. The rider had dismounted and was hitching his buckskin mare and a blood bay gelding packhorse in front of the veranda by the time Doc reached the steps.

"Good afternoon, sir," said a soft voice betraying just the slightest trace of southern heritage.

A lean man, who stood a good six feet tall, stepped out from behind the horse. Instantly, Doc judged him a colored man despite skin hued light mahogany that betrayed ancestry that included Europeans, not unusual, of course, among many folks who were labeled Africans or Negroes.

"Hello there, welcome to the Triad."

"Triad. I am where I was hoping to be then. You wouldn't be Doctor Roman Hayes, by chance?"

"I am. You can call me Doc."

"I am Henry Flipper. I am an engineer and land surveyor. My friend, Conor Byrne, sent me a telegram in El Paso and said you had work for me."

"I certainly do." Doc stepped over and extended his hand, receiving a firm grip that left his fingers stinging. "Why don't you come up on the porch, and we can talk a spell. Can I get you a glass of water or a cup of coffee, maybe some ginger cookies? It's just past time for lunch. I can fix you up with a roasted beef sandwich. You've been riding. I'll bet you haven't eaten."

"Sandwich, coffee, and cookies would be welcome. No, I didn't stop to eat lunch, which would have been hardtack and beef jerky that I have pretty much been living on the past few days and have lost my appetite for."

"You can come in my residence and eat at the table if you like, but given the breeze and shade out here, it is a good deal warmer."

Flipper gave an easy smile. "I don't need it warmer. Right here would be fine. Can I help with anything?"

"Nope, you are my guest, and I've got a young lady who has taken over my kitchen and has everything where I can find it. She's with Conor at his place several miles east of here right now, helping set up things for your stay there."

Flipper said, "East? When I was on top of a knoll trying to get a fix on your place, I saw smoke to the east, and there's not much to burn on this land."

"How long ago?"

"A good hour now, I would guess."

"I will round up something for you to eat. You just sit back and relax a bit. If Conor and Kat don't show up by the time you've eaten, we might just mosey over that way."

"You're worried. We can head out now, if you like."

"No. We should give it a bit of time. If anything has happened, it is too late to change the outcome by now." That is what he hoped anyhow. Regardless, Flipper's news killed his own appetite for lunch.

When Doc returned with a tray of food, he asked Flipper to pull up one of the small cedarwood tables scattered about the veranda for customer convenience and set the food and coffee on it. "More cookies inside if you want."

"I'm sure this will be more than ample. This is a banquet compared to my fare the past three days, and I don't get service like this at the hotel in El Paso. Of course, it takes a lot of imagination to call that place a hotel."

"I am curious," Doc said. "How did you become a surveyor and engineer? Conor said you were in his class at West Point. I assume you received training there."

"I did, and I had planned on a military career. I got a lot of newspaper attention for being the first colored graduate from West Point. That cuts two ways. With some it helps advancement, and with others it works the opposite. It didn't matter to me. I just wanted to be the best and let the dust settle where it would."

"But you left the Army?"

"Conor didn't say anything?" He smiled. "On second thought, that would be Conor. A man could not have a better friend in this world than Conor Byrne."

"I have learned that."

"Anyway, you should know that I was booted out of the Army. Court martialed and found guilty of conduct unbecoming an officer and a gentleman. The other charge was embezzlement of government funds. I was found not guilty of those charges. That ended my military career, though. I have lawyers trying to clear my name, and I will never quit till that is accomplished. In the meantime, I am establishing a new career, and I intend to make a success of it. There is a huge demand for services like I can provide in Mexico and the Southwest."

Doc liked the man's confidence and determination. Flipper was not a man who wallowed in self-pity. He simply moved on to the next challenge. "I predict you will do very well," he said.

While Flipper ate, Doc told him the story of his property purchase and the challenge that had been laid down by Emilio Ortiz, the lawyer who represented an informal group called the Santa Fe Ring. "Apparently, these men in Santa Fe acquired a deed from someone who claimed to be the heir of a land grant of which my land was a part. My lawyer wants me to establish a proper legal description for my land and the tracts I have agreed to transfer to others. That is why you are here."

"That makes sense. This should be an interesting project. I will need another man to help. Conor suggested he could assist. It will be good to work with him again."

"Otherwise, there are several among the Mexican families I could recruit, I am sure. I must warn you, though, the job might carry some risk." He told Flipper about the attack on Kat and the man following Conor to Santa Fe. "They have watchmen posted in the mountains, and I am concerned they will start evictions when they learn I am not walking away."

Flipper ate the last of three cookies and finished his coffee. "I charge five dollars a day. I could be here as long as two months. You will get a long day's work from me."

"That will be fine. Tell me when you want some money."

"When I am done, or weekly, whatever suits you. Do you see the dust moving this way from the east?"

Doc looked out onto the desert. "I don't see anything."

"You will. Can I put my horses up somewhere for now? If it is Conor, I doubt if we will be moving out right away, and I should water and feed the critters and give them some rest. I will need to unpack my surveying gear, too."

"We have an empty stable right now that would hold a herd. I've got some grain and plenty of hay in the loft."

Chapter 32

HENRY OSSIAN FLIPPER liked Doc Hayes. This was a man to be trusted who offered an opportunity that could lead to other survey work. He knew that the demand would be insatiable in the years ahead. Countless properties had been acquired with boundaries marked by trees now dead and disappeared or stones long since moved. In many instances no paper had changed hands as proof of ownership, or no proof of a seller's rights had been established. Land records were nothing if not chaotic. The prospect of danger simply added a bit of excitement to a job that sometimes became too routine. He would not mind seasoning his work with an adventure or two.

Doc and Flipper finished getting the horses settled a few minutes before the buckboard pulled into the yard. Flipper saw his old friend sitting next to the driver, who at first glance he would have taken for a boy if Doc had not told him that a young woman had accompanied Conor. As soon as the mule team slowed to a near halt, Conor leaped out and trotted over to greet Flipper, first shaking his hand like a pump handle and then giving him a quick embrace.

"Flip. It's been too dang long, buddy. I'm glad I found some bait to pull you up this way."

"My pleasure, Con. And, yep, I am looking for work, so you had the right bait. Now, are you going to introduce the young lady?"

Kat had slipped up behind Conor, and Flipper could see that the newcomer was being appraised. There was no welcoming smile, but he did not sense hostility, either. Darn, there wasn't much to her, but there was plenty enough to turn any sane man's eyes her way.

Conor said, "Sorry, Flip. Kathleen, I would like to have you meet my good friend and West Point classmate, Henry Flipper. Flip this is Kathleen Ryan, a daughter of Ireland, new Triad resident, and Doc's good right hand."

"My pleasure, Kathleen," Flipper said, doffing his hat.

Her lips did not part, but Flipper caught traces of a smile and a twinkling in her eyes.

"A gentleman," she said. "That's rare out here. Most call me 'Kat.'"

"I prefer Henry. Conor, though, ignores preferences."

And Conor called her "Kathleen." Interesting. Maybe he liked the Irish sound. Other than her name, Flipper did not see a hint of Irish in Kathleen Ryan beyond her eyes.

Flipper said, "I saw smoke to the east when I was riding in."

Doc interrupted. "You've got a corpse in the buckboard. What in blazes have you been up to?"

Conor said, "Kathleen added another notch to her gun. This man and two others burned down my house and stable. I am hoping you will put me and Flip up in the stable loft."

"You could stay in the hospital room till that law wrangler shows up."

Flipper said, "The loft would be fine. Better than I am accustomed to. But I would like to hear more about your ranch house being burned down."

"My ranch house was a small two-room cabin barely fit for habitation. Kathleen would vouch for that, I'm sure. That's why she insisted on cleaning it up for a guest."

"Well, I appreciate the thought," Flipper said. "But why would someone burn you out?"

"I have a bad feeling the evictions are starting, and I was chosen as an example. The so-called enforcers are sending a message." He turned to Doc. "I wounded one of the men—I don't know how badly. It is possible, I suppose, he could show up here, but that would be the same as turning himself in. He was able to ride away with the other, but he was hurting and leaning forward in his saddle. Or his friend may finish him off. Hard to say. We don't know how many men they have down this way. I'll bet the Ghost does. I wish we could talk to him."

Flipper said, "Ghost? What are you talking about?"

"How would you like to help me bury this fella in the horse lot. I will tell you about the Ghost while we work."

"Okay. I'll help you out today, but any more burying will be on my surveying bill."

"That's fine by me. Doc's paying the bill."

Chapter 33

KAT WAS SURPRISED when Flipper insisted on helping her prepare supper, but she accepted the offer without hesitating. There was something about the man that fascinated her, and he was such a gentleman, soft spoken and unfailingly kind. She was uncertain whether he was consciously trying to charm her or if that was just his natural way. She had to admit she liked him from the moment they met.

Doc and Conor were in the parlor talking about the salt business. It seemed that Conor had returned from his Santa Fe trip with some ideas of expanding the salt delivery enterprises—some notions he had picked up at the Roswell Trading Post. He talked about processing salt for commercial and home use in addition to the raw shards they had been procuring for ranchers to distribute to cattle herds. He also spoke of providing jobs for the local families that might also bring in a few new folks as well.

"We have got plenty of beans," Flipper said on inventorying the cupboards, "and I suppose most things we are short are right next door. But meat. What do we do about meat?"

"That's always a challenge, because it only keeps so long. Most of our stuff is smoked and salted and kept in a steel box buried down by the stream just above the underground water level. That keeps a good spell. What would suit you?"

"Dried beef?"

"I will get some. You can get started."

"I don't suppose you have milk?"

"Yep. One of the Mexican families delivers goat's milk every other day. That's in the cold box, too. I am after Doc to find us a milk cow. I like to milk, and I don't have a taste for goat's milk for drinking."

"This will be for gravy and the biscuits."

The four ate their fill that evening on beans with fresh biscuits smothered in dried beef and gravy, topped off by cherry cobbler made possible by a big can of cherries Kat had retrieved from the store. How could she struggle so much to gain weight with a general store accessible by opening a door?

Later they all sat on the veranda to discuss the next day's plans. Flipper said, "How far is it to the Pecos River from here?"

Conor said, "Miles, I don't know. About a two hours' ride at a steady pace without pushing the horses."

"I will need some help. I operate the theodolite on the tripod and enter all the notes, but I want someone to hold the rod I use for alignment and assist with the hunt for landmarks and such. We are very near the Texas border. The south mountains are split by the New Mexico Territory and Texas boundaries. I have been told that there is a government survey stake on this side of the river where it intersects with the Texas border. That would be a godsend. If not, I will start from the river's center, not my preference because the channel shifts."

"I can get you to the Pecos," Conor said. "I am guessing we will need to stay a night or two."

"Make that three or four. I want to work my way back to the stone outcropping that Doc's drawings show to be the southeast corner of the property. Then we will have established our starting place—the most important part of the survey."

"How do you measure all this?" Kat asked. "Doesn't this survey have to be reduced to feet and angles, that sort of thing?"

"That is where my theodolite and other instruments along with plain old geometry come in. I must allow for mountains, canyons, and other places I cannot measure in my calculations. Someday, there will be instruments and techniques that will be more accurate, but I will be very close. There is a long history that helps. The ancient Egyptians were doing this back in 2500 B.C. Some folks ridicule the knowledge of past ages. I think we should be humbled by it."

Kat marveled at this man's mind, and he was a handsome devil, too. She had not known more than a few colored men who were laborers in town, hard workers as near as she knew, but lived in clusters among their own kind like Mexicans and other cultural groups. This man certainly did not fit the image Louie had painted of the Negro, and she was curious about him, wished she could question him about his past without being rude.

Conor said, "I can help for the first week, at least. Diego Munoz will work when I have tasks elsewhere. There is nothing back at my place that can't wait. Critters are in the pasture with water from the mountain stream passing through, and the spring calving and foaling is done. After we get back from the Pecos, I should spend some time getting the salt business started up, but none of it matters if we lose this land. I would like to see as much of the survey done as possible before the lawyer shows up—if she is crazy enough to travel this far."

"She is not crazy, Con," Flipper said. "Disputed land titles are becoming a huge business. I am betting my future on it. Every success this Danna Sinclair has will bring more clients. She will not have enough hours in a day to handle the demand and will take on more lawyers."

Kat said, "Henry, I hope you won't take offense, but I have a question."

"Go ahead. I promise it is very difficult to offend me."

"Well, you are a colored man . . ."

He chuckled. "You noticed?"

"Aren't you afraid there are folks who won't do business with you because of that? There are some who don't like colored people."

"Oh, I know that, but there is something I learned from my father. He was a slave, you know. For that matter, I was born one, but that was over by the time I was eight or nine years old. My father was a leather craftsman. My father's owner started preparing many of his slaves for freedom long before the war. He sent Pa off to another town to learn the leatherwork before my folks were married. When he returned, there were things he was expected to do for the owner, but mostly he worked for others who paid him, and his owner received a commission. He did that with others who learned carpentry and the like."

"I never heard of such a thing."

"There were others who did that with their slaves but no doubt more who did not."

"Anyhow, Pa saved his money. He married Ma who was a nearby preacher's slave, and my little brother and I were born while she belonged to the preacher. Well, it's a long story, but Pa's owner decided to move to Atlanta, and while he was sympathetic about breaking up the family, he did not have the cash to purchase Ma. Pa solved the problem. He loaned his owner the money to buy Ma and the two kids, and we moved to Atlanta as a family, and I had three more brothers born there."

"What about the business?"

"Pa found a shop there and started up again, paying his owner the commission. He was good at what he did and word got around. White folks who wouldn't eat across a table from him came to his shop and paid premiums for his work. Freedom came and the owner's commissions ended. We never starved and now I have a brother working with him. They have a lucrative business, and most customers are white. The other brothers are all in college now, and I look forward to seeing what they become."

"You were telling me this as a lesson."

"Very simple. Learn to do something. A skill, a trade, or whatever that folks need. Be the best you can be. It's funny how folks become blind to color when you have got something they want, maybe must have. People don't care if you are green or purple when that happens."

It occurred to Kat that out here in the remote desert beneath the Guadalupe, she was encountering far different men from those she had previously spent much of her life with.

"When you get back this way and can do your work with day trips, I would be glad to help you with your work if you need it."

"And I would welcome your help."

Chapter 34

WHEN THEY REACHED the Pecos River, Conor and Henry Flipper dismounted and looked out over the muddy waters funneling through the river's steep banks. "Somebody's prayers were answered upstream," Conor said. "It took some gully washing rains to raise the water this much. John Chisum likely got his share. I traveled through his river bottom land on the way to Santa Fe. Ten acres would support a cow and calf on what I saw. Takes more acres as you move west anyhow. It takes a hundred outside the canyon and foothills areas here. The Triad's canyon would likely match the Chisum river bottoms."

Flipper said, "I've heard of Chisum. Foxy devil, they say, but honest as a looking glass."

"Doc and I have been selling salt to his outfit. I haven't met the man himself. My dealings have been with a brother, and he has been a straight shooter."

"Well, Doc's not paying me to worry about Chisum. Let's head south along the riverbank and see if we can find the Texas border."

Conor said, "Have you noticed we're being followed?"

"Nope. Your enforcer friends?"

"I can't imagine who else. I am getting damned tired of being followed everyplace I go."

"How many?"

"I can't say. There has been only one within sight. He might be on his own. It depends on whether they're just curious or have decided to get rid of us. If it is the latter, there would likely be others trailing behind. Either way, I don't like it."

"Should we wait and have a chat with the fellow?"

"Nah, not now anyhow. Men like this aren't likely to cause trouble in daylight. Night is when we need to take precautions."

An hour later, Flipper reined in his buckskin. "I think we should hitch the horses. See the stubs on the trees along the bank where limbs have been cut?"

"Yeah. It has been a good while since the cutting was done, ten, even twenty years, I would guess."

"Surveyors will do that kind of cutting when they're wanting to sight and measure. If they were trying to do the state boundary line, the surveyors likely had a big crew, maybe some Army guards, too. I am hoping to find a steel stake or even a concrete monument. Let's look around."

After hitching their mounts and the packhorse to some hanging cedar limbs, Flipper coordinated their pacing to cover every inch of ground within a radius of fifty feet. Conor discovered the quarry when he almost stumbled over an iron rod imbedded in crumbling concrete and protruding several feet above ground level. "Flip," he called, you had better come take a look at this."

Flipper joined him and knelt to examine the find, brushing away the dirt and residues that had accumulated over the years. "Eureka," he said. "I can make out 'Tex' scratched into the concrete surface. We have found the border. We start here, but first I want to get some backup measurements. Then we will begin working our way back to that stone outcropping we passed under this morning. I am guessing it will take us a few days to get there. We will need to do some staking along the way. I want to follow the Pecos bank until we make our turn west. Then it might not be so easy."

"You are the boss."

"That's a change, since you always tried to do the bossing during our West Point and Army days."

"I was just trying to keep you out of trouble."

"Yeah, and I guess occasionally you did. Well, let me get a pencil and paper and my theodolite and other gear off the packhorse, and we will see what we can get done before sundown. We had better keep our eyes open for a place to camp."

That evening, Conor chose a clearing at the base of a sheer wall on the northeastern face of the Guadalupe for a camping place. The stone wall assured they would not be surprised by intruders from that side. One side dropped off into a steep canyon, and another opened onto the desert from which they had come. They were vulnerable from the northeast, however, by a strip of dense growth of willow and cottonwood that bounded a weak stream that trickled down from the rocks above.

The location was precisely what Conor had been seeking. He preferred a single point of vulnerability. They built a fire, making no attempt to hide their location and staked the horses out near the canyon side of the camp. There was little grazing here, but the men had walked their route here as Flipper set up his equipment and did his sightings along the way. Conor mostly led the horses, took the sledge to long steel surveying stakes, and hoisted the rod when Flipper requested. He quickly determined that he had no interest in pursuing a livelihood as a surveyor.

They warmed up beans and biscuits from the previous night's meal at the Triad, and even enjoyed a serving of the left-over cobbler. They would be eating a lot of jerky and whatever else they could put together from here on.

They sat by the dying fire as the night chill crept in, enjoying hot coffee prepared by Flipper. Conor said, "Good coffee, Flip. You always had a knack for the cooking end of camping."

"I had to when I was with you, Con, if I didn't want to gnaw my way through burnt crusts of things."

"Never claimed to be a cook."

"That little gal at the Triad—Kat. She seems to know her way around the ovens."

"Yeah, I haven't seen much she can't do. She clerks in Doc's store, helping with his inventory and books, and other times she cleans stalls. That's between shooting fellas or hammering heads with an axe."

"You like her, don't you?"

"Sometimes. Others, she annoys the hell out of me, but I remind myself that she has been through a lot in her life."

Flipper grinned. "Yeah, but I see the way your eyes follow her. It's hard for a man not to look at her. I wouldn't call her a beautiful woman exactly, just different."

"I would call her exotic."

"Hah. You have been thinking about her."

"And so have you, obviously. Just don't be trifling with her."

"Me? Since when do I trifle with ladies?"

"Since I've known you, and the ladies like you and you leave them broken-hearted. I don't know why, but some find you a handsome cuss."

Flipper shrugged, "I am what I am."

"Yeah, most of the time that's alright, but take care with Kathleen."

"I think you are staking a claim on her. Don't worry, I won't be trying to charm her away from you. Of course, I can't be responsible for any attachment she might get for me."

Same old Flipper. A man of his word but careful about his promises. Well, he was not courting Kathleen and had no intentions of doing so. He just did not want to see her hurt by a man again, although he knew it was not in Henry Flipper to physically harm a lady.

A wolf howl broke the stillness of the evening, as the last traces of sunlight disappeared behind the mountains to the west, and a dusky curtain descended on the desert. But the howler was not a wolf. "Get away from the firelight, Flip. I think we have got company."

"The wolf howling. Apache?"

Conor spoke in a near whisper now. "I think we are being told we've got company coming. The wolf howl was a warning, and it came from not more than a hundred feet up in the rocks above us. It's not likely a wolf would come in that near until the fire was out, and it was full darkness. I suspect it was the Ghost. I will explain later."

"That would be right kind of you."

"For now, get your Colt ready. I think somebody is going to be breaking through the trees in the next half hour. We ought to feed the fire a bit more wood, so they can find our camp. I suggest we each search out some cover at the edge of the tree line and just wait."

"Are we looking to kill?"

"Not if we can avoid it. A prisoner would be fine. Maybe we can learn a thing or two about their plans."

Twenty minutes later, he heard the crunch of twigs and the rattle of stones as footsteps crept snaillike through the trees. He guessed there were two men, certainly no more than three, approaching their campsite. Soon, a tall, bearded man emerged from the trees, his eyes sweeping the campsite, pausing to check the vacant blankets spread out on the opposite side. He started backing his way into the trees again when Conor stepped out.

"Drop your gun, mister, or you are a dead man."

The intruder swung around to fire, and Conor squeezed his Army Colt's trigger, breaking the silence like a clap of thunder. The man dropped his gun and pitched forward, but two more quick gunshots cracked following his own. Conor tumbled backward as he felt the force of a slug drive into the right side of his chest just an instant before another entered his upper left arm. As he went down, he heard two more shots, and then all was quiet.

Blackness overtook him for a time—he did not know how long. A voice carried him back from oblivion, and his eyes opened. Flipper was bent over him, and he could feel his friend's fingers working at his chest. The pain was excruciating. "Hey, Flip, have mercy, will you?" he said with a weak scratchy voice he did not recognize.

"Conor, thank God, you're awake. I'm staunching the bleeding and trying to plug the hole with cloth I've ripped off your shirt. I've already got a tourniquet on the arm wound. It was spurting blood like a geyser."

"I think I'm going to die, Flip. Thought I would be more fearful, but I just want to sleep, stop the hurting."

"I am not about to let you die, Conor, so get that notion out of your head."

Conor looked up, and no more than a half dozen paces behind Flipper, he saw a giant of a man, his face almost hidden by a mat of shaggy white hair and a long beard that fell below his chest. He carried a big bow, and a quiver of arrows was slung over his shoulder, but he did not have an arrow nocked in the bowstring.

"Flip, got company," he said before he faded away to welcome oblivion again.

Chapter 35

FLIPPER FELT GOOSE bumps on the back of his neck at Conor's warning, and now he sensed the presence of someone behind him. His hands were blood-soaked, and his Army Colt holstered. It would be suicide to go for his gun, draw, and seek out his target if the visitor meant him harm. He was already a dead man if that was the case.

He continued his work until he was satisfied he had ebbed the blood flow. Many such wounds signaled near-instant death. He clung to hope that the fact Conor still breathed meant that the slug had not struck something vital. The entry wound was high, and he considered that positive, but he had to get his wounded friend back to the Triad where a doctor's help awaited. But how? Conor certainly could not sit a saddle. Regardless, he must deal with the man behind him first.

He lifted himself from the ground and turned to face the man, instantly surprised by his stature. Flipper was a bit over six feet, but this man was at least a half foot taller. His shaggy white hair and beard gave him the look of an old man, but he stood erect, and the bare arms and shoulders, revealed by a deerskin vest he wore, were thickly muscled, his biceps bulging like a blacksmith's. Knee high moccasins and loose cotton britches, like Apache males sometimes wore, suggested that an Indian faced him, but this was no Apache, and he made no threatening advance.

Flipper said, "I am Henry Flipper. I must get my friend to a doctor. Can you help me?" He figured the man's answer would tell him what direction this encounter was going to take.

The visitor did not speak, but he shook his head affirmatively and began swinging his arms and hands with his fingers pressing into his palms as if holding an object. An axe. He was pantomiming the swinging of an axe. Flipper said, "Yes, I have an axe." He walked over to the stack of supplies they had unloaded from the packhorse and retrieved the big axe they had brought with them for clearing survey obstacles as well as cutting firewood.

The man stepped forward, hand outreached, and Flipper handed him the axe. The giant disappeared into the trees, and soon he could hear him chopping. Flipper returned to Conor and did not like what he saw. His friend's breathing had shallowed like he was slipping toward the end, but from experience he knew it was difficult to tell. He might just have descended into a sound sleep, and that would not be a bad thing under the circumstances.

Soon, the giant returned, dragging two poles and one arm wrapped about a collection of smaller pieces. A travois. He was going to construct a travois on which to carry Conor, of course. He scolded himself for not instantly thinking of the solution. He had a lariat and several rolls of smaller rope he used for aligning survey stakes. He got up and gathered them, and the two men began working to fashion the stretcher to drag behind one of the mounts, probably Conor's Stoic.

In a bit over a half hour, they crafted a sturdy travois, which he would cushion with blankets from the bedrolls. When the travois was anchored to the horse and the packhorse and his own mount readied, the silent man helped Flipper lift Conor onto the crude stretcher and bind him to it. Conor moaned several times but did not wake up.

The Samaritan took the lead on foot as they headed for the trail that led back to the Triad. He waved to Flipper to swing his mount nearer the mountain base briefly and pointed to a body lying face down in the dust, an arrow protruding from his back. He raised his hand exhibiting three fingers. Three men. The Samaritan had disposed of one, and he and Conor had downed the other two.

"What about the horses?" Flipper asked.

He led Flipper to a spot where saddles and tack were stacked, raised his hand in the air and swept it in all directions. He had turned them loose. They would turn wild, he supposed, or show up at somebody's house, a gift that would amount to no small amount of money.

He figured that moving the horses at a fast walk, they faced a three- or four-hour ride to the Triad. He wondered if the big man intended to go with him. He should have held back one of the attackers' mounts for the journey. He heard Conor moan and tossed a look over his shoulder to confirm that his friend was not resisting the bonds that held him to the travois. His question about the Samaritan was answered when he turned back and realized that the man had disappeared into the darkness like some apparition. Had this been a visit from the Ghost to which others had been alluding?

He did not give a whit who the man was. He had likely been the one who warned them of the approaching killers and then rushed to come to their aid at a critical time. He hoped for an opportunity to give proper thanks someday.

Now he must focus on getting Conor to the Triad while he still breathed.

Chapter 36

KAT WAS YANKED from a deep slumber by Loafer's barking from the parlor. Then she heard the frantic rapping at the front door. She wormed her way into a flannel robe to cover her nakedness and grabbed her Colt revolver from the bedstand. She went into the parlor and saw Loafer, still barking, facing the door.

"Who is it?" She hollered to the person on the veranda side of the door.

"It's Henry. I've got Conor with me. He's been shot and is in bad shape."

She slipped the bolt back from the lock catch and pulled the door open, finding a sober-faced Henry Flipper struggling to hold onto his usual calm. "Get Doc. Conor has taken two slugs, one in the chest. It could be too late."

She whirled to go roust Doc and almost collided with him when he emerged from the darkness. "Doc, did you hear?"

"I heard. Let's get Conor inside."

She placed her gun on the lamp table, and they both joined Flipper outside, descending the steps and walking barefoot to the rail where the horses were hitched before making their way to the travois. Doc bent over Conor's still form, placed his fingers on his young friend's neck, and pressed his hand to the chest.

"He bled a lot?" Doc asked.

"Yes. The arm wound pumped five times as much as the other. The slug passed clear through the arm, but I am guessing it hit an artery. I finally got it stopped, but I know he was close to bleeding out."

"We've got to get him inside to the surgery. Get this thing unhitched from the horse, and if you can handle one end, Kat and I will try to take care of the other."

It was a struggle, but they got the travois through the hospital door and into the surgery. The worst part was hoisting Conor onto the surgery table, and Doc bent over, catching his breath for a few minutes after that effort.

Doc said, "Kat, why don't you go make yourself decent? I won't need your help for a bit."

She suddenly realized her robe had opened and slid down her shoulders while moving Conor, exposing her breasts to the world. She flushed and snugged the robe about her body. "Yes, of course, I should do that."

She hurried out of the room. At least Doc had slipped on britches and a shirt. She was mortified. She had not left much to the two men's imaginations. Doc was family, and she was not so troubled by his observation, but Henry—how could she look him in the eyes after this. She was comforted some by the fact he had always seemed a gentleman and likely would not mention her exhibition.

In her room, she snatched up her denim jeans and a long-sleeved shirt and slipped into moccasins, which she still preferred over boots. She wished she could wear a flour sack over her head to hide her embarrassment, but when finally dressed and her body well-covered, she returned to the surgery where Doc and Flipper had stripped Conor down to his undershorts and covered his lower extremities with a sheet.

She noticed that the arm wound was gauze-wrapped now, with a few spots of blood seeping through. She assumed that the bandaging there was temporary, and that Doc's attention was focused on the chest wound which seemed to be to the right side of the torso. Doc appeared to be absorbed in gently removing the packing Flipper had applied to the entry, and blood was oozing out as he worked.

"Doc, what the hell are you doing here?" It was Conor's weak and scratchy voice.

She could see that Conor's eyes were glazed and puzzled, but it was the first time they had opened since his arrival, and she welcomed the confirmation that he was alive.

Doc said, "You are in my hospital at the Triad, Conor. You went out and got yourself shot without my permission. Now, I've got some patching to do."

"Am I dying, Doc?"

"Nope. What kind of doctor do you think I am? My patients don't die. Now, I am going to use some chloroform to put you out, so you won't feel a thing when I'm working. And I can't have you moving around." He turned to Kat. "You have done this a few times now. Can you handle the anesthetic?"

"I don't see why not." She went to the cupboard and removed a bottle along with cotton and a thick cloth.

"You're letting her put me out?" Conor said.

"She has done it before."

"She doesn't like men. Shoots them. Hammers them with axes. I know folks have died on a table because of chloroform."

"Kat has got the knack for it. She's not going to kill you," Doc turned to Kat. "Are you, Kat?"

"Not if he behaves, anyway." She spread the cotton out on the cloth, and carefully dripped the chloroform on it. "Henry, would you hold his shoulders to the table while I do this? He might struggle some."

"Yes, ma'am. I can do that."

Doc laid out his forceps and other surgical instruments on a counter within easy reach while Kat and Flipper tended to Conor. When the patient was asleep, Doc moved to the table. "Now, Kat, you focus on his breathing, ease up if you are concerned, add more chloroform if he starts moving around on me. I am thinking his weakness is coming mostly from loss of blood. I've got to do some probing to find the dang slug, but the entry wound is a bit high for a lung shot, although the lead often makes detours once it gets in there."

An hour later, Doc removed the slug. "Closer to the collarbone. It headed upward. He's lucky. Nothing vital."

"Thank God and Doc," Flipper said.

"I want to do some cleanup work, be sure there is no fabric to taint the wound. A few stitches maybe, but we will leave an opening for drainage. Then I'll tend to the arm. You can lighten up the anesthetic some, though, Kat. We have had him under about as long as I like."

Later, after Conor was moved to one of the beds in the two-patient hospital room, Doc said, "You did a fine job, Kat. Do you mind being the nurse to this guy for a week? Unless infection sets in, we should have him out of here in that time."

Kat said, "There is a lot I would rather do, but I can look in on him from time to time, I guess. What are you going to do about an assistant for Henry? I was thinking I could do that."

"Maybe later sometimes, but I need you here now. Sunup will be here in a few hours, and Henry has had a long night. I am thinking he might use a day off. I need to speak with Diego and Lucia Munoz. I thought I might ride over to their place later this morning and see if I can hire Diego to help Henry for a spell."

Kat shrugged. "You are the boss." She could not explain why, but she wanted to get to know Henry Flipper better and was disappointed at the lost opportunity.

Chapter 37

MIDMORNING DOC WENT to the stable to retrieve a horse for the half hour journey to the home of Diego and Lucia Munoz. He was surprised to find Flipper with a pitchfork in his hands cleaning stalls.

"You are supposed to be sleeping," Doc said.

"I grabbed a few hours' shuteye, but I have never been much for sleeping daylight hours, and I have got to keep busy with something."

"I understand that. If I don't get my sleep at night, I generally don't get it, but this old man's strength is flagging some, and I will grab a nap before the day is gone."

"I was wondering if I might use the desk in your private office later. I need to do some drawings of the work I have done so far, set out the measurements and such. Most couldn't make sense of what I scribbled on paper sitting on my lap or a big rock. It helps to keep up as I move along while my memory acts as a check on what I've done."

"Of course. Take over the office if you want. I go days, sometimes weeks, without using it. I am not much dealing with paper. That's why I surrendered the store books to Kat. She doesn't seem to mind that sort of thing, halfway enjoys it, I think."

"She is a remarkable young woman, isn't she?"

"Yep, but don't tell her. She doesn't know it yet. I don't want her to get a big head and run off someplace looking for better things." Doc wasn't sure what Flipper meant by his comment. He hoped the surveyor was not talking about the female attributes Kat had unknowingly displayed earlier.

"She is quick as her namesake in her head. You can almost see that brain calculating constantly. I don't think she gives her head much rest."

"I wouldn't argue that."

Flipper said, "Another question. That fella I told you about who showed up last night—the tall man with the long hair and beard. Is he the Ghost you folks keep talking about?"

"I've never seen the Ghost, so I can't rightly say for certain. If he was the Ghost, it appears you might be the only man alive who has ever seen him. But, yeah, I would guess that you were visited by the Ghost. I suppose he came out of hiding because it was the only way he could help you."

"Nobody really thinks he is a real ghost then, a spirit of some sort?"

"Some think so. The Apache bands generally stay clear these days because they think the Guadalupe are haunted. The mountains were formerly a favorite lair for the Mescalero. I haven't seen one here for several years. I used to harvest good money trading with the Indians in these parts, and for the most part we never had as much as a scuffle. They were glad to have access to my merchandise. Some had gold coins—never asked where they got them. Others had furs and other things I could market. Anyhow, I think the Ghost helped keep me and mine safe most of the years I've been here." He did not mention the one occasion when the Ghost apparently arrived too late.

"Well, I owe him for certain and so does Conor."

"I would like to meet the feller. Talk to him some."

"I told you he doesn't talk—or can't, didn't I?"

"Yeah, I've been thinking on that."

Later, when Doc rode into the Munoz farmstead, he saw both Lucia and Diego on hands and knees in the garden. They were probably weeding, and all the little ones seemed to be helping, too, even the youngest who had not been walking all that long. He was confident that Diego would not turn down an opportunity to escape the garden or any other work that Lucia would have him doing here, and Lucia would not resist the cash money.

When they saw Doc, the entire family hurried out to greet him. He dismounted and unfastened the straps on his saddle bags. He dug into the pocket and fished out a small paper sack of hard candies and handed them to Lucia when she arrived. "For the kids. Madre will hand these out later." The twin boys, who at six years of age looked mildly disappointed, obviously did not want to depend on their mother's rationing. The five-year-old daughter seemed more accepting, and the two-year-old boy did not understand it all yet.

"Gracias, Doc," Lucia said, "you are so generous."

"I am not finished." He plucked another sack out. "A few soft candies for the little one, and saltwater taffy for the family, and finally a Peter's milk chocolate bar for Madre. I've got a pound of coffee to add to this, and a special gift for Padre when he stops by the trading post."

Lucia wrapped her arms about him and kissed him on the cheek, almost toppling him. "We love you, Doc. You are so good to us." Then she stepped back, and her dark eyes narrowed, and her voice took on a scolding tone.

"But this special gift for Diego, why did you not bring it with you?"

She had him cornered now. "Alright, you've got me. It's a bottle of whiskey. I thought you might prefer that the children did not see it."

"No, you thought I would take the bottle and toss it away."

It appeared that Diego was not going to engage in this dispute. "Lucia, Diego is not a drunk. He will stretch a bottle of whiskey for weeks. But he enjoys a sip of whiskey now and then. And I have work for him that will bring cash to the family."

Her mood switched, and now she smiled. "Maybe I will forgive you for this. Tell me about the work. What does it pay?"

"One dollar per day. He will be assisting a surveyor." He continued, explaining what the surveyor was doing. "This is important work for all the people here. You have been visited by men who are saying you must move, haven't you? This will help the lawyers I have hired."

"We had the visit, and we are not leaving."

"I worry that it might not be safe here. If you are threatened with violence, I want you to leave and bring your family to the Triad till this is settled. We will build temporary shelters."

"I will not leave my home and my garden."

"Think of the children."

"Maybe I will bring them and return here."

Doc did not know what he would do with four children, but he intended to get the same message to all the families and maybe others would help. "Anyway, I would like to have Diego come by the Triad after sunrise tomorrow to start work."

"He cannot."

"Why not?"

"You are a generous man with your gifts, but they do not buy you cheap workers. He must have a dollar and a half a day."

"You are a shrewd businesswoman, Lucia. Very well, a dollar and a half." He had planned on two dollars and would give Diego the extra for his personal hideaway.

"And I know what you are doing, Doc, you scoundrel. You give Diego extra money to hide from me, but I will find it. I have ways."

Doc looked at Diego, who shrugged and grinned sheepishly. He changed the subject. "I will see Diego in the morning. Now before I leave, I need two witnesses for some legal papers I brought with me. I have ink and pen in my saddlebags. Can you help me?"

Lucia said, "Of course. We will go into the house. Diego makes a beautiful signature even though he will not let me help him to read and write when I teach the children. It does not matter. He has many other skills." She winked.

Diego grinned again.

Chapter 38

"YOU MUST DRINK," Kat said, pressing a glass of water to Conor's lips. "Doc says you may eat when you say you are hungry, but you must drink whether you are thirsty or not. Do you still feel sick?"

"Not so much now."

"Doc said the chloroform will do that. You look much better now, not so pale. You will probably live."

"Thanks for the encouragement."

"I thought you were a dead man last night, Con. I feared I was bringing you back to bury you."

Conor looked up and saw Flipper in the doorway leaning against the doorframe. He took the smile on his face as a good sign. "Flip, what are you doing here?"

"Doc loaned me his office to work on my drawings."

"What happened last night?"

"You ought to be resting, catching some sleep."

"I've done nothing but sleep for hours now. Come in and tell me about it."

Flipper looked at Kat. "Is that okay with you, nurse?"

"I am not a nurse. I am more of a conscripted servant. I've got work in the store. You can have him for as long as you want. See that he keeps drinking that water. I've got a pitcher full on the side table. If he needs to piss, there is a chamber pot under the bed. You help him. I don't want any part of that."

After Kat departed, Flipper asked, "Is she always that grumpy with you?"

"Pretty much. I did see her smile once. Maybe she is just not cut out to be a nurse. She might make a better gunfighter."

Flipper said, "You are a little grumpy yourself. The two of you seem to make a good match."

"Two bullet holes don't bring out the cheerful side of a man."

"I guess that is understandable."

"Now tell me what happened. You can spare the details. I would just like to fill in some gaps."

"There were three men. Do you remember taking one down?"

"Yeah. And then those shots came from the tangle of trees and undergrowth. That's about all I remember—except for a time or two when you were trying to do some patching."

Flipper said, "I was late on the trigger but got the one who shot you. The third was further behind, and he never reached the camp. He went down with an arrow in his back."

"An arrow? Apache?"

"It came from a friend who probably saved your life last night." He told Conor about the appearance of the bearded giant who had helped construct the travois and position him on it.

"The Ghost, of course," Conor said.

"I guess you can call him that, but he was a man, not a ghost. Of course, I guess I've never made the acquaintance of a ghost, so what do I know?"

"And he could not speak?"

"I don't know that for sure. Maybe he didn't want to talk."

"I would bet he got his tongue cut out."

"Not a pleasant thing to ponder. Anyhow, that is pretty much the story." He took the water pitcher and filled another glass. "You had better keep drinking or we will be in trouble with the boss lady. Do you want me to hold this up to your mouth?"

Conor slowly reached out with his right hand and took the glass. "I can handle it."

"And you were letting Kat hold your head up and putting the glass to your lips. I think you were taking advantage."

"Letting her practice her nursing."

Flipper returned to Doc's office to continue his work, promising to return periodically to pour a glass of water from the pitcher. Conor instantly dropped off to sleep, not waking till he felt a hand gently tapping on his shoulder. His eyes opened, and he saw Kat's face only a few inches above his own.

"For a minute, I feared you were dead. You need to drink your water. Henry let you sleep longer than he should have."

She poured a glass of water and handed it to him. "I saw you drinking by yourself when you were talking to Henry. The invalid game is over."

He took the glass. "I never said I couldn't hold a glass. You never asked. There is something you could do for me, though."

"What is that?" she asked, her tone suspicious.

"My pistol—the Colt. It must be here someplace. I would feel more comfortable if I had it on the table beside me."

"It is holstered and hanging on the gun belt in Doc's office. You can ask Doc about that when he gets back. Do you need another dose of laudanum for pain?"

"No, not now. Thank you for your kindness." He hoped she detected the sarcasm. He put the glass down and closed his eyes, feigning sleep, hoping she would leave, yet knowing he would miss her nearness. Kathleen Ryan was becoming an unsettling problem in more ways than one.

Chapter 39

A WEEK LATER, CONOR was back on his feet, but with a tender left arm and a gimpy shoulder from the more serious wound beneath the collar bone on the right side, he was not yet strong enough to rein a horse. The confines of the four walls of the hospital room had him on the brink of insanity, and this morning he was moving back to the barn loft he shared with Flipper.

He figured he could find some chores he could help with around the place while he mended a bit more. He expected to be back in the saddle in another week. Kat had softened a bit as he improved and had been noticeably more kind the past few days. Maybe she just wanted him out of the Triad. It seemed like she was taking over the place, and Doc did not seem to mind being supplanted as commander. Of course, Kat was always deferential to her friend and mentor. Why would she not be when he spoiled her like a child? Even Loafer seemed to have shifted loyalties some and followed on Kat's heels whenever she left the Triad.

Kat had disappeared with Loafer an hour earlier without any indication of where she was going. Sometimes, she rode her mare in the canyon for a spell, and he suspected that might have been her destination. She felt no responsibility to report her whereabouts to him. Any request for her to do so would have inspired the bite of her sharp tongue.

Kat and Conor were the only occupants of the Triad this morning, since Doc had joined Flipper and Diego for the day on a trek to all the farmsteads carved from Doc's original land. Doc was to confirm the boundaries established by natural landmarks, stacked stones and the like. Flipper would make notes and sketches to assist with the surveyed legal descriptions he would create. The three men would not return till nightfall and would likely require yet another day for the task.

Conor had been uneasy the past few days. It was too quiet, like the calm before the storm. He was certain the Santa Fe Ring would not have surrendered so quickly on the land grab, and he supposed the so-called enforcers were aware of their missing cohorts by now. Flipper and Diego had gone to the site of the bloodletting when they embarked on their first survey trip together a day later. Flipper had decided it would be best to bury anything that was left of the corpses, thinking that it would be desirable to plant seeds of doubt regarding the fate of the three men. The bodies had disappeared, however, and they assumed that the Ghost had relieved them of the task.

Conor was getting ready to take the remainder of his personal belongings to the stable when he heard the bell clanging from the trading post. He put down his light load and headed to the closed door that separated the store from the residence. He had assisted several customers yesterday and was glad to do something useful, but he knew he was not cut out to be more than an occasional storekeeper.

When he opened the door and entered the store, he was met by two men standing at the counter, one a hulking man with a scraggly beard and red-scarred pit in his forehead and the other a shorter man gone to fat with a salt and pepper, untrimmed mustache that fell over his upper lip. Both were dust-covered and reeked of stale sweat, obviously having spent many days in the saddle and avoiding soap and water on their journey. He recognized both from his visit to Albuquerque and had hoped their paths would never cross.

The hulking man spoke in a needlessly loud voice. "Are you the owner of this place?"

"No, sir. The owner is out for the day, but I am helping him out. What can I do for you?"

"We might buy a few supplies, but, first, we're after information."

"Well, I will help you if I can."

"My friend here is deputy city marshal up in Albuquerque. We're looking for a criminal. Buford's got his badge pinned on his vest. You can see for yourself."

Buford Walters just nodded repeatedly and pointed to the silver badge on his vest.

"Just who is this criminal you are after? How dangerous is he?"

"Ain't no 'he.' We're trying to chase down a 'she.' She's a sneaky killer given the chance." He rubbed the disfigurement on his forehead. "She done this to me. Took an axe to my head while I was sleeping. No cause. Just for the pleasure of killing. I'm damn lucky I ain't dead. She is my woman. Common law married, we are. I'm going to take her home, help her with her law problems if she behaves decent."

"So that's why the law is after her?"

"Oh, that ain't the end of it. She escaped jail and rustled Buford's horse. Stole saddle and tack with it. Lots of money worth of stuff there. Serious business."

"So, you have got a warrant for her arrest?"

"Don't need no warrant." Gaynor looked at Buford. "What do they call that, Buford? Pursuit? We are in pursuit. Charges will be filed after an arrest."

Conor said, "I haven't seen anybody for months but folks who live around here. What's this woman's name? What does she look like in case I see her?"

"Her name is Kat Gaynor. I'm her husband, Louie. She always claimed to be Ryan, though. I doubt if she would be using either name on the run the way she is. She's a little mite of a thing, scrawny but a pretty morsel if a man takes a second look. Her pa was Irish but takes more to the look of her Mexican mama in her hair and fine bones and such. On the lighter side for a greaser."

Conor prayed that Kat did not show up while these men were here. If she did, folks would die, and it was anyone's guess who that might be. "What makes you think she might have turned up in these parts? We're miles from a settlement. There are still a few Apache that have jumped the reservation that come by here, outlaws. A lone woman could starve or die of thirst getting here from Albuquerque."

"None of your concern, but she was tracked to the stretch of the Guadalupe west of here. We saw this place and figured it was a likely stop."

"She is probably dead." He saw Walters ease his pistol from its holster.

"Possible. But we ain't gonna quit looking for the little bitch anytime soon. And there is something about you, mister, that makes me think you know more than you're letting on."

Conor was the first to admit that he was a lousy liar. Flipper had often joshed him about it. "Think what you will, but I can't help you. Now you said you might need supplies."

Suddenly the door opened, and Kat, with Loafer trailing, walked in. Conor yelled, "Kathleen, run."

She froze, her eyes staring in disbelief at the visitors, before she whirled and darted out the door. The dog stood fast with bared teeth and growling threateningly, blocking the doorway to Gaynor who charged after her with six-gun raised. Gaynor did not hesitate. He aimed his pistol at the dog and fired, the explosion deafening in the room. The dog yelped, staggered ahead a few steps and collapsed. Gaynor stumbled over the dog but regained his balance before charging out the door.

Conor slipped his Colt from its holster, seizing the opportunity while Buford Walters was distracted by the chaos. When Walters turned back to him, pistol ready to fire, Conor figured there was no point in attempting a discussion with a voiceless man, he squeezed the trigger, the weapon's kick sending stabs of sharp pain to his shoulder, before driving a gut shot into the man's big belly. Walters moaned, lowered his own weapon and stared in astonishment at the blood seeping through his shirtfront before raising his gun to retort. Conor delivered another slug to the so-called deputy's throat before the man crumpled over and landed on the hardwood floor.

Conor heard gunfire outside and raced to the doorway in time to see Kat, mounted on her red roan mare, headed toward the Guadalupe in the direction of the long-abandoned Butterfield stage trail. Louie Gaynor had just burst away on his own mount, now out of pistol range, from the Triad. It would be difficult for Gaynor to catch her soon with his bay horse carrying extra weight, and Toughie was fast as the wind. Kat was smart to head for higher ground. Conor was confident Kat carried her Winchester in a saddle holster, and it would help to gain the elevation advantage. But the terrain was rough, and, according to Doc, the stagecoach company gave it up after a six-month try and established another route.

Regardless, there were a dozen ways Gaynor's chances could more than even up.

He turned back into the building. He need not examine Walters to confirm that the man was either dead or dying. It was over for that no-good, and Conor could feel no remorse.

He knelt beside Loafer expecting to verify the dog's death but found that the valiant canine still breathed. He searched out the wound and found a gaping hole at the juncture of the dog's neck and shoulder. He felt flesh surrounding the slug's entry opening, and Loafer whined, lifting his head slightly and looking up at Conor with pitiful eyes. Fortunately, the bleeding was not profuse, but only Doc could help the creature, and time was wasting. He would be far behind, but he needed to get to Stoic in the stable and take up the chase.

He hurried to Doc's surgery, rifling through the cupboards for materials. Then he returned to Loafer, applied a compress to the wound and wrapped gauze about his torso and looped it about the injured shoulder, hoping it would stifle bleeding till Doc returned later. He could not move the big dog to a more comfortable location given the state of his own injuries.

After he had tended to the dog as well as he could, he wrote a note for Doc, leaving it on the office desk. He was confident Doc and Flipper would search it out after they discovered a dead man and wounded dog in the store and learned that he and Kat were missing.

He quickly packed his saddlebags, retrieved his rifle, and headed for the stable to commence his journey into the mountains.

Chapter 40

I T WAS MIDAFTERNOON now as Kat urged Toughie higher into the Guadalupe, following the faint trail left by the temporary stage road. She had not made this journey previously and was surprised at the contrast from the semi-arid land below. There were pine, oak, and many trees she could not identify, as well as berry bushes of assorted kinds. Some places, steep stone cliffs framed the trail of an unknown destination. She came upon a spring dripping from the face of one of the stone cliffs just off the trail and noticed it was forming a pool below. She reined in the mare so she could water both horse and rider.

She had an empty canteen from the morning ride, so she filled that before letting the mare drink. Then she clambered over some rocks that took her to an outcropping that she thought might give her a view of the trail below. As she gained her footing and stood there, she was surprised to see the Triad in the distance and a lone rider departing and angling southwest in the direction of the Butterfield trail. She could not make out the rider's features, but he appeared to be astride a light-colored mount, probably a gray. It had to be Conor Byrne.

She gave a sigh of relief. She had heard the gunfire from inside the trading post as she was riding away from the Triad. Conor had survived. She hoped that meant that Buford had not. She worried about Conor's endurance for a frantic ride considering his injuries. Certainly, the pain would be significant. He was far behind, but the thought that he was on his way revived her spirits. She searched the trail behind, but its snakelike twisting at some places made it difficult to locate Louie. She knew that he would not give up till one of them was dead.

Finally, she saw him several hundred feet below, emerging from behind a bend in the trail. She still had a good lead, but he was narrowing the gap between them. She returned to her horse but paused before mounting, studying Toughie's left rear fetlock. Was she limping? Did she see some swelling? She bent and grasped the hock and hoof, lifted and bent it so she could examine it. There was a small gash in the fetlock and it was swollen slightly. She released the leg. It appeared the injury was recent, likely the result of a sharp stone. The cursed rocks were like scattered horse traps all over the trail. No wonder the stage line had been unable to operate here. Hoping that the injury was not serious, she decided to continue slowly and keep an eye on the mare's response.

Fifteen minutes later, she knew she would be forced to abandon her beloved Toughie. The limp was worse now, and the poor mare could not handle more stress on the leg. What would become of her? She dismounted and unsaddled the mare, tears streaming down her cheeks, more for the fate of her horse than from fear that Louie would now run her down. Before removing bit and bridle, she pressed her face softly to Toughie's cheek. "Goodbye, dear friend. I must leave you now. Go home, if you can."

She took her rifle and cartridges, leaving the saddle and tack off to the side of the trail. She started walking, knowing she would be forced to abandon the trail soon if she were to have any chance of evading Louie. If nothing else, she must find a place to either hide or provide her with a defensible position.

As she made her way up the slope, she heard the rattling of stones on the trail behind her. She levered a cartridge into the Winchester's chamber and swung around, ready to get off a quick shot, and then she relaxed. Toughie. The horse was struggling to follow her. She walked some ten paces back to the horse and stroked her on the neck and withers. She sighed. "I won't leave you behind. I will find a way to kill the bastard. Then we will take a slow walk downslope and make our way home. Doc can fix you." Home. Yes, the Triad was home, and she prayed that it would be for the remainder of her life if she was granted more time on this earth.

Kat considered her dilemma. She dared not retrieve her stake-out line and anchor the mare someplace to await her return. There was every possibility that she would not make it back and then the poor animal, if unable to break free, would die of thirst or starvation, or weaken to be easy prey for a mountain lion or some other predator. No, she must abandon the horse again and hope they could reunite later. She would retreat into the rocks above where Toughie could not follow.

She turned away and broke off the trail, scrambling up a steep incline that was cloaked with shale that made footing a challenge. Her eyes were focused on a stone landing above that promised a route along the cliffs that appeared to cut between craggy crests. Of course, it could easily dead-end and leave her trapped. She searched for a natural fortress where she might garner some protection from Louie's gunfire if he caught up with her. She reached the ledge and stepped onto solid rock just as a rifle cracked and splintered stones from the cliff wall burned her cheeks. She turned and looked down upon the old trail nearly a hundred feet below. Louie with Toughie on a halter and tied to a tree limb. The rope and halter must have been taken from her own tack pile. His bay was probably tied out of sight back down the trail.

"Afternoon, wife," Louie yelled. "You make a nice target there. That was a warning shot. I can take you down whenever it suits me now. I'm gonna give you a chance to live, though. I just want my woman back doing her wifely duties. You just slide your pretty ass down those rocks, and we'll be heading home. If you don't, you get to watch this lame critter die and then take your turn."

She had no choice, and she was not without hope. Conor was trying to catch up with them. If she could buy time, he might yet arrive or meet them going back down the trail. "Don't harm my horse. I'm coming down."

"Not your horse, honey. Our friend, Buford's . . . remember? You stole it from him. He will be wanting her back."

Buford was likely dead since she had seen Conor leaving the Triad, but it was better that Louie remained unaware. She dropped off the ledge and sat down on the shale, sliding her way to the bottom, still clinging to the Winchester that had a cartridge in the chamber. She might find an opportunity when she got solid footing again. He would try to relieve her of the weapon, but before he did, she just might be able to get off a shot.

She held no illusion that Louie intended to take her back to Albuquerque as his wife. He would kill her, but not before he pleasured himself for as long as it suited him. He would be wary of her now since their last encounter. Unfortunately, she would be bound by rope or rawhide now, for he would not dare close his eyes to sleep or he would never wake up again.

He was waiting less than five feet away when she landed on the trail and struggled back to her feet. "The rifle, sweetheart," he said. "Little girls shouldn't play with such things."

She swung the barrel around to fire just as he whipped the barrel of his own rifle around and slammed her on the side of her head. Her knees buckled, and she collapsed, aware first of the overwhelming pain and then the blackness overtaking her.

Chapter 41

CONOR WAS PERPLEXED when he came upon Kat's saddle and tack along the side of the trail but no sign of the red roan mare or rider. He rode on ahead, however, and found a cluster of fresh horse apples and traces of shoed hoofprints in the dust that told him horses had passed that way.

He reined in when he saw a spent bullet casing lying in the dust. He dismounted and picked up the casing, realizing his examination would tell him nothing. A horse whinnied behind him and startled him. He turned and saw the roan mare emerging from the trees on the opposite side of the old road, limping noticeably, favoring a back leg. That explained the saddle on the trail. His guess was that Louie Gaynor had caught up to Kat. If she had been killed here, however, there would be a body. He shuddered at the mere thought.

He readied to mount and forge ahead when another form appeared from the trees behind the horse. A tall man with long white hair and beard. He had only a hazy recall of briefly glimpsing the visitor during his ordeal over a week ago, but he knew instantly he was seeing the Ghost. "Greetings," Conor said. "Have you seen a young lady, one you likely helped before?"

He nodded and waved for Conor to follow. The Ghost took Toughie's lead rope and headed back in the direction from which he had come. Conor followed, leading Stoic.

They walked higher on a narrow trail just wide enough for a horse to clear most of the pine branches and undergrowth. Their destination appeared to be a high-reaching bluff outlined against the fading blue of a late afternoon sky. Conor stopped suddenly when he saw a lonely, dead tree not more than fifty feet distant on the slope. Louie Gaynor was suspended from an arching naked branch, a rope cinched about his neck, his dangling feet perhaps a foot off the ground. It was an eerie sight, one Conor knew would never escape his memory.

The Ghost looked at him with the palest blue eyes he had ever seen and swept his hand outward as if saying, "It is done."

Conor, not knowing what to say, just nodded.

They continued on the trail for another twenty minutes until they came to a little clearing at the base of a bluff—a man-made clearing that extended for some distance on both sides of an opening in the bluff wall. He led Conor some fifty feet south of the wall to a small stretch of grass that lined a narrow stream fed by water that trickled off the craggy limestone wall, where a bay gelding, he assumed Gaynor's, already grazed. There he pantomimed that Conor should unsaddle his horse.

Conor said, "Do you expect me to stay a spell?"

The Ghost pointed to threatening thunder clouds and lightning moving in from the west portending rain for the mountains if not for the flatlands below. Also, it would be dark soon and foolhardy to embark on a journey down the mountain slope.

Conor said, "Kathleen, the young woman, is she here? Is she alright?"

The Ghost nodded and pointed to the opening, which was apparently the entrance to a cave. The Guadalupe mountains were noted for their many caves, some of which were thought connected to the great caverns to the north. Men were said to have died trying to prove that rumor.

When the horses were staked out, Conor followed the Ghost to the cave opening. They had to drop to their knees to crawl in, but inside they could stand easily with several feet to spare. They were greeted by a warm fire that sent its smoke through a fissure in the stone ceiling to a source of air through an opening probably hidden many feet beyond.

The light in the room was supplemented by a kerosene lamp that was suspended from a rough stone that protruded from one wall. Kathleen Ryan sat on a bearskin rug, leaning against the wall on one side of the cave, and the Ghost gestured for Conor to join her. Then he signed with his compressed right hand, passing the tips of his fingers to curve downward past his mouth several times, after which he raised his hand with the universal "wait" sign. They would eat but would need to wait. From his experience with the Army scouts, Conor now realized the Ghost was communicating largely with Indian sign language, much of which could be interpreted by common sense.

Conor nodded that he understood. The Ghost disappeared into another chamber of the cave, and Conor saw the place fill with light. He wondered how far the cave extended. He looked at Kat, who sat beside him, only a few feet separating the two. She stared hypnotically at the fire as if unaware of his presence. Her head was wrapped with cloth strips, and it was swollen beneath one side of the binding. She had obviously been injured, but the Ghost had tended to the damage. Kat seemed to have a knack for getting her head pounded.

"Kathleen, are you okay?"

She continued to gaze at the fire and spoke softly and numbly. "Yeah, Louie gun-whipped me with his rifle, but the Ghost showed up and carried me here. He hogtied Louie and brought him along slung over the back of his horse. Toughie followed and then fell behind. I think he planned to go back and find her, but I am not certain."

"She is outside, staked out and grazing with the other critters."

"Did you see Louie?"

"Yes, I saw him."

"I watched. I didn't want to, but I did. I hated Louie, but I didn't want him to die like that. The Ghost looped the rope around his neck and dragged him over to the tree, then tossed the end over the branch. After that, he untied the bonds—I think so he could watch Louie struggle and dance. He pulled Louie off the ground, and poor Louie screamed and fought. I begged him to stop, even said I would go away with Louie. He did not seem to hear me. Louie strangled; he did not hang. He suffered to the end."

"But you are safe now. I think he wanted you to know that."

"And I am haunted. Can I ever erase that memory?"

"No, but it will dull and fade."

"This is why you gave up soldiering, isn't it?"

"Yes."

She still had not looked at him. "What happened to Buford?"

"Dead."

"You killed him?"

"Yes."

"I heard gunshots. I feared for your life."

"No need."

"And Loafer is dead?"

"Not when I last saw him. I did what I could, but I had to get on your trail. I think there is a good chance Doc can patch him up. I have got hopes anyhow."

They lapsed into an uneasy silence. When the Ghost returned, he was carrying a Dutch oven. He scraped coals to the side of the fire, then set the oven with its contents on the coals before using a hand scoop to drop a scattering of red-hot coals on the lid. It occurred to Conor that the man did not seem to suffer much from lack of life's amenities, partly due to his visits to Doc's trading post. He apparently had a kitchen of sorts in the other chamber. For all he knew, the stone mountain bluff contained a palace within its cavities. And he suspected that he and Kat would visit nothing beyond this room.

He tossed a look at Kat again and saw tears streaming down her cheeks. He risked scooting nearer to her and placed his arm about her shoulders. He felt her tense at his touch, and then she relaxed and turned toward him, her green, tear-filled eyes looking up at his. She started sobbing and buried her head in his chest while he held her close. Minutes later, the tears stopped as abruptly as they had started, and she pulled away, turning her face toward the flames again.

The next time the Ghost appeared from the chamber, he carried a pan of batter, and using an iron hook to lift the oven lid, poured the mix over the contents before dropping the cover back in place.

Returning to his chamber, he soon emerged with two thick quilts and a buffalo robe in hand and placed them next to Kat. He pointed to Conor and Kat indicating they should share. A noticeable chill was settling in, and nights tended to cool significantly on the desert below, and he knew from Army experience that mountain heights had a way of turning downright cold even during the hottest days of summer. Now he heard muffled rumblings of thunder outside. The horses had some tree covering they could edge into, so he was not too worried about them. He and Stoic had endured far worse.

In a short time, the Ghost served up two generous platters of venison and potato stew intertwined with biscuit strips. Greens were included, but Conor could not identify the kind. He suspected they had a wild source. A pot of coffee was on the fire now, and soon the guests had steaming cups at their sides. The Ghost took the Dutch oven and disappeared again, presumably to eat alone. He was obviously not a social person.

Both Conor and Kat ate ravenously, and he savored the coffee. When the Ghost came out the next time, he offered each more food and coffee. They declined the food, but accepted the coffee, both thanking him and praising his culinary skills. Then the Ghost left and returned with another blanket, this one in a roll. He dropped it on the floor in front of the guests and pointed to his head, leaning it to the side over pressed-together hands. Conor took it that the blanket was intended as a pillow. "Thank you," Conor said, uncertain how the sleeping logistics would be negotiated.

On his way back to what Conor took to be the Ghost's private chamber, he paused to turn out the lamp, leaving the room in darkness except for the light furnished by a dying fire. This was fine with Conor. There was a stack of wood in one corner for feeding the fire during the night if they chose, and the front chamber's dimensions would be less than ten by twelve feet, he figured. All he knew was that he had suddenly become dead tired.

He turned to Kat. "I am about to drop off sitting here. Can we share this bearskin? Or I could move off the bearskin if you prefer and wrap the quilt around me—make it into sort of a sleeping bag."

"I wouldn't feel right about that. We can share the bearskin and the blanket-pillow—it's wide enough—and then each take one of the quilts to wrap around us."

"That's more than fair."

They began laying out the quilts, when Kat stopped. "Conor, I've got to pee."

"It's raining."

"He didn't leave a chamber pot. The bearskin will be wet if I can't go soon."

Her words triggered his own urge. "We'll both go out. You turn right, and I will go left. I will not turn around until you tell me you are finished. I would allow ten feet from the opening. Rain will flush it away."

He got up and instinctively reached for her hand, then was going to pull it back when she grasped it. He led her through the opening, and they each tended to business and returned to the bearskin, where he pulled off his boots and she, her moccasins. He laid his gun belt with the holstered Colt within reach, and they each nested into their respective quilt cocoons before pulling the buffalo robe over them both, Kat facing his back in order to share the improvised pillow. Conor fell instantly to sleep.

Conor slept through the night and did not awaken till he heard the Ghost at the fire, where he was already baking in the Dutch oven, biscuits, Conner guessed from the redolent smell in the air, and, of course, coffee. He started to roll over, but stopped when he felt the pressure against his back. He looked over his shoulder and saw that Kat was wedged against him. He could make out her closed eyes barely above her quilt. Not a bad sight to wake up to, he thought.

He moved away from her and wormed his way out of the quilt and buffalo robe and pulled his boots on, flinching at soreness about his wounds but grateful that no real harm had been done to interfere with healing. The Ghost, noting his awakening, lit the lamp and turned it up enough to allow some light in the chamber. He nodded at Conor, who replied, "Good morning."

He saw Kat stirring beside him and soon her head popped out from the quilt. She gave him a sleepy smile, of all things. Biscuits, honey, and coffee brought them fully awake. After they had eaten, the Ghost knelt beside Kat and removed the head wrap. The side of her forehead was red and swollen only a bit, on its way to turning blue and purple, but there was no evidence of a cut in the scalp. The wrap was not replaced.

"Is it still raining outside?" Conor asked.

The Ghost shook his head, indicating his answer was "No." After turning up the lamp, the Ghost stepped over and handed Conor a sheet of paper. Conor held it out so Kat could see. Written in elegant, penciled script, was the Ghost's message. "You will leave now. The horse should remain here. I will return her to your stable when she is well. You will forget this place exists and not return here unless your lives are in danger. Now tell me about the men who have visited and now watch the doctor's property."

Their host was obviously telling them that their visit was concluded. Conor told him about the land grant dispute and Doc's legal efforts to protect his ownership and that of those who had acquired parcels from him. He also explained the reason for the land survey that Flipper was doing and how important it was that the surveyor should not be deterred from completing his work. "There will likely be more violence and bloodshed. We are preparing to fight to hold the property until the courts decide. The lawyer seems confident we can win the battle there."

Kat said, "I just want to thank you, sir, for saving my life—twice now, it seems."

Conor added, "And for helping to save mine."

The Ghost waved his hand forward as if to say, "It was nothing" and then turned and walked back into the other chamber. Conor took that as a signal they should depart.

"Time to go, Kathleen," he said, getting to his feet and giving her a hand to lever herself up.

When they stepped outside, he was not entirely surprised to find that his gray gelding and the late Louie Gaynor's bay were saddled and hitched to a nearby tree limb, ready to ride. "Seems like the Ghost has had enough company."

"Seems so," Kat said. "I hate leaving Toughie behind."

"You risk permanent damage to that leg if you try to take her with us. Are you worried he won't bring her back?"

"No. She will show up in the stable when he decides she is ready."

"Then let's get you home."

Chapter 42

DOCTOR ROMAN HAYES struggled to help the lame shepherd out onto the veranda. Loafer would love basking in the sun this morning. He wasn't eating yet, and the stiffness and soreness in the damaged neck and shoulder kept him from putting weight on the left leg. That would work its way out when the dog started eating and moving around a bit. He expected improvement to start before the day was finished. With Henry's help he had put the dog out with ether less than ten hours earlier. It took a spell for an animal to gain its appetite back after that.

He scooted Loafer onto the blanket and dropped down on the rocking chair beside him. He was sweating profusely, and the sun had not even made its full appearance yet. The pain that had stabbed his chest yesterday and sent shocks from his neck and shoulder down his left arm was gone now, leaving him with barely enough energy to stand. Henry had noticed his discomfort and asked him several times whether he would like to quit early, but Doc had declined. Henry and Diego would not need him today, though, and he was glad of that.

Of course, nobody would be working on the survey if Kat and Conor did not turn up. He was sickened at the thought that harm might have come to Kat—Conor, too, for that matter. But Conor's message had assured him that he was fine after the altercation in the store. He hoped this was the last killing to stain the floor of his trading post. Henry had buried the man Conor identified as Buford Walters in the horse lot last night, and Kat could scratch another problem off her list. But Gaynor was after her. He would have shown no mercy if he caught up to her.

He saw Henry making his way toward the Triad from the big stable. He was sauntering along like he did not have a care in the world. Flipper was an unflappable sort, it seemed, and he had grown quite fond of the young man. He would be going places regardless of his color or any unpleasantness with the Army.

"Good morning, Doc. You and Loafer are out early this morning. I thought you might sleep late."

"Not me. Loafer and I like to watch the sunrise. Besides, with Kat and Conor out there, I was lucky to catch any shuteye at all. I've been wondering if we shouldn't mount up and start a search. Is Diego coming by to help survey this morning? He's a tracker. Maybe we can pick up a trail and figure out where they headed."

"Diego will be over. I told him to get some rest and that we wouldn't start work till midmorning. I have some paperwork that needs attention first. And, Doc, you aren't feeling so well. I think you should stick with Loafer in case Kat or Conor show up while Diego and I are out. We will ride out and see what we can pick up, though, if they aren't here by the time Diego arrives. Now, you just stay where you are, and I'll go in and see what I can scrape up for breakfast."

Doc was not inclined to protest. He just did not have the gumption to climb out of the chair right now. He had intentionally buried Ruth and the kids on the long outcropping that edged the mountain face, so he could view the little cemetery from the veranda. How he missed them every day, never more so than this morning as he saw the sun rays begin to bathe their gravesite. Life goes on, and there are still some joys to be snatched now and then, but it is never the same. Thankfully, Kat had brought him a taste of family again, and he would be forever grateful for that. He closed his eyes to savor a morning breeze and to bask in the warmth of the fragments of sunrise that crept under the veranda roof at this early hour, and the sleep that had eluded him during the night suddenly captured him, and his chin dropped to his chest.

He did not know how much time had lapsed when he was awakened by Loafer's whining and opened his eyes, confused at first as to where he was. He looked down at Loafer and saw that the dog was gazing to the west. Dust clouds, not more than two riders, but he could not make them out. He started to get up and summon Flipper, but the chest pain struck him again, and he thought better of it. He had no weapon nearby, so he called for Flipper.

Chapter 43

FLIPPER HAD STARTED a small fire behind the Triad and was baking biscuits in the Dutch oven and boiling a healthy batch of cornmeal mush. The coffee at the fire's edge was already brewed and hot. It was going to be too damn hot to use the inside cookstove this day. When he heard Doc calling from out front, he took the boiling mush pot off the fire, quickly checked the Dutch oven, and seeing that the biscuits were far enough along to finish with the oven's heat, he pulled the black iron kettle away from the coals. Then, patting his Army Colt reassuringly, he rushed around the house.

When he reached Doc, he noted that the man had not moved from the rocking chair. "What is it, Doc?"

Doc pointed westerly. "Riders. I can make them out now. Two. I think one is Conor's gray. I don't recognize the other, but it could be—"

"It is. Conor and Kat." He stepped out into the yard and waved. Several minutes later, his friends reined their horses to the hitching rail and dismounted. He extended his hand to Conor. "Welcome back, Con. I was going to ride out for a search when Diego got here. You saved me a workday by showing up."

Conor took his hand in a firm grip, but not so challenging as usual. He supposed the gimpy shoulder restrained his friend a bit. Kat had already rushed past him and up the steps to Doc. When he turned around, he saw that she was bent over the doctor, squeezing him, and brushing his cheeks with soft kisses.

"Oh, Doc," she said. "I was afraid I would never see you again. I love you, Doc. Know that. I love you like my own father."

Doc had his arms wrapped awkwardly around her, hands patting her back, his own eyes glistening with tears.

"I've got breakfast out back. Conor, if you will get the tables scooted between some chairs, we can eat out here."

"Well, Kathleen and I both had breakfast at the hotel, but I am good for another round, and I am betting she is too."

"Hotel?"

"I will explain when we get together for breakfast."

Later, after they all had eaten their fill and Kat and Conor had told the other two an edited version of the previous day's adventures, they sat on the veranda clustered about the tables discussing plans for the day. Doc said, "Kat, are you sure your gun whip doesn't need more attention?"

"Not even a headache, Doc. I'll have a nice bruise to decorate this beat-up face for a spell, but I'll be fine. You can look at it later if you want. What do you think we should do about reporting the deaths of Louie and Buford to the law?"

Flipper thought that most women would kill for a beat-up face like Kat's. Strangely, she probably believed her description. "I never saw or heard of anybody named Louie and Buford," Flipper said.

"Who are they?" Conor said.

Doc nodded in agreement. "I don't recall any men by those handles ever dropping by the Triad. I don't know who would be asking about them anyhow. Where are you working today?" Doc asked.

"The east property line. I've got to get the outer boundaries first. Then I can finish with the legal descriptions on the tracts you agreed to sell to others. Doc, this is a challenge, I will probably be another month yet. That's the best I can do. I'm sorry."

"I know you are doing the best you can. I want these titles nailed down if it takes a year."

"Neither of us can afford a year." He tossed a glance off to the east. "Diego's coming. I'd better get saddled up and my gear loaded. Do you suppose you might help me, Con, while you are putting up your horses?"

"My pleasure."

The men got up and headed down the steps, and Kat called after them. "I'll be along in a few minutes. I can put the bay up."

"Not this time," Flipper said. "We'll handle the critters. You stay and help Doc get the trading post ready for business and let him look at that head bruise."

As they led the horses to the stable, Flipper said, "You look like you are hurting, Con. You are hardly moving that right shoulder."

"Nothing that time won't fix. I might have overworked it some yesterday. I'll see later if Doc wants to redress the wounds. They've been healing, but I've got a bit of blood seeping through on the bad one."

"Con, I'm worried about Doc. I know the concern about Kat was dragging him down, but it is like all his strength has been sapped away. He is moving like a snail, and I know he was hurting yesterday. When we dismounted to check corner markers on the parcels and had to walk any distance at all, he kept having to stop and catch his breath, and he bent over once like his chest was hurting. He was hurting this morning, too. That's why I brought breakfast out. Kat should be alerted to keep an eye on him."

"If he is sick, I don't know what to do for him. We are days away from another doctor. If he would fess up and tell us what to do, maybe we could help him."

"I just wanted you to know. It seems like this has come on suddenly."

"Not necessarily. When I look back, there have been clues. His stamina for outdoor work hasn't been much during the few years I have known him. He has always been slow moving, but I figured that was just his pace. He might have had some breathing problems all this time. Doc's just not a complainer. I like to moan a bit and talk about my aches and pains. Of course, out here I am mostly complaining to myself."

"Yeah. I used to have to listen to you grumble about your sore ass and back when we spent a few extra hours in the saddle."

"You didn't have to confirm it. But I've got to admit I never hear you complain about anything, not even back at the Point, and you sure as hell had stuff to complain about."

"Would it have done me any good?"

"Nope."

"That's why."

Chapter 44

AFTER FLIPPER AND Diego departed, Conor returned to the Triad, where he found Doc and Kat in the trading post cleaning up the mess left by the assault a day earlier. Loafer lay near the interior doorway observing the others, and Doc was at the counter and seemed to be drawing something on a sheet of parchment. Kat, with a bucket of water and a jar of white powder that he assumed was soap of some kind, was on hands and knees scrubbing at the dried blood spots on the floor, mostly permanent stains by now, he thought. He thought she should be resting after her ordeal, but he was not about to waste words with the suggestion.

Conor said, "It's a losing battle, Kat. If it's a worry, you will need to paint the floor brown."

She looked up, her brow furrowed in annoyance. "Did I ask for your opinion?"

"Sorry."

Upon hearing Conor's voice, Doc looked up. "Conor, I've been wanting to talk with you. We need to step into the parlor and sit down. Kat, I want you to join us."

"But, Doc, I have got a mountain of things I need to be doing."

"I told you that you should take it easy today. There is nothing on the list you are keeping in your head that can't wait till tomorrow or the day after . . . or a week or two, for that matter."

She lifted herself off the floor and followed the two men into the parlor. After they were seated, Doc got right down to business. "Conor, you are planning to rebuild the house that burned down, aren't you?"

"Yes, of course."

"I have a proposal. Build over this way near the Triad. I have a stable so big, most of it is wasted space. And the warehouses . . . you had plans for those if we get seriously into the salt business. Everything would be handy."

"But I want to build on property I own."

"You would. I will sell you that property on higher ground above the stream that comes out of the canyon. You and Henry have engineering backgrounds, but besides the stream access, I am betting you could get a well there, pipe water into the house. Build a stone house big enough for a family. The stream almost splits the canyon.

I will sell you everything on the east side of the stream. That would be over two thousand acres, I am thinking. With good grass. It would pasture two or three times the cattle and horses your place would hold, but you would keep that, too, of course. This would be your headquarters place, though."

Conor was momentarily overwhelmed by the proposal, but the idea was more than attractive. "I don't know, Doc. The money—"

"A dollar an acre. Just what I paid for it. I'll take your note just like on the other. I've got a selfish motive, Conor. I want the safety that goes with another home nearby, and I am getting on in years and may be needing another man available to help out more. And if we are going into the salt business together, think of the convenience. We would have Henry survey it out while he is here doing the other properties. We wouldn't need a fence between us, but I am learning that it is dang important to know who owns what."

"You have been thinking about this a spell, haven't you?"

"Yep. I've even got something I wrote up for us to sign until the lawyers can get everything formalized."

Kat had been sitting next to Doc silently, but Conor could tell she was understanding it all. Her poker face, though, revealed nothing.

Doc turned to her now. "What do you think, Kat?"

"It is none of my business."

"It is your business. You said you don't want to leave this place. This will be your home for a lifetime if you want it. I promise."

Conor thought that was a mighty serious promise for a man forty some years older than the young woman.

She frowned and said nothing.

"Be truthful. Do you object to Conor being a neighbor? I can still pull back the offer."

She shrugged. "I suppose we could do worse, and what you are saying makes a lot of sense for both of you. If you are wanting my approval, you have got it."

Conor understood now, although he did not think Kat did. Doc had made some kind of legal arrangements that would assure Kat's residency in case of his death. He suspected the documents he had brought back from the Santa Fe lawyers' office had something to do with that. Doc wanted her to have a neighbor close by in case she needed help. He wondered if the wily old devil might even be trying his hand at matchmaking.

He admitted that his thinking had evolved since Kat's arrival almost two months earlier. He would not deny that she had started to incite thoughts that kept him awake nights, and he had become fond of her unpredictable and outspoken ways. He had also started to see through that tough exterior and liked what he was discovering. Any romance in their future was no more than speculation now, and, of course, it took two to make a romance. Regardless, the least he could do for Doc was to live nearby where he would be available to help on short notice.

After an awkward silence, Conor spoke. "Everything you say makes sense, Doc. I would be a fool to turn down this opportunity. Yes. I will buy the land and build here."

Doc smiled. "That pleases me, Conor, more than I can say. The paper I wrote up is in my desk drawer. We can go in there and sign right now."

Chapter 45

JOSH RIVERS HAD not known, of course, that Danna Sinclair, his partner in the Rivers & Sinclair law firm, had once been intimate with his brother, Cal Rivers, when he had insisted that Cal accompany Danna and Jael Chernik Rivers on their journey to the Guadalupe Mountains. He had questioned in the first place why two firm lawyers had to be absent for the case.

His point was well taken. The absence of both was certainly not an efficient use of the firm's resources, but this was Danna's case, calling upon her expertise, and she had no choice. Jael, on the other hand, had lived among Quanah Parker's Comanche for many years and was itching for adventure. She loved her husband deeply, but he knew that in the end he must give her free rein.

Certainly, given their history, Danna would have refused to travel alone with Cal. He was married but estranged from his wife, Erin McKenna Rivers, who resided on her northeastern New Mexico ranch with his step-daughter Willow and son Zack. The handsome rascal, in his early thirties with seductive, clear blue eyes and straw-colored hair, was near impossible to resist when he put his mind to it, and he was prepared to do just that at the mere hint of a female's interest. She needed Jael as a chaperone to keep her faithful to her fiancée and lover, Doctor Micah Rand in Santa Fe, as much as to discourage Cal's approaches.

They had been on the trail for five days now. Cal, a former Army scout, had promised that he knew a shortcut to their destination, having stopped at the trading post during scouting days for Colonel Ranald Slidell Mackenzie. If so—and Cal was rarely wrong about such things—their journey should be about finished.

She pulled the brim of her Plainsman hat down on her forehead to ward off a glaring, early morning sun. Astride a sorrel gelding, Danna wore a long-sleeved shirt and faded denim britches with boots that boosted her height to nearly six feet. She turned when she heard Jael ride up behind her, leading Cal's pack mule, Sylvester, a cantankerous creature inclined to bite if one stepped to within its mouth's range. She still had a sore butt cheek from when she learned her lesson the first day out. Cal adored the critter and seemed to be inoculated against its bite.

She slowed her mount to a walk when Jael edged her buckskin gelding up beside her. "Have you seen any sign of Cal?" Danna asked.

"Not since breakfast. He says to follow this dry creek bed, and we will stay on target."

"He promised we would be at the Triad by midafternoon. That would be not much more than five or six hours away. Why can't he just stay with us?"

"He's got a reason. He will tell us when he is ready. That's Cal."

Jael preferred calf-high moccasins but was otherwise attired much like Danna. Jael's lightly bronzed skin did not appear to suffer from the sun's rays, unlike her own fair skin that Danna feared was matching her hair color by now.

Danna said, "I get a bit annoyed at the man. He never tells us anything and he is off on his own half the time."

"He was an Army scout. He wants to be certain there are no surprise threats out there. I don't like to admit it, but Josh was right to insist he join us. I feel safer. You seem to be carrying a grudge against Cal. I thought you hardly knew him."

Her eyes narrowed, and she looked directly at Jael. "I know him better than you might think."

Jael burst out laughing. "You and Cal? I can't believe it. You seem such an unlikely pair."

"I didn't say anything happened between us."

"But it did. Don't worry. I won't tell Josh—or anybody else. I am your friend, you know." She shook her head in disbelief.

Danna sighed. "Yes, you are, and I value that."

They moved the horses into a gallop now, always keeping the dry creek bed in sight. They came across a water hole near a solitary cottonwood shortly after noon and reined in their horses and dismounted. The water source was not obvious, so Danna assumed from the clear water that it must be fed by an underground spring. From the mass of animal tracks, it was obviously a social center for all the creatures of this arid land. Cal was likely aware that they would pass this spot when they needed it.

There was a scattering of grass and horse edibles near the watering place, so they staked out the two mounts and pack mule. Their saddlebags contained jerky and a few leftover biscuits from the previous night along with a few dried apples. Danna hoped that their hosts would have a better offering of culinary delights during their brief stay. They each claimed one side of the tree to lean against as they ate their meager fare.

Danna watched the critters graze as she ate. "I am surprised that Josh let you ride Chief on this trek."

"He insisted, as a matter of fact. He loves that horse and trusts him. He didn't think any other would do. I am glad to have him."

"You are raising a few other buckskins, aren't you?"

"Josh is partial to buckskins, has been for as long as I have known him. He still tears up some when he speaks of Buck. He had loved that horse for twelve or thirteen years when the beautiful animal was impaled by a buffalo's horns and saved my life, probably Josh's, too. The two of us buried Buck. Josh could not bear the thought of buzzards and coyotes and other animals shredding the horse's flesh. I'll tell you the whole story sometime, if you like."

"I would love to hear it."

"Much of it is recited as fiction in Tabitha Rivers's book, The Last Hunt, the story of Quanah leading his band to the reservation at Fort Sill."

"I am guilty of having never read the book. Now I will search it out and do so as soon as we get back to Santa Fe."

"Danna, I see Cal headed this way—across the creek bed."

Danna looked to the southeast. Yes, there was no doubt about the identity of the slim rider, more than six-feet-four-inches of him, at this distance seeming to dwarf the black-spotted white gelding he rode. "He doesn't seem to be in a hurry."

"That means nothing with Cal."

"Yes, I guess that is true enough."

They quickly finished eating and were off the ground by the time Cal reached them. He dismounted, and said, "Howdy, ladies," before promptly leading his horse to the water. "I was hoping I might find you here. I think you should be on your way. Trouble brewing out there."

Danna did not like the somber tone of his words. "What kind of trouble?"

"I ain't sure, but there's a couple dozen men—gun-slinging types—setting up camp along the west slope of the Guadalupe. I don't know exactly what you two are doing down this way, but it is starting to look dang risky. That sort ain't gathering for a dance."

Jael said, "We must get word to Conor Byrne and Doctor Hayes about this."

"We ain't more than two hours ride away from the Triad. I suggest you saddle up and we get moving."

Chapter 46

I T HAD BEEN a good week since her escape from Louie and encounter with the Ghost. Kat had relished the relative quiet of the days that followed. She had been busy in the trading post all morning with a few passerby customers and several from the nearby ranchos stopping in. For the local folks, her Spanish-speaking ability was proving to be an asset, and she sensed that her fluency in the language and the obvious Mexican ancestry in her features was earning the trust of the women who came to trade produce for goods and food supplies.

Only occasionally did she receive cash, but it turned up often enough to provide funds for replenishing. She felt she was getting the knack of the trading business now and always ended up with enough surplus for their own table. She found that she enjoyed the work and was looking ahead to the possibility that the salt business might attract more workers and families to the area. At her suggestion, Doc had asked Henry to plot and survey a dozen two-acre lots some hundred yards north of the Triad for possible construction of homes for occupants who would then become customers of the trading post. Perhaps, they would lie dormant, but she thought it best to be prepared for the opportunity.

Sometimes she had to force herself to remember she did not own the place. Doc did not seem to want to be bothered with decision-making these days and had turned the management of the trading post over to her by default. She worried about him, observing the lack of energy in his movement about the place. He rarely made visits to the stable and had willingly allowed Conor to handle the few livestock chores, since he was residing in the loft anyway.

Conor, at least, was on the mend and only occasionally limited by his healing wounds. She was pleased that she could think of him as a friend now, and it seemed they had left the previous uneasiness between them behind when they departed the Ghost's cave. She trusted him, not an easy thing for her to do when it came to men.

She looked up from her bookkeeping spread out on the counter when the door opened, and a very tall man and two women walked in. Her first instinct was to reach for the pistol under the counter, but she relaxed upon seeing the friendly smiles of the two women. The man was giving her a quick study, but did not appear threatening, and she found that she was becoming less hostile to such scrutiny, realizing that most of the foolish creatures could not help themselves.

"May I help you?" she asked.

The tall woman with strawberry blonde hair stepped up to the counter, towering over Kat. "My name is Danna Sinclair. I am a lawyer from Santa Fe." She nodded toward the black-haired woman. "This is my partner, Jael Rivers, and the gentleman with us is our escort, Calvin Rivers, who happens to be Jael's brother-in-law. I think Doctor Roman Hayes and Conor Byrne have been expecting us."

Kat smiled now. "They certainly have, and they will be more than pleased that you have arrived. My name is Kathleen Ryan, and I . . . work here. If you don't mind waiting a few minutes. I will see if I can find Doc. Conor is probably working around the stable or in the warehouse, but Doc should be close by."

"A few minutes is nothing in our long journey."

Kat left the store and entered the living area. She knew exactly where Doc would be—in his bed partaking in an after-lunch siesta which had become a recently acquired habit. She tapped softly on the door, and when he did not respond, opened it and stepped in. She was relieved when she saw the rise and fall of his chest. She had feared the worst several times this week when she had found him sleeping in a chair and unresponsive to her voice.

She stepped over to his bedside and bent over, placing a hand on his shoulder and shaking it gently, "Doc, wake up. We have got visitors."

Doc's eyes opened slowly, and for a moment he seemed confused. Then, he looked up at Kat. "Visitors?"

"The Santa Fe lawyers. Two females and a man who came as their escort."

Doc nodded. "That's good news. Why don't you invite them into the parlor to sit. I won't be long. Do you suppose you can round up Conor? He should be here and so should you."

She returned to the trading post and invited the guests into the parlor. Calvin Rivers declined. "If you can spare a horse, I would like to be getting reacquainted with this country for a spell yet, and my critter could use a rest."

"I am sure we can help with that. Let me get the lawyers comfortable, and I will walk you over to the stable. You can meet Conor Byrne."

"Lieutenant Conor Byrne? I know him. The gutsiest officer I ever rode with during my scouting days. Likely the smartest, too."

"I don't know about 'lieutenant,' but he must be the same man. Conor was a cavalry officer, and his would not be a common name. Perhaps you know Henry Flipper, as well? He is doing survey work for us."

"Flip? I sure do. I scouted for him a few months when I was assigned to the Ninth Cavalry buffalo soldiers. He was the only colored officer to ever lead a troop. I heard he got a bad deal from the Army. He would have been playing against a stacked deck. Don't matter none, old Flip will make his way through this world and come out standing tall."

"Well, he will be back before sundown. You do the same, and you Army folks can enjoy a reunion."

After she seated the two women in the parlor, she met Cal Rivers on the veranda and helped him lead the mounts and pack mule to the stable. She was not attired for handling horses but was glad she was wearing a dress. Somehow, Cal Rivers made her want to look like a woman again. It occurred to her then that she was changing. She was starting to care about how men saw her and no longer flinched when Conor offered an admiring glance, rather liked it to tell the truth. She was basking now in

Cal Rivers's obvious interest. That did not mean either man's touch would be welcome, but the truth was that she was not blind to a male's physical attributes, either. Mostly, she was rather taken with the notion that she might not be as ugly as she had once thought.

"Do you still scout for a living, Mister Rivers?" she asked.

"Nah, Miss Ryan. Just a hobby, you might say. This trip is a favor to my brother. I do some ranching up in the northeastern part of the territory. I was in the freighting business for a spell but sold out to my Colorado brother. Now, let's say, I am looking for new opportunities. Ham—that's my brother—is in banking and wants me to come back and handle the day-to-day stuff for the freight outfit. I don't know—ties a man down. And call me Cal."

"And everybody except Conor calls me Kat." She was curious about this man. "But you have got a ranch to tend to."

"Not really. It's my wife's ranch, and I ain't welcome. I'd never go back, but Erin's got our two kids up there. I like them to know now and then that they got a dad."

"You are married then?"

"I suppose the law would say so, but I don't think of myself as married."

She was suddenly wary. She could not help but like this man, but he spelled trouble for someone like her. And she had spent almost two years with a violent man who insisted they were married, but the law would say they were not. She doubted this man would strike a woman, but he could sure as blazes break her heart.

When they led the horses and mule into the stable, they came upon Conor sitting on a wooden chest braiding rawhide strips into a narrow rope. Conor looked up, and, seeing Cal, set his project down and jumped up to meet him. He stepped toward Cal, smiling, and with hand extended. "Cal Rivers. I must be seeing things." He took Cal's hand and grasped his shoulder firmly. "I doubted our paths would ever cross again. What brings you here?"

"I brung you a feisty pair of lady law wranglers."

"Rivers. You are related to the lawyer?"

"Jael is my brother Josh's wife—dang it."

"A lady at the bank in Santa Fe told me her story. She was taken captive by Quanah's Comanche band and grew up to be Quanah's counselor and interpreter. She spoke a half dozen or so languages fluently, and they called her 'She Who Speaks.'"

"Yep, that's her. The language business is mighty handy for a woman in Santa Fe."

"I look forward to seeing her again. I assume Miss Sinclair is here, too?"

"Yeah, she didn't want me to come, but Josh insisted."

"I won't ask why, not in the presence of a lady."

Kat interrupted the reunion. "Maybe you two can catch up some while you put up the critters. Conor, Cal needs a fresh mount. I was sent to summon you to the Triad to meet with the lawyers. After you are done here, Doc would appreciate it if you would come on up. We will be in the parlor."

She caught Conor looking at Cal and rolling his eyes. Cal responded with a grin. She supposed she was getting bossy again and didn't care.

Chapter 47

WHEN CONOR WALKED into the parlor, he found the two lawyers already engaged in serious discussion with Kat and Doc. He had already met the visitors at their Santa Fe offices, so he simply nodded and claimed a chair.

Doc looked at him and said, "Conor, we haven't got to the legal business yet. Danna and Jael have brought some worrisome information about men gathering on the west side of the Guadalupe, further north, it appears, where they would have several possible passes through the mountains. The mountains would slow them some, but they likely wouldn't be more than four or five hours away. I don't like it."

"Cal already told me about it, and he is going to be doing some more scouting. I don't like the numbers. I am guessing that it is a show of force for now. They might even be hoping for discovery. Otherwise, they will be out to enforce an exodus of the occupants of the Triad and the ranchos. I can't believe the killings would help their legal position, but I will let the lawyers advise us on that. I am betting we will have contact within the next few days."

Danna Sinclair spoke. "What you say makes sense, however, one never knows. I assume you will have a strategy to deal with attacks."

"I don't think we need to waste time on the details here. I would like to speak with Henry Flipper when he gets back from surveying, and, of course, Cal. I must say that I am very grateful you brought Cal with you. That was a nice surprise. We have worked together before. He will be a big help."

Danna said, "I will leave the issues regarding enforcers to you. I am not a military strategist. You should be aware, however, that Jael and I have brought our rifles and Colts with us and that we can handle weapons as well as any man, better than most."

The woman was not given to modesty it seemed. "We may need everyone who can handle a gun."

"Let me summarize our legal position, which I frankly find very encouraging."

Doc said, "Please do. Some good news would be welcome here."

Conor was encouraged that Doc appeared stronger and more alert this afternoon. Maybe the arrival of the lawyers would pull him out of the malaise he had been in the past week.

Danna continued. "First, we have identified the person who is claiming the land grant rights. His name is Angel Mendoza. For him to pursue any rights, he is required to file a claim of interest in the territory land office. Emilio Ortiz did that on his behalf. Our investigation of Mendoza indicates that it is very unlikely that he is the heir to any land grant rights. He is spending most of his time in Santa Fe taverns these days, a convenience for our investigators to initiate conversations with him. Someone is obviously paying him to make the claim. He has probably already signed a contract to sell his rights to several Santa Fe Ring members if his claim is successful."

Kat said, "So he is a Santa Fe resident?"

"A very recent one. He speaks no English and appears to have journeyed here from El Paso. The Ring would have contacts there. I am confident his story would collapse under cross-examination. I would ask Jael to do that considering her fluency in Spanish. It may never come to a trial. I am hoping the Ring would back off if they cannot force the occupants to leave."

Doc said, "But how can we be certain this will not happen again?"

"I want to file something called a quiet title lawsuit on your behalf. For this we should have a surveyed legal description for the land you claim. You, of course, have already commenced that process, and I look forward to meeting with Mister Flipper about this. The territory's laws are vague on this type of legal action, but there are several centuries of case law—the common law—that say open, notorious, and adverse possession of property for more than ten consecutive years will establish ownership."

Doc said, "The legal talk is starting to make my head ache."

"I apologize. In a nutshell, you have held this less than perfectly described land for over fifteen years under the deed on file in Santa Fe. We cannot find a record of Hiram Zimmer, who deeded it to you, ever acquiring it, but there are few records preceding that period. As near as we can determine, the last Mendoza with recorded ownership died over a hundred years back. Of course, that was long before New Mexico became a territory. Yours would be a landmark case in the territory, and I am excited to make this happen."

Conor was glad somebody was excited, because her explanation was putting him to sleep. Oddly, Kathleen appeared to be entranced, hanging onto every word. She was a strange one, still a mystery to unravel.

Doc said, "You just tell us how we can help."

"You will be the most important witness and will eventually need to travel to Santa Fe for any trial or hearing. That would be six months or even a year away."

Doc said, "What if I am not alive?"

"You must stay alive. As near as I know, you are the only one who can personally testify regarding the length of your occupancy of the land."

Doc seemed genuinely concerned about the question, and Conor wondered if there was something Doc was not telling them. Kathleen had a look of horror on her face.

"I had better start figuring out supper," she said, rising from her chair. "After I get things started, I can show you both your lodging. It is a hospital room with two beds. I hope that will be satisfactory."

"Any bed will be welcome after sleeping on hard ground these past days. I will probably oversleep in the morning," Danna said.

"No such thing as oversleeping here," Doc said. "Get up when it suits you."

Jael said, "I am going to see if I can help Kat with supper." She got up and headed for the kitchen where Kat had disappeared.

Doc said, "Can the rest of your legal stuff wait?"

"Of course, we can be here three days, four, if necessary. I hope I can speak with your surveyor tonight or tomorrow. I would like to ride out and get an overview of the land sometime."

"I don't know how much riding I would do with those enforcers closing in." Doc said.

"Cal will know what we can do. He can be useful for such things."

To Conor it sounded like she complimented Cal grudgingly. "I will be interested to hear what he reports tonight." He turned to Doc. "You will want that dining table pulled away from the wall and the leaves put in. We will be having a crowd for supper. I will take care of it before I go back to the stable. Is there anything else I can do?"

"Maybe round up enough chairs. There are extras in the hospital area. What about Cal Rivers? Where are we going to put him up?"

"He has already tossed his bedroll in the stable loft."

Doc said, "I think I will nap just a few minutes before supper. I feel like I've been worse than Loafer lately."

"You have had a lot to deal with, Doc. You are entitled to be tired."

"Yeah, I suppose."

Conor was certain Doc had another diagnosis, and he was not optimistic about what it might be. They were going to have a talk within the next several days, certainly before their lawyers departed for Santa Fe.

Chapter 48

"WELL, CAL, HOW about telling us about the visitors collecting out by the west mountains," Conor said. "We have got just enough time before supper."

Cal had come across Flipper, who was finishing up a day's surveying work and the two had returned to the Triad together. The horses had been grained and turned out in the small, enclosed pasture adjacent to the stable, and the three old comrades now leaned against the plank fence talking about old times for a spell. But Conor had more immediate concerns and was itching for a report from Cal.

"Well, I didn't ride over to the gathering I saw earlier, or I wouldn't be back yet. But I saw something interesting headed in that direction. I was on high ground with my spyglass and picked up two chuckwagons with three outriders. Appears like those gents are planning on staying a spell."

Flipper said, "They are probably going to try to chase the families off the ranchos by threats and intimidation first. If that doesn't work, the killings will start with the idea of showing they mean business. They wouldn't be settling in like this if they thought they were going to get the job done overnight. I would be expecting a warning, the Santa Fe Ring would not want the attention that a community slaughter would bring. The army would show up for sure, and they would be risking national newspaper headlines. That doesn't mean they won't resort to that if slaughter is what it takes. They will be sending someone out to talk a bit more."

Conor was inclined to agree. "I think I had better join you and Diego on the surveying crew. You might need another gun or two."

"Let me go for the few days I'm here anyhow," Cal said. "I don't want to be just sitting around this place watching that little so-called Irish gal. She's a temptation, I tell you, and I don't think she trusts me much. There are only two things I'm scared of: being left afoot and a decent woman. I fear she's decent, and them kind and me don't work out so good. The minute I let it slip I had me a wife, I could feel a freeze come on. Didn't matter that me and Erin don't share a house, let alone a bed these days."

Flipper laughed. "You come help me. Con needs to stay close to the Triad, and you're risking your balls if you cause Kat Ryan any trouble when Con is nearby."

Cal looked at Conor. "You got a claim on her, Conor?"

"No, I don't have a claim."

"But he would like to," Flipper said. "I just don't think he has quite admitted it to himself yet."

"Let's go eat. After supper, I want to talk about some ideas I've got."

Supper at the Triad turned into a celebratory affair. There was no mention of legal strategies, or the pending danger presented by the enforcers. Danna Sinclair and Jael Rivers were engaging conversationalists. Cal, the master storyteller, kept the diners laughing. Conor noticed that any freeze that Cal had sensed with Kathleen had obviously thawed, because the devil had her mesmerized this evening. But it was not his concern. Or was it?

He really wasn't worried about Cal. His old scout would keep a healthy distance and likely settle for affirming that he had a chance at seducing the little lady. Still, he would not risk rejection or loss of a friendship.

As the meal ended, Doc, looking very drained, asked Conor if they could speak privately in the hospital office.

Conor told Cal and Henry he would meet them at the stable later.

Flipper said, "We might just relax with a smoke on the veranda and chat a spell before we head back to the loft. Doc gave us a couple of cigars and a half bottle of whiskey. Knowing you don't hold your whiskey so well, we'll see that there is none left."

Conor just shook his head, unable to deny the truth. He enjoyed a drink now and then, but he had learned that it was best that he keep his distance from the demon most of the time.

Cal said, "Well, I guess Flip's got the bottle to hisself. I been on the wagon more than a year now, and I'm working at staying there. But I would be glad for a good cigar."

The three women had pitched in to clear the table. Conor's offer to help had been brushed aside. He would not battle for the opportunity to wash dishes. They seemed to be making fast work of things, and Kathleen had broken out a bottle of wine that awaited their completion of the task. All but Doc and himself seemed to be in a party mood.

Doc was already seated when Conor walked into the office and signaled for him to close the door, a rarity for the physician. It was cooling some outside, and a nice breeze drifted in the open window behind the desk, so the small room was not uncomfortable. Conor sat down and looked expectantly at the older man. "You wanted to talk, Doc?"

Doc, looking so weary Conor wondered if he could stay awake, said, "You are my best friend, Conor. I think of you as the kind of man Joseph might have been, and I thank the Good Lord for the day you came here. I am not thinking so clearly the past few weeks, and I must drop some of the burden on you."

"I'm honored to be your friend, Doc. You know I would do anything for you. Tell me how I can help."

"I think my time is short, Conor. My heart is failing, and there is not a damned thing to be done about it. Death stalks all of us, but he is breathing down my neck now. I can feel it. How long do I have? I can't even make a good guess. It might be a day, a month, or a year, certainly not two years."

"I . . . I don't know what to say."

"Nothing to be said. I am ready to join Ruth and the kids up on the hill and hope for a reunion out there somewhere. I have seen worse deaths, I assure you. I want to live to see this battle over the land grant through. When the lawyer said my testimony as a witness in the court case might be critical, I almost keeled over. What if I don't live to do that or am not fit to testify?"

"Your life is all that counts, Doc."

"My life is nothing if the place where my loved ones are buried gets in the hands of strangers. And there is Kat. And you. If the two of you can hold this land, it will be like a part of me remains. Otherwise, my life here has been for naught. That's the way I see it anyhow."

It would be pointless to argue with him. "I will do whatever you want, Doc."

"First, look after Kat. That's one reason I wanted you to rebuild near the Triad. She can take care of herself better than most folks, but I want somebody here to back her up if she stays on alone. I know you two didn't get along so well at first, but you seem more than civil now. I won't presume to write a script for your lives, but I would sure like to. Just be here. Be her friend."

"Done."

"Prepare her for this. I just can't do it. I'm a coward."

"You are not a coward. I will speak with her soon."

"After you tell her, talk to the lawyers about what I have said. Maybe there is something that can be done to help the case if I am not here to testify. You may alert Henry if you wish. I have been paying him each week, so he won't need to worry about his money."

"I can do these things."

"Your job won't be over when I die. You already have the combination to my little safe. So does Kat. The papers you took to the lawyers in Santa Fe contained instructions for a will. You brought the document back, and I signed and had it witnessed. You will find it in the safe. You are named executor. Your debt will be cancelled on the parcels you have agreed to buy from me. The debt is also canceled for those who purchased the rancho properties. Nobody had the money to buy outright. The Triad, the remaining land, and any money go to Kat. You will be holding everything in the estate for at least two years, so she will have time to prepare for management. I daresay she is already well on the way."

"I'm a bit overwhelmed, Doc, but I will carry out your wishes. You can count on that."

"I know, son. About the salt business. You and Kat will need to work that out. While I am still kicking, I will back whatever she decides for my part."

"Understood."

"Now, I am going to make my way to bed. I hope what I have told you doesn't keep you awake tonight."

Conor did not think there was a chance he would sleep.

Chapter 49

FELIPE SANCHEZ HAD just left the trading post with a buckboard load of supplies when Conor walked in. His face had a grim set to it this morning, so Kat decided he deserved a friendly greeting. "Good morning, Conor. I missed you at breakfast this morning."

"I helped myself to a biscuit and coffee while you were setting up in here. Doc's still in bed?"

"Yes, he said he might sleep late."

"Did you look in on him?"

"I did. He was snoring softly, and Loafer was snuggled up against his back. That dog has really been tagging Doc lately. I guess I was just a flirtation."

"Did Flip tell you about the new arrival at the stable?"

"A foal?"

"No. A red roan mare."

Traces of a smile appeared on the somber face. "Toughie is back?" She could not restrain her laughter and relief. "The Ghost came last night."

"It appears so."

"I've got to see her now. Come with me." She grabbed his hand and led him back out the door. She released his hand only when they reached the bottom of the veranda steps, and she suddenly became acutely aware of the contact of his flesh. It was not the least unpleasant, but she found herself surprised at the naturalness of her gesture. She liked this man. She really liked him.

During their walk to the stable, Conor said, "I saw Felipe pull out with his wagon. He's around early this morning."

"Sofia sent him for flour, and he picked up a week's supplies while he was running her errand. They have lunch guests. Henry is surveying the Sanchez tract today, so she and Maria are feeding the whole crew. That includes Cal and Jael. He said it was Maria's idea."

Conor was silent a moment. "Cal."

"What do you mean?"

"Cal. Maria's got her eyes on Cal and a ticket to Santa Fe."

"You are a suspicious man."

"I know Maria."

"I suspect you do." She waited for a retort but got none and remembered that his sense of humor was likely absent today.

Inside the stable, she rushed to Toughie's stall and wrapped her arms about the mare's neck. She could not keep the tears from rolling down her cheeks as the horse nuzzled her neck, and it occurred to her tears seemed to come easier these days. Finally, she stepped back and looked at Conor, who was smiling now and nodding approvingly.

"She's glad to see you, too," he said.

"The only good thing I ever got from Buford Walters was this mare, and I had to steal her."

"I wouldn't make horse rustling a habit. It can be hard on the neck, I am told."

"Has she been out of the stall? Is she limping any?"

"I led her up and down the alleyway a few times. She seems fine. I thought I would turn her out with the canyon critters, but I figured you might want to see her first."

"Yes, of course. And thank you. I'm sure she still shouldn't be ridden for a spell."

"Kathleen, before you head back to the store, there is something we need to talk about." There was something ominous in the way he spoke that made her apprehensive.

"I am listening." She stepped out of the stall and closed the gate behind her, joining him in the alleyway where he was leaning against the gate of the adjacent empty stall. She walked toward him, stopping when she was not more than a yard away and looking up into his hazel eyes, seeking something that would ease her apprehension but finding nothing.

"I want to talk about Doc," he said.

"I thought so. You were with him a long time last night."

"He is very ill, Kathleen. He says it is his heart."

"But can't he fix it?"

"No. His time is running out. But he could have a year, maybe two. He seems to be expecting much less."

"He is going to die, and I just found him. Oh, my God." She began to sob, at first softly and then uncontrollably.

Conor stepped forward and took her in his arms, continuing to hold her as she began to regain her composure and speaking softly. "I don't know why he wanted me to tell you. He just wasn't up to it, I guess, and there were business matters to discuss with me. I can tell you this. He loves you like a daughter. His death will not force you to leave the Triad. It is important to him that you remain here for as long as you choose, your lifetime if you wish. I am building my house, and I am not leaving. I hope he is wrong and that he is alive ten years from now. I promise I will be here to help you care for him, regardless."

Conor's gentle embrace was like a soothing balm, and somehow, she drew strength from it. She had never experienced this with any man, and it left her confused. She stepped back. "I must come to terms with this yet but thank you for telling me."

"I will be discussing this with the lawyers, too, but Doc thought you should know first."

"Things haven't been right with him for the past month. Who knows how long he has been dealing with this. You have confirmed the worst I feared. I can only do my best to care for him. You will join us for lunch, of course."

"Certainly."

She turned and hurried away.

Chapter 50

EMILIO ORTIZ HATED this part of his job. The members of the Ring treated him like a hired hand and seemed to forget that he was a distinguished lawyer. He vowed that this would be his last case. He had to admit the Ring had paid him well enough, and he had ample money set aside with their payments and what he had been able to skim in their assorted ventures. He could walk away from all this now.

He planned to pack and escape to California and enjoy a life of luxury. To remain in the territory would be signing his own death warrant. He knew too much for the Ring to allow him to live outside their organization, and he intended to disappear. But he had this job to finish, and he did not intend to wait months, perhaps years, for the courts to resolve the dispute. His case was a fraud, and he knew it. Mendoza had been a mistake. He would not withstand scrutiny as a witness, and that damned Danna Sinclair probably already knew it.

It was his bad luck that Roman Hayes had stumbled onto that witch. She was the acknowledged expert on land law in the territory, especially Spanish grants. Worse, she was ruthless, like a lion with prey grasped in its claws when she went after a client's opponent. He was not about to be torn apart by that woman.

Calhoun and Marx joined him now at the chuckwagon. Calhoun, a bear-like, black-bearded man was generally the spokesman, but Marx, a lanky, balding man with billy-goat chin whiskers, seemed to be his equal partner.

Calhoun, in a growly voice that fit his appearance said, "Men are getting restless. We need to give them some work, and we ain't going to be able to hold them for a month. They're uneasy about this place, and we are, too."

Ortiz said, "Why would they be uneasy?"

"I told you that we've had seven men disappear now. One by one, the posted guards went down. Nobody would take on the jobs again. Three men who were to take down the surveyor just up and floated away, it seems. These gunfighters ain't deserters. They would have stayed around for their money, if nothing else."

"How many men do you have now?"

"A few more than twenty not counting us."

"That should be plenty. I am still hoping we won't need them, and I don't intend to wait long. Tomorrow morning we visit the Triad and give Hayes notice that folks start moving out within two days or we begin burning them out. I want to get back to Santa Fe."

"Do you have our money?"

"It is nearby. I am not fool enough to tell anybody where it is at. Incentive for you to keep me alive."

Chapter 51

KAT SPRUNG OUT of bed before sunrise, pausing in front of the open window to let the gentle breeze caress her naked body. The intensity of the late July heat had dispensed with the need for bedclothes even with cooling evenings, and she savored being freed of binding cloth. She went to the little doorless closet space. Dress or britches today?

She guessed she would not be riding considering Doc's fretting about the enforcers camped not far away. She had two dresses now, and she chose the green, cotton garment. She expected to be in the store most of the day, and she was convinced that the customers, especially the ladies, preferred dealing with a woman who looked like one. She was allowing her hair to grow again, any need for a masquerade having passed and never worked in the first place.

She plucked her undergarments from the chest of drawers and dressed quickly. She would visit the privy and then, after looking in on Doc, she would get breakfast started. Cal, Henry and Conor would show up shortly after sunrise. Jael would likely join the men for breakfast, but she was staying at the Triad today. She and Danna evidently had legal matters to discuss, but Danna had suggested an extra gun on the premises might be desirable.

Danna refused to rise before seven o'clock. Jael had explained that her friend generally worked long into the night and said Danna insisted she would not get up before the birds unless she had cows to milk—and that would never happen. Kat had milked a cow mornings until her father's death and had always rather enjoyed it. One of the Mexican families sold them goat's milk now, and she had still not acquired a taste for the stuff. She rather enjoyed the cheeses, though, and goat's milk was fine for cooking. Someday she would have a milk cow.

Before she started breakfast, she peeked into Doc's room, and satisfied he was still sleeping, she went to the kitchen. She had told Doc yesterday of Conor's disclosure of the health problem. They did not discuss it further. She just said, "I am going to do everything I can to make your gloomy predictions outlandish."

Doc just nodded.

Conor had also discussed the state of Doc's health with the two lawyers the previous evening. Kat suspected that might be one reason Jael was remaining at the Triad today.

She was not surprised when she found Jael already in the kitchen. From the moment of her arrival, Jael had been anxious to pitch in and help. She supposed her years with the Comanche had established enduring work habits and that idleness was difficult for her. Kat could relate to that. Jael, too, in contrast to Danna, was a woman who enjoyed interaction with people and found it easy to converse with strangers. From their first meeting, she had put Kat at ease.

"Good morning," Jael said. "What can I do this morning?"

"Well, I am thinking hotcakes and fried eggs this morning. I traded for four dozen eggs yesterday, so I should start putting them to use. With this heat, I don't want to fire up the cookstove, so I think we should get something started in the firepit. And we will need coffee, of course."

Jael said, "Let me do the fire. Keep me away from the coffee, or the men will be spitting it out. I will try to scrape out some coals for the coffee pot as soon as I can. I will leave the batter to you, but I can help with the griddle and frying pan."

"That would be fine by me. I don't like the fire building that much. Conor has kept us supplied with wood of all sizes."

"He seems like a good man."

She hesitated. "He is. Yes, he is a very good man."

Jael said, "One thing before I get to work. After what Conor told us about Doc, Danna believes we should ask Doc to sign a sworn statement about his history of occupying the land."

"A sworn statement?"

"Yes. Danna would spend time with him, getting his story of how he came to be here and what things he has done to show his possessory rights over the years. If we cannot take him to Santa Fe to sign, we would arrange for a notary public or other official to come here and witness his signature."

"That sounds like a lot of trouble."

"But it could be very important. Such a statement under territorial law can be used when a witness is either deceased or for good reason not able to be physically present to testify. Even a signed statement without the official swearing could be valuable, and Danna intends to work with Doc on that. Acceptance of such a statement by a judge would likely be routine in an uncontested case, which Danna still has some hope for if the Ring backs away."

"Is there anything I can do to help?"

"Yes, if we bring someone this far to take an oath, it would be nice if we could find another witness who could testify or sign a sworn statement regarding Doc's period of possession. Doc says he cannot think of any other witnesses. All who reside here have done so for less than the required ten-year period. Again, even an unsworn statement could be valuable."

"Most residents have been here only five or six years, I think, certainly none not more than eight."

"Perhaps you and Conor could ponder this. I know you have not been at the Triad long, but you have come to know the people here. Or Doc may have mentioned a name and since forgotten about it. He has obviously had much on his mind lately. To be honest, he almost reacted as if he knew such a person but was reluctant to disclose his or her identity. Danna thought it was my imagination."

"I will think on it." And she knew who Doc was thinking of.

Chapter 52

I T WAS ALMOST noon when Emilio Ortiz rode up to the Triad accompanied by the same two thugs who had visited last time. Loafer had barked an alert before their arrival, and Kat could see that Conor was standing at the veranda corner nearest the trading post, Winchester cradled in his arms.

She was ready to race into the parlor where Doc was speaking with the lawyers and alert them to the visitors when she saw Conor walk along the veranda's edge, looking down at the visitors below. She could not hear what he was saying, but the men remained next to their horses while he turned away and came into the store followed by Loafer.

He closed the door. "You saw our visitors? I told them to stay where they are at. Ortiz wants to speak with Doc. I don't think they have a clue that the law wranglers are here. If you want to alert Doc and the lawyers, they can decide how to handle it. Let me know what they want to do, and I will tell Ortiz the rules."

"I have my rifle under the counter. I will tell Doc and the others and let you know what they plan to do."

She hurried into the parlor, where Doc was sitting in his rocking chair talking to Danna and Jael. Danna was busy with her pencil writing furiously in a bulky notebook but paused when Kat appeared.

Kat said, "We've got company. Ortiz is here with his two enforcers. Conor doesn't think Ortiz is aware that your lawyer is here."

Danna stood. "He will shortly. Jael, you might want to fetch your rifle and stand by. Doc, you stay put. This is lawyer business."

"But—"

"Lawyer business."

Danna followed Kat back into the store where Conor waited. Jael caught up with them, a rifle tucked under her arm. Both lawyers still wore britches and trail clothes, the long horseback trip having made it infeasible to pack something less practical. Danna said, "Kat, do you have a gun handy?"

"Under the counter."

"I would like you and Jael to each take one of the windows. Push the rifle barrels through the openings but try to stay out of sight. I just want them to see that guns are backing me up. I don't anticipate that you will need to use them. Conor, perhaps you would join me on the veranda."

"Yes, ma'am."

The two stepped outside. Kat watched and listened from her window station and saw the disbelief on Ortiz's face when he saw Danna. Conor stepped off to one side of Danna.

"Hello, Emilio," Danna said. "You are late for breakfast and too early for lunch. I understand you asked to speak to my client. You do recall, do you not, that it is unethical for a lawyer to speak to another's client without his lawyer's consent or presence?"

Ortiz said, "I cannot imagine what you are doing in this godforsaken place, and I had no reason to be aware that you were Roman Hayes's legal counsel."

"Please do not take me for a fool, Emilio. I spent some hours at the recorder's offices searching the title history for this land. Your spies there informed you within fifteen minutes after I walked in the door and announced what I was looking for. Now tell me what you were going to discuss with my client and then be on your way."

Kat could see that Ortiz was struggling to contain his anger and frustration. "Very well, your client and other occupants of the lands here have been notified previously in writing to vacate this land on which they are trespassing. Two days. If the trespassers are not vacating their ranchos—and that includes this so-called Triad—they will be forcibly removed."

"You are a fool, Emilio. I have investigated this Mendoza, your pretend client. He is a fraud, and I will make a fool of both of you in a courtroom, and you know it. Your true clients, members of the Santa Fe Ring, don't have a chance of winning the case, and I will commence a quiet title action to seal my client's claim. If you resort to violence, you and the Ring will be flooded with publicity that will drive the lot of you out of the territory, if you escape the penitentiary. Now, get your asses out of here."

Ortiz and his men mounted their horses, but before he reined his mount away, Ortiz said, "Twelve o'clock noon, two days from now, and our enforcers start their work."

Chapter 53

AFTER SUPPER THE day of Ortiz's visit, Conor called a meeting on the veranda of all the Triad and stable occupants. It had been at Flipper's urging he had assumed command. He was never comfortable with limbo, and he had been itching to respond to the threat facing the settlors.

Out of deference, he had procured Doc's approval, and his old friend, who had become uncharacteristically indecisive in recent days, had seemed relieved to turn responsibility over to Conor. Flipper had cancelled future surveying plans until safety could be assured, agreeing with Conor that this was no time for separation.

The suffocating heat had eased with sunset, and a soft breeze drifting off the mountains made the veranda more amenable to a group than the residence. Chairs were arranged haphazardly at the trading post end of the big porch, and Conor stood before the curious faces. He spoke slowly and deliberately. "I asked for everyone to meet here, because I think we must take seriously Emilio Ortiz's threat to evict folks here and on the surrounding ranchos. This will not be a peaceful exodus, and I would not be surprised if Ortiz hasn't decided it would be in his interest to see every last person at the Triad dead."

Kat spoke. "Shouldn't we warn the people on the ranchos?"

"That is where I was this afternoon. Diego Munoz was out with Henry on the survey, of course, but I spoke with Lucia. They will be bringing their family here tomorrow." He smiled. "She has probably informed Diego by now."

"You couldn't have reached all the families in that time."

"I also stopped by the Sanchez rancho. Luckily, Cal happened to be there. He and Felipe took on notification of those families furthest out, and everyone should be aware of the deadline now and the invitation to come here for sanctuary. I fear some won't budge, though." He did not mention that Cal was at the rancho talking with Maria, having detoured from the survey route since Flipper had Diego available to assist. Several had likely figured that out anyhow.

Kat said, "So we are providing sanctuary. Where will put all these people?"

"The warehouse. The stone walls will protect in the event of gunfire, shelter from any storm. The doors on each end can be left open for air but closed in case of danger. Cookfires can be built outside. It won't be like setting up a new campsite."

"Yes, I suppose we could make that work, but I worry about those who refuse to leave their homes."

"I think we can help with that."

"How?" Kathleen always wanted answers. She took little on faith, and neither did he.

"We will lure the enforcers here . . . if they have not already decided to attack the Triad first."

Kat was incredulous. "Why on earth do we want to bring those men here? Over twenty of them, Cal told us. We are outnumbered."

"That means nothing if we are prepared. The Triad, all the buildings here, were built of stone only partly because of convenience, I am guessing. It was a fortress to defend against hostile tribes. The warehouse loft with its narrow windows, as well as the Triad were all constructed with defense in mind. Starting tonight the three of us in the stable will commence guard shifts just in case the enforcers have thoughts of an early surprise. Those sleeping in the Triad should keep guns handy. If you hear gunshots, grab your weapons and head for a window.

Keep the doors barred unless you confirm that one of us wishes to enter. Do not go outside."

Jael said, "I would like to take a guard shift."

Conor thought a minute. "I don't see why not. First two-hour shift at ten o'clock. Be here with your weapon, and I will tell you where to position. Tomorrow night, we will double post, but we should have a few more recruits by then."

Danna said, "I can take a shift tomorrow."

"Me, too," Kat said.

Conor said, "We should be fine then. I know we can count on Diego and Felipe. There may be others."

Kat said, "So, you are going to lure the enforcers here. With what? Cookies and pie?"

"We are going to attack first, as soon as the enforcers give some indication they are going to move out. Starting tomorrow morning, I would like to have Cal set up camp within spyglass distance of the enforcer encampment and head back here the instant he sees a sign they are moving out. Hopefully, by that time we will have a few extra men, and we will join up with Cal and try to intercept the bunch before they split up, which I assume they would do to run off families at the individual ranchos. Folks will die if that happens, and the deaths are not likely to be those of the enforcers. We will launch our own attack to divert them and hopefully draw them after us."

Kat said, "And what if they take you down before you get back here?"

"This won't be close in fighting. We will have a big edge because we know what we are going to do. They must get reorganized. Regardless, they will get the message that we are not going to lie back and let them attack any of these people without making them pay. The bosses, whether that is Ortiz or one of his thugs, will decide they must deal with us first. Questions?"

He looked around at the grim faces, barely discernible in the dusk now. He noticed that Doc just stared ahead as if he had detached himself from it all. Kathleen sat beside Doc and stood. "Doc needs to go to bed." She helped the physician to his feet, and they disappeared into the Triad.

After the group broke up, Conor entered the residence. He saw Kathleen standing in the hallway that connected to Doc's bedroom staring pensively into the room. She did not appear to hear him as he approached, so he spoke, softly. "Kathleen?"

She turned and looked at him with the sad eyes of a forlorn pup. She stepped toward him. "He's getting weaker, Conor, and I can't do a damned thing about it.

I saw this when Mama died. I remember those last days like yesterday. The Angel of Death is lurking here, waiting. I just know it. I am sitting up with him tonight and every night. He will not die alone."

He took Kathleen in his arms and held her for some minutes. She clung to him but did not cry. Before she gently slipped away, she whispered, "Thank you, Conor."

Before he departed, he moved the rocking chair from the parlor into the bedroom, hoping it might allow her to capture snatches of sleep during the night. He offered to stay with her, but she shook her head negatively. "You have work to do," she whispered. "Doc wants you to tend to that. I know he does."

Conor walked out onto the veranda and sat down on the steps and gazed at the starlit sky while he waited for Jael to take first watch.

Chapter 54

DOC DID NOT die alone. Kat would always be grateful for that. He had awakened in the middle of the night and given her hand a feeble squeeze, sighed, and closed his eyes. His breathing was very shallow after that, and she had not released his hand until he died an hour later.

She was glad Conor appeared at the residence early, so she could tell him first. "I feared that would be your news this morning," he said. "Are you alright?"

"I guess so. I was losing him a bit day by day. I will save my tears for later. There are things that must be done."

"This heat. You understand that he must be buried soon? No time for a funeral. Maybe we can do something with the community later."

"I do understand what must be done. Can you and Henry dig a grave next to Ruth's? Doc wouldn't want a formal gathering. Deep down, I don't think he ever wanted much other than to be with Ruth and his children again. Folks go on after losses like that, but it is a journey with a big burden on their shoulders."

"Cal will be heading out on his scout soon. He will likely stop by to beg some grub."

"I will put together a few things for him and then I will find a blanket for Doc. I am going to try to get some decent clothes on him. I simply won't bury him in just his undershorts."

"Jael will be up anytime now. I'm sure she will help with these things. I've got a feeling that she has seen worse than either of us has during her years with the Co-manche."

By midmorning, Doctor Roman Hayes was buried in the plateau cemetery. Besides Kat and Conor, the two Santa Fe lawyers and Henry Flipper were present at the graveside. The women watched solemnly as Doc's blanket-wrapped body was lowered by Conor and Flipper into the grave.

When the grave was covered, Kat thought somebody should say something, but she found herself unable to call up any words. She was relieved when Conor, who stood on the opposite side of the grave, spoke.

"I am sorry I only came to know this fine man during the last years of his life. Few knew of him beyond this lonely land, but he was a great man of the kind I can only aspire to be. I learned little from his words, but his quiet, unheralded examples made him a rare teacher of a life well-lived. He deserved far better than what fate handed him, but he refused to complain. He trudged on, doing good when he could. The Stoic Marcus Aurelius said that life is the sum of all our acts, and that we should be judged by that totality and not by our worst performance. I cannot imagine Roman Hayes not tallying a positive balance in the end. A person's life is like a book with many chapters between the first page and the last. Doc's book was too short for those who knew and loved him, but I thank God that he shared with me the last several chapters of his life. I learned so much from those final pages." Conor looked directly at Kat. "That is what we should be grateful for."

Kat found herself entranced by Conor's words and mesmerized by his soulful eyes. The man speaking those words was not an ordinary man. He was as far from a Louie Gaynor or Buford Walters as a man could get. She realized now that Doc had not left her alone.

Flipper said, "Why don't we recite the Lord's Prayer together?"

And they did.

Chapter 55

EMILIO ORTIZ WAS not about to spend another night near the Guadalupe Mountains. He intended to finish his work here, head back to Santa Fe in one of the wagons, and make secret arrangements to depart for California. Mid-morning, he summoned Calhoun and Marx to the chuckwagon that had become his command post.

"The cooks will have grub ready before noon," Ortiz said. "Order your men to be ready to ride after that. We've got work to do today."

Calhoun said, "What kind of work?"

"Evictions, starting with the Triad. We do that, and everything else collapses. The Mexican families will desert that land like rats from a sinking ship if the Triad is wiped out. Why waste our time hitting each little rancho when we can have it done in a single strike. Eventually, we would have to hit the Triad anyway."

"I suppose that makes sense, but don't he got till noon tomorrow?"

"Do you think they are going to move out?"

"Ain't likely. But you said—"

"Surprise. They aren't moving. Today, they will be caught up in making preparations to resist."

"You ain't going to give them a chance to leave first?"

"That would be stupid. I want everybody dead, and the buildings gutted by fire."

"We ain't cold-blooded killers, you know. We generally give folks a chance to move on."

"Oh, come now. Please do not tell me you have not killed people."

"Yeah, we kilt people when they didn't do what they was told. Tried not to kill women and kids unless forced to."

"There is a bonus for the two of you. Five hundred each if you don't leave anybody alive."

The men looked at each other before Calhoun spoke again. "Are you riding with us?"

"Well, no. I planned to wait here."

"Nope. You ride with us to see we done our job. You can stay back a ways if it suits you, but you ride with us, or we ain't riding."

Ortiz was getting very tired of this son-of-a-bitch and his belligerent ways. He would be glad to be rid of the whole outfit. "Very well. It doesn't matter, I guess. It might be entertaining."

Two hours later, Ortiz and the enforcers rode away from the camp, beginning the four-hour journey to the Triad. Ortiz had informed the two cooks to plan for a late supper, probably well after sundown. When the task was done, he planned to remove the box of gold coins from the hidden compartment beneath the headquarters wagon bed, settle with these no-goods, and be done with them.

An hour into their journey, Marx, who had been riding some distance ahead signaled a halt. When the others reached him, he pointed to an outcropping nearly a hundred feet high off the east slope of the Guadalupe.

"What is that?" Ortiz asked.

"A feathered lance. Likely Apache," Marx said.

"So what?"

Calhoun said, "That wasn't there when we rode past yesterday. Sometimes it's a warning. Any word of Apaches around these parts?"

Ortiz said, "They are all on the reservation."

"Ain't true. Lots of the Chiricahua ain't gone in. And there's always reservation-jumpers going in and out. I don't like this. I didn't bargain to fight no Apaches."

"They've got no part in this, and they wouldn't want to take on a near-army of men for no purpose."

"I still don't like this."

A half hour later, they came upon another lance planted in the sand along the side of the trail. Calhoun remarked, "If we see Injuns, we're outta here."

Ortiz did not argue this time. He wanted no part of Apache.

Chapter 56

WHEN CAL RODE into the yard shortly after two o'clock, Conor, returning from the warehouse where he was settling the Munoz and Sanchez families, intercepted him. Cal dismounted, and Conor noticed that Cal's horse was breathing hard and sweat-soaked. Cal had been pushing the critter. "Trouble?" Conor said.

"Yep. A whole passel of it. You had it figured. They're headed this way. At their present pace, I would guess your guests are about an hour and a half behind me. No reason to ride out and bait them."

"I will alert the ladies in the Triad. I think Flip's there, too, meeting with Danna. Why don't you put up your horse. On the way, you might stop at the warehouse and tell the Sanchez and Munoz families to get ready for an attack. Diego and Felipe know that they are to position in the warehouse loft. I would like you to go with them. Di-

421

ego has ridden as a scout with the cavalry, so he has been under fire plenty of times. I don't know about Felipe. Lucia Munoz can handle a rifle, so we might position her someplace."

"Is Maria there? She claims to be a dead shot with a Winchester."

Conor doubted the claim, but even if she was not, the extra noise could be useful. She would likely be positioned within arm's reach of Cal, but he did not care. At least she was speaking to him now, even with a congenial tone. He suspected Cal was performing well.

He told Kathleen about the approaching visitors, and she commenced closing down the store and barring the doors. Flipper was in Doc's office with the lawyers, his survey drawings spread out on the desk when he interrupted. "They're coming, Flip. We need to get that wagon turned over. Danna and Jael, you know what to do. Kathleen has already started."

Flipper and Conor went to the warehouse where the wagons were stored, and with the help of Diego and Felipe pulled and pushed a buckboard out into the yard and then pushed it over on its side about fifty feet from the Triad's front.

Cal said, "And what if somebody circles and comes at you from your backside?"

Conor said, "You've got a clear shot from the ware-house loft. It's your job to take care of that."

"I don't like being cooped up there one bit. I like my fighting face to face."

Flipper said, "Conor, we could use another man here."

Conor knew Flipper was right. "Okay, get everybody positioned in the loft and then head down here."

Cal grinned at his victory and winked at Flipper. "I'll be back shortly."

"Bring your spyglass, would you?" Conor said.

After that, the hardest part came: the waiting. There was not a hint of breeze, and a clear sky allowed the sun's rays to turn the ground below into an oven. Conor checked his timepiece several times to find that only minutes not hours had passed since his last confirmation.

Finally, they caught sight of the enormous dust cloud rolling in from the west. At least this dust-carpeted land would not let riders sneak up on you, if a man kept his eyes open. Conor said, "The spyglass, Cal."

He pressed the telescope to his eye and focused. It was like viewing the riders through a veil of smoke, but he could make out the skinny man named Marx in the lead. He thought Calhoun and Ortiz might be in the next tier of riders, but he found it difficult to believe that Ortiz would come this close to the gunfire. As the riders drew

Ron Schwab

nearer, he saw one veer off from the mass and move in the direction of the mountain slopes. Ortiz, obviously choosing to observe from a safe distance.

They came into the yard with pistols firing. Fools, Conor thought. Hitting a target from a moving horse was not impossible but gave the intended victim a huge edge. Just before he directed his comrades to fire, one of the enforcers dropped his pistol, straightened in the saddle, and grasped the base of his neck where the feathered fletching of an arrow protruded. He tumbled out of the saddle. What in blazes?

"They're too close for comfort, fellas. Choose your targets. Cal, you start from the left; Flip, you from the right."

The men raised their rifles and commenced firing. This would be the signal for the others to start. He did not fire his own rifle, concentrating on evaluating the effectiveness of their action, readying to make a run to back up the Triad if necessary. But the attackers were caught in a rainstorm of lead, their bodies starting to clutter the yard. He saw an arrow plunge into Marx's shoulder, and before he plummeted from his saddle, another struck below the breastbone.

Calhoun at first headed his mount toward his fallen partner, then having second thoughts, swung the horse around and headed away from the Triad in retreat. The survivors, including several who were obviously wounded, wasted no time following. The smaller dust cloud had reversed directions and was headed west now.

Conor raced around the toppled wagon bed and grabbed the reins of a bay gelding wandering aimlessly about the melee, confused by the loss of its rider. He stepped into a stirrup and lifted himself into the saddle, galloping the horse after the quickly fading dust cloud. He could hear Flipper hollering after him.

He soon changed direction. He, of course, did not want to catch up to the whipped enforcers. Ortiz was his quarry, and in mere minutes he saw a riderless horse not more than fifty feet from a prone form sprawled out in an agave patch.

He dismounted, hitching the horse to a small scrub oak that would not survive another summer. He walked over to the body, the pallid face seemingly frozen in terror, drying eyes wide open. The arrow had struck the left side of Ortiz's neck and dug its way through the flesh and muscle till the tip of the arrowhead emerged on the right. A powerful man had loosed that missive.

He reached for his holstered Colt when he heard a rider coming up behind him and wheeled in readiness before he relaxed at the sight of Flipper. "Flip, you should have called out. You're lucky I didn't shoot you."

"I wasn't worried. You are too dang slow on the draw. I've seen you in action, you know. And I didn't even see you pull a trigger today."

Conor pondered a moment. "Darn, I guess I didn't. I think that ought to get me out of burial detail."

"Don't bet on it. There is too much burying to do."

Flipper dismounted and nodded toward the body. "I guess Ortiz is out of the game. The Indians must be on our side."

"I doubt if it was Apache. It had to be the Ghost. I just don't see how he killed Ortiz and got to the Triad fast enough to down a few more."

"Ghosts can do such things."

Chapter 57

TWO DAYS AFTER the enforcers' attack, Flipper led his mount and packhorse up to the Triad. It was a rigorous three-day ride to El Paso, and he had told Conor that with an early start, he hoped to spend only two nights on the trail. Conor waited at the hitching rail as his friend approached and stepped out and shook Flipper's hand.

"I'm going to miss you, friend. Stay in touch and let me know where you are at."

"I will do what I can, but you need to petition the government for a post office here. Kat could handle the postmistress's job with the trading post."

"Jael is going to help us with that. She wants us to collect signatures from all the folks around here, including Pablo Torres's little colony to the east. She thinks we can easily qualify for weekly service. For now, though, send mail to the Roswell Trading Post. They've got service, and they aren't more than a year from telegraph service, thanks to old Chisum's influence. Maybe we can even tag onto that one day."

"Put that task in Kat's hands. That lady will find a way."

"Yeah, she just might."

"When do you expect to marry that gal?"

Conor was caught off guard. "Who said anything about marriage?"

"She suggested you move into the Triad."

"In the hospital room after the lawyers leave tomorrow."

"And then it will be Doc's old bedroom, and after that you will draw straws and decide if you share her room or Doc's."

"I am going ahead with plans to build a new house."

"Yeah, three bedrooms you wanted."

"I hope to have a family someday."

"Helps if you got a woman. I would highly recommend one that lives in the Triad."

Conor decided to ignore him. "I've got your address. Still in care of Renata Aguilar in El Paso, right?"

"I will let you know if it changes. I expect to be doing a lot of traveling. El Paso should be the home port for a spell. Don't count on a fast response. I will likely be off to Mexico a lot."

The trading post door opened, and Kat appeared and hurried across the veranda and down the steps. "Henry, darn you. Were you trying to sneak out on me?" She stepped over, grasped the surveyor about the neck and kissed him smack on the lips. Conor thought the kiss lingered well beyond propriety and was relieved when Kathleen stepped back.

Flipper looked at him with what Conor took as a taunting smile on his face. "Don't forget my recommendation," Flipper said. "If you don't take it, I might think on it myself."

"Goodbye, Henry," Kat said. "You will come back and visit, won't you?"

"I expect so, sooner or later." Flipper mounted his gelding and headed west, the packhorse trailing behind him.

Kat looked up at Conor. "You look so sad. Henry is really a special friend to you, isn't he?"

"Yeah. It's strange because we are so different."

"You mean your color?"

"No. We just approach life so differently. For instance, the roaming life has no appeal to me. I am not a nomad. I came here because I wanted someplace to sink roots. Like Doc, I want to be buried right here near the Guadalupe. I doubt if Flip will ever sink roots. He will carve out his own place in this life, but he will cover a lot of territory in his journey."

"You are probably right." She paused. "I want roots, too."

Chapter 58

"CAL IS GETTING everything ready for us to ride out in the morning," Danna said. "Maria Sanchez will be riding with us. I have spoken with her at length and set some conditions. One is that she will be staying at my home until she finds a suitable, permanent situation in Santa Fe. She is a pretty thing and appears quite bright but seems to have little notion of what life is like in a place like Santa Fe. There are opportunities there, but not all are the right kind."

The two lawyers, Kat, and Conor sat at the dining room table after clearing the lunch dishes. Kat was relieved that Maria would receive some guidance and supervision. Maria was about her own age but had lived a somewhat sheltered life. Cal was not a bad man, but he would be a terrible influence on Maria. He should go home to his wife and children and straighten out his own life, whether that meant a stable marriage or divorce. She had to laugh at herself. Here she was creating scripts for other lives when she had not figured out her own yet.

Danna continued, "As you know, we planned to leave several days ago, but circumstances changed that. It is important that we spend some time together this afternoon. We have a basketful of legal matters to discuss. First are the procedures concerning settlement of Doctor Hayes's estate. I reviewed the terms of the will that Conor took from the safe yesterday. It is very simple. Conor, as executor, will carry out Doc's wishes, but first the will must be probated in the territorial court in Santa Fe, since there is no organized county here. We will take the will with us and see that it is filed with the court along with the appropriate paperwork. Conor, I would like for you and Kat to travel to Santa Fe two months from now, so we can take care of your official appointment. Can you do that?"

He looked at Kat. "Will that work?"

"It is not as if I had other travel plans. Lucia has expressed interest in helping with the trading post, and I am sure Diego would see to livestock chores."

"We will be there," Conor said.

"Good. We will have the documents ready to commence the quiet title action as well. Conor, you will need to sign as executor, and Kat, you will sign as the sole beneficiary of the will. We must first establish title to the land in Kat's name. Henry Flipper left a legal survey with his signature suitable for filing and recording. There has been nothing recorded regarding all the tracts Doc agreed to sell or transfer. Since his will provides that all agreements are to be honored, once title is established in Kat's name, we will have her sign deeds transferring those tracts to the entitled owners and file those surveys."

"This is mind boggling," Kat said, "but, of course, I will do whatever it takes to honor Doc's wishes. Will there be a problem with the court action?"

"We will be prepared for the worst, but I expect it to be routine now. I think the Santa Fe Ring folks will stay as far away from this as they can."

Jael interjected. "We cannot legally or ethically hide what happened here. There is a mass grave containing nine bodies. This must be reported to the U.S. Marshal in Santa Fe. I will give him Emilio Ortiz's name and that of someone with the last name of Marx. I doubt if anyone will wish to exhume the contents of the grave, but there may be further inquiries. I will make the marshal aware of your availability when you visit Santa Fe. I cannot imagine him making the journey here."

Kat wondered what Jael would say if she informed her of the other bodies scattered about. No, things were already complicated enough.

Conor said, "You once told us that you would need Doc's sworn statement or personal testimony for your legal action."

Danna said, "I worked with him for the better part of two days during the week before his death. He wrote and signed a statement. If it is not challenged, I am confident the judge will admit it into evidence, and as I said, I see the possibilities of someone contesting the case as very remote."

Kat said, "Would it help if I obtained another statement that could at least verify the length of Doc's residency here?"

"Do you know someone?"

"I cannot tell you more yet, but if it would help, perhaps you can tell me the things that should be recited in such a statement."

Danna eyed her suspiciously. "We can talk after our meeting here."

Danna and Jael spent almost two more hours with Conor and Kat asking questions and one or other of the lawyers responding with more detail than Kat cared about. She guessed they made their living with words.

She wondered if they were like farmers and producing more words was like growing more corn.

When Danna adjourned the meeting, she and Kat went into the hospital office to create more words.

Chapter 59

A WEEK AFTER DEPARTURE of their guests, Kat shrugged off Conor's assistance and saddled Toughie. Conor was not pleased with her decision to leave him behind.

"You said you would fix supper tonight, Conor. I will be back to eat. You know you can count on that. Don't worry so much."

"You have a knack for causing me worry, Kathleen."

"Well, you are not going. I don't think the Ghost will give me a bit of trouble. He might resent that I felt it necessary to bring a guard."

Conor shrugged and walked away, as she led her mare out the wide entrance, mounted, and headed for the old Butterfield trail. As she nudged the roan up the trail at a relaxed pace, she thought about her new living arrangement with Conor. She missed Doc so much she could not hold back the tears some days. She supposed it would get easier, but it would be a spell.

Conor's presence in the Triad helped for the most part. She did not want to live alone in the sprawling building. Still, his presence could be unsettling at times. She thought about him too much, wondered what was to become of them. She doubted they could live as brother and sister for forty or fifty years. Could they even make a year? She had come to like it when he was near, even when they had nothing to say. His mere presence lifted her spirits. She had never felt like this before.

And that dream last night about the two of them lying naked on a bed, his hands moving to forbidden places, his lips pressed to hers, and her fingers responding in kind. She had never once behaved like that with Louie. She had been like a rag doll, spreading her thighs on demand, and then, thankfully, it was over quickly, unless he decided to beat her for her passivity.

She forced her thoughts away. She had business to tend to this day. Less than two hours later, she found the trees that hid the pathway to the Ghost's cave. She reined in and pondered her strategy. Suddenly, the tree branches parted, and the giant stood there. His pale blue eyes seethed with anger. Of course, he had been following her trek into the mountains from above somewhere. He missed nothing. And he had guessed her destination.

She said, "I know you do not want us coming to your home, but this is very important. Without your help we may be forced to move from this land."

His eyes softened, and he waved to her to follow him. He turned away, and she dismounted, leading her horse up the trail behind him. She was glad when they approached the cave that there was no sign of Louie's remains hanging from the tree. She supposed the vultures would have cleaned his bones until they fell apart and dropped to the earth for some other creature to carry off.

When they reached the cave, he signaled her to sit down outside on a big stone not far from the opening. She removed her saddle bags from the horse, and he took Toughie's reins and led her off to drink. She guessed he must have staked her out in the grass because he returned without the horse.

The Ghost squatted on his haunches in front of her and pointed toward his lips, which she took as a sign to talk.

"You do know that Doc died, don't you?"

He shook his head in the affirmative.

Of course, he would know. He knew everything that happened on their land at the base of the Guadalupe.

She sensed that he would be impatient with a long tale of woe, so she quickly explained their dilemma.

"The lawyers are confident we can win this case and establish our claim on the land, but a written statement from you about your knowledge concerning Doc's time of possession could be critical." She reached in the saddlebags and plucked out a sheet of paper, handing it to the Ghost. "This is a list of the information that would be important. This was compiled by our lawyer." The Ghost frowned as he studied it.

"I know she is asking for information you do not wish to divulge, but your statement will not help without it. It must be written with pen and ink. I have brought those things with parchment. You may think about this. We would not be taking the document to Santa Fe for almost two months."

He stood and entered the cave. She waited for a quarter hour before he returned and handed her a note. She read it silently. "I will think on this. Do not return to this place. The statement will be delivered to you if I choose to do it. Leave your paper, pen, and ink at the cave entrance."

He turned away and retrieved her horse. When he passed her the reins, she said, "Thank you."

The Ghost nodded.

Chapter 60

A MONTH HAD PASSED with no statement from the Ghost. Conor and Kat sat side by side in rocking chairs on the veranda like an old grandma and grandpa, he thought. Loafer slept on a rug not far from his feet. They had settled into a routine the past few weeks of doing this nightly. Sometimes they just sat silently, and others they would talk about the new house, the canyon, and the business enterprises, even sharing bits and pieces of their pasts. Kat was unusually quiet and pensive this evening, it seemed.

"Are you worried because the Ghost hasn't left his statement yet?" Conor asked.

"A little."

"Be patient. We have another month."

"I don't always share your patience."

He chuckled. "That's true enough."

"You haven't said anything about the salt business lately."

"I am still thinking it out. But I can't go much beyond thinking. What if we lose the case? I don't have the warehouses available. Also, Doc was going to be my partner. It was going to be his seed money that started the company."

"He left us his money, and as we go through his things, there seems to be much more than I would have imagined. Over two thousand dollars in gold coin in the safe. Healthy bank accounts in El Paso and Santa Fe. We've added a fair number of horses lately. You said they weren't breeding stock, mostly geldings, but they could be sold to the army."

"First, Doc did not leave us the money. He left you the money."

"I guess I never thought of it that way."

"Are you serious?"

"I am. It's strange, I suppose. I have started thinking of everything as ours."

Conor thought for a spell about what she had said. "I think it is time for a serious talk that I have been trying to work up the nerve to have with you."

"Please don't say that you have decided to pack up and leave."

He reached across the rocker's arm and took her hand in his. "Never."

"Never?"

"Never. But I am tortured living the way we are. I dream about you, Kathleen, and I wake up, and sometimes it makes me crazy that you are so near, yet far away."

"You could take Doc's room if that would help." She was teasing him now. And he was not about to follow Flipper's script. He was determined to skip a step.

"It would not help. Kathleen, we have been living almost like husband and wife this past month and just the two of us here most of the time. Well, almost isn't enough anymore. I meant it when I said I would never leave you, but I am thinking that it might be best for me to move back to the stable."

"Don't be silly."

"Do you know we have never even shared a kiss?"

"Yes, I know that. You never so much as suggested you wanted one."

"I want everything." He released her hand and stood before kneeling in front of her chair and taking her hand again. "I want you to marry me. I am asking you to marry me, Kathleen."

"Before we have even shared a kiss?"

"Yes. I don't care if things are out of order. Will you marry me?"

"Stand up."

He got to his feet, and she arose from her chair, lifting her face toward his.

"Kiss me," she said. And their lips met, first gently and then hungrily. He could feel her breathing heavily against him, matching his own urgency before she pulled her head back. "Yes, I will marry you."

"You don't want to think about it?"

"I've done enough thinking about it."

"We will find a judge or preacher when we go to Santa Fe."

"So long as the honeymoon starts tonight."

"But—"

"I don't give a damn about things being out of order, either."

He swept this woman, who was light as a feather, off her feet and lifted her into his arms.

"Conor," she said, "what are you doing?"

"I am carrying you across the threshold." He looked down at Loafer who was eyeing them suspiciously. "And, Loafer, I will let you know when you can come in."

Chapter 61

I T WAS THREE days before they were to depart for Santa Fe when Conor woke to a rapping at the residence door. Kathleen, sated from a busy night, lay naked beside him, seemingly oblivious to the disturbance. He swung his legs out of bed and sat on the side of it a moment to clear the fog from his head. He stumbled around the room in the darkness a few minutes before he found his undershorts and britches. Bare-chested, he snatched up his Colt from the lamp table and headed down the hall toward the door.

Loafer was sitting at the door, his eyes fixed on it with interest, but he seemed undisturbed, which Conor took as a good sign. "Who is it?" he called when he reached the door.

No reply.

He released the bolt on the lock and opened the door slowly, pistol readied. He lowered the weapon when he saw the Ghost standing there, two envelopes clutched in his long fingers. The Ghost handed him the envelopes and then turned and disappeared into the night like his namesake. Loafer slipped through the half-open door, and went onto the veranda, likely deciding it was cooler there.

Conor held the bulky envelope up close to see if he could read anything with the moonlight sifting through the window. He saw the word "Kathleen" written in perfect script on the envelope and decided to place it on the kitchen table where she would find it first thing after sunrise. The other small envelope bore his name. He opened it and found a gold band that would not fit over the joint of his little finger. He stuffed the band and envelope in his front trousers pocket, returned to bed, and fell instantly to sleep.

Kathleen was already up when he next awakened with the sun almost fully above the eastern horizon. This woman was wearing him out, but there were far worse reasons to be tired. He got up, dressed, and went into the kitchen where Kathleen was sitting at the table, sheets of parchment in her hand.

"I see you found it," Conor said.

"Yes. You knew? He didn't just slip in here?"

"He was rapping at the door. You didn't hear, and I hated to wake you."

"You can read this whenever you wish, but I can tell you about it for now. His name is Andrew McAllister. He was born in 1825 in Philadelphia. He was a history professor at Harvard and came to the Southwest following the Civil War with several associates to study the Spanish venture into what was then a part of Mexico. Chiricahua Apache killed all his party but him. The Apache cut out his tongue and because of his size kept him as a slave, using him much like a pack animal."

"But how did he come to be here?"

"Within a year, he was traded by the Chiricahua to the Mescalero who spent much of each year in the Guadalupe. Shortly after that, he escaped from the Mescalero. He hid in the mountain caves and stole from the Mescalero villages when he wished. They thought it was a spirit and soon they came to fear him. Doc settled in the Triad only a few weeks after his escape, and the Mescalero and other bands did not disturb him because of their need of his trade goods."

"But why on earth did he stay?"

"He says he made a new life here and decided he would never leave; like us, I guess."

"Not much of a life, living in a cave."

"I suppose a professor who could not speak would have difficulty finding a position."

"His mind is obviously good. I just don't understand it."

"Let's be grateful that he stayed and will apparently continue to do so. He obviously found a treasure of doubloons in a cave that makes his life easier. At least we have the document Danna wanted. It is signed and even dated. I suppose he can determine dates from the calendar in the store. I would not be surprised to learn that the Ghost has a diary of his life here, but I suspect he would never share it with the world."

"Well, his secret is safe with us, and we certainly don't want others to know there could be a treasure hidden in the Guadalupe. I have got chores to do. I will read his statement later."

"I will have breakfast ready when you are finished."

He kissed her before he left the kitchen, marveling again at the hold this young woman had on him.

Later, as they ate breakfast, Kat hit him with another thought. "I assume you will allow me to move into the new house with you when it is completed next spring."

What now? "Get to the point. You have done more planning for the house than I have."

"The Triad will be vacant."

"You will still have the store there. We will think of some new use for the hospital area, perhaps make that and the residence area into rental spaces for folks that pass through, or guests."

"I think a family should be there. Doc would like that, and I would, too."

"You will own the place. Do what suits you."

"No, everything will be ours."

"Tell me what you have already figured out."

"Lucia and Diego and their family. She would be perfect in the store, and you have said you plan on having Diego play a big part in the salt business and any other enterprises. This would be convenient for us all, and the Triad would be a palace for the Munoz family compared to that cramped, board shack they have been living in. We would not want to give up ownership just yet, but they could live there rent-free."

He had to admit she had come up with a good plan. "You have got my vote if you really think you need it."

"Wonderful. Lucia is excited about doing this and is already planning where to stake out a garden."

Chapter 62

JAEL RIVERS ARRANGED for a justice of the peace to preside over a brief morning wedding and promised to see the marriage properly registered in the territory records. Jael and Danna were the witnesses. The first surprise to Kat was the placement of a simple gold wedding band on her finger by Conor. The band fit perfectly, and she could not imagine when he would have had time to purchase it. And know precisely the right size. The ring had not been important to her . . . until now.

The second was the unexpected appearance of a Mexican violinist, who following the official declaration that they were husband and wife and Conor's tender kiss, played a beautiful song she had never heard before.

"It is called, *I Will Take You Home Again Kathleen*," Conor said. "It has been around five or six years. The lyrics refer to a return to Ireland. But I will be taking you back home again tomorrow."

She kissed him again. "Yes, below the Guadalupe. That is my home. But the band. When did you buy it? I have been with you every moment here, and how did you know the size?"

"I have friends, Kathleen."

THE LAWYERS HOSTED the newlyweds at a Mexican lunch before they made a final visit to the law office, and now they sat in the Rivers & Sinclair conference room. Danna said, "We will send all our mailings to the Roswell Trading Post until you have your own post office."

"With all the signatures you brought in," Jael said, "I think you will have mail service within three months, certainly no more than six. I will do everything I can to expedite it."

"That will bring a big change to our lives," Conor said. "This could be critical to some of our business plans. Will we be needed for testimony at the court hearing?"

Danna said, "Yes. I will give you ample notice. Your presence will only be required for a few hours at most. As I told you, I am confident that Professor McAllister's statement will seal the case. After my report to the marshal, I cannot imagine the Ring coming anywhere near the case. Title to the land will be quieted in your name, Kat."

"Kathleen Byrne?"

"Yes, that is how you just signed your name on the petition. A few typing corrections on the text will be necessary before the court filing. You caught me by surprise with your marriage plans."

"Very well," Kat said, "we will be leaving early morning. We expect to honeymoon the remainder of the day in Santa Fe."

After the meeting with the lawyers, they stepped onto the boardwalk outside the office building. Conor asked, "So we are honeymooning in Santa Fe. Where are we going?"

"Foolish man. The hotel room, of course. We are newlyweds, you know."

"Oh, I guess that's right."

"And tomorrow, you will take Kathleen home again."

Author's Note

Henry Ossian Flipper (1856-1940) in this novel was, indeed, the first black graduate of West Point. He was a prolific engineer and writer, who had a fascinating career outside the military. To learn more about Flipper, the following reading is suggested:

Henry Ossian Flipper: West Point's First Black Graduate by Jane Eppinga

The Colored Cadet at West Point by Henry O. Flipper

Black Frontiersman: The Memoirs of Henry O. Flipper by Henry O. Flipper

The Fall of a Black Army Officer by Charles M. Robinson III

Acknowledgments

My thanks to Leafcutter Publishing Group, Inc., which currently via its Uplands Press imprint, has published all of my novels. Without Leafcutter's guidance and expertise in the packaging and promotion of my books, they would never have reached the reading public.

Leafcutter's Mike Schwab acts as final editor and handles formatting of the manuscript and steers the book through the process that gets it to our readers. His input as the novel progresses is essential to the completion of a novel that, hopefully, readers will enjoy.

As usual, my world keeper, Diane Garland, helped straighten out timeline and character discrepancies with skill and professionalism. Her work has been invaluable to the production of my novels.

As always, the assistance of my wife Bev Schwab is an in-home treasure. She works on editing at multiple stages and is my sounding board and good right hand on all phases of each novel's production. Moreover, she listens to my daily grumbling without complaint.

This novel, as do many of my stories, presented various legal issues, and I have been fortunate to have Judge Linda Bauer available for counsel when I request her opinion. Judge Bauer is also a part of the editing team and unearthed valuable research information for this novel.

The input of attorney Ben Murray regarding several legal issues presented in this novel has also been appreciated.

About the Author

Ron Schwab is the author of several popular Western series, including *The Blood Hounds*, *Lockwood*, *The Coyote Saga*, and *The Lockes*. His novels *Grit* and *Old Dogs* were both awarded the Western Fictioneers Peacemaker Award for Best Western Novel, and *Cut Nose* was a finalist for the Western Writers of America Best Western Historical Novel.

Ron and his wife, Bev, divide their time between their home in Fairbury, Nebraska and their cabin in the Kansas Flint Hills.

For more information about Ron Schwab and his books, you may visit the author's website at www.RonSchwabBooks.com.